THE
TWELFTH
VICTIM

By

Michael Clark

DEDICATION

To all those people who have heard about this book.

CONTENTS

ACKNOWLEDGMENTS

Thank you to Nigel Mynard
for proofreading the first drafts.

SUN SIGNS AND DATES

Sun Sign	From	To
Aries	March 21	April 20
Taurus	April 21	May 21
Gemini	May 22	June 21
Cancer	June 22	July 22
Leo	July 23	August 21
Virgo	August 22	September 23
Libra	September 24	October 23
Scorpio	October 24	November 22
Sagittarius	November 23	December 22
Capricorn	December 23	January 20
Aquarius	January 21	February 19
Pisces	February 20	March 20

PROLOGUE

He pushed the door closed, allowing the darkness to fold around him. He flicked on a torch and pointed the beam down a flight of uneven stone steps hemmed in by an arch-shaped tunnel. At the base of the steps, he entered a slender entrance and walked at a brisk pace through a narrow shaft until the temperature dropped, making the hair on his arms stand on end.

A large fracture in the solid rock served as an entrance to what he called the 'Dead Zone'. Once inside the spacious cavern with its high dome-shaped ceiling, the distinct change in atmosphere was clear. The cavern's colder dry environment contradicted the constant temperature in the tunnel.

Sweeping the torch beam along the chalk floor, from right to left, the discoloured faces of the mummified bodies lying on the chalk floor lit up, staring back with eyes long faded.

Whispering hello, he stared wide-eyed toward the dome-shaped ceiling. A brief pause followed until orbs of light floated upwards. The silence became a hive of echoing voices calling for 'vengeance' against the men who offered opportunities to work in London. There would be good pay and conditions, grand houses, grateful bosses who would look after their workers. There was no shortage of takers who jumped at the chance of expecting the best.

However, within days of arriving, their dreams lay shattered. Promises became a denial. The traffickers controlled all lives; violent men who would silence anyone who spoke out of turn. Their loyalties lay with darker sinister forces whose grip on the establishment extended beyond all that was decent and democratic. Their purpose was to silence dissenters. If you broke the rules, you paid with your life.

The deceased once lived with dreams and aspirations until they had the misfortune to meet men who ran a business trafficking people.

He sauntered to the stone steps thinking about the day ahead. Today was a full day. He skipped two levels at once and entered a dark, cramped space, and closed the door. Raising his foot, he stamped down on a metal lever – seconds later clunking gears filled the quiet space. To his right, a shaft of sunlight appeared that widened with enough space to squeeze through.

He side-stepped into a sizeable bare-walled reception hall. Streaming through windows sited in the high ceiling were warming rays of sunshine touching his arms and face.

There was one further task.

He heaved open a nearby trapdoor and let it smash against the floorboards. Echoes bounced around the house like a ghost announcing its haunting presence. Highlighted by the shifting beams of sunlight, he gazed at the plumes of dust stirred from the floorboards to linger in the still air.

…How I'll miss this place, despite the memories…

He stepped down onto a well-worn and smooth circular wooden stairwell and hurried downwards. He strolled to the walk-in refrigerator and placed his ear against the door and tapped twice.

All was as it should be.

At last. Onwards to new beginnings.

CHAPTER 1

1974 | Moscow | A new-born

After seventeen years of a marriage that had produced four boys, the Soviet army Colonel Valentin Lenevski and his wife Irina were due for a surprise. For more than a month Irina, fearing the worst had put off a visit to the doctor with stomach pains. However, when she saw the doctor, the relief was immediate; Irina was pregnant.

While relieved at the news, being pregnant raised a serious question, would Valentin want another child?

Valentin was a man of custom. On Thursday evenings, after dinner, he listened to an opera or classical concert. During the interval, he opened a bottle of vodka and enjoyed a glass or two until mellow and moving with the music.

Thursday was Irina's chosen day.

Irina picked the moment and sat opposite her husband. Time to tell him. His nature was to take notice of any news and decide before reacting. *Tell him!*

"Valentin, I have something important to tell you," began Irina, waiting for the usual nod which meant he was listening. Taking hold of his hands, she continued.

"The doctor told me some unexpected news."

Irina's hand holding and mention of the word 'doctor' prompted Valentin to open his eyes and shuffle forward in his chair. With obvious concern, he asked, "You are not well, is it something urgent?"

"No, nothing like that," she replied, thinking, *Tell him.* "I'm pregnant with our fifth child."

Valentin smiled and uttered the word, "Pregnant?"

"Three months pregnant, yes."

"Why did you not say sooner?"

Irina looked on as Valentin threw up his arms to hum 'Hava Nagila' complete with an on-the-spot jig. Then cupping Irina's face to kiss her forehead, he whispered, "I like this news because we will now have our girl. I know this to be a certainty. At last, a daughter."

Six months later, Valentin rushed Irina to the clinic where she gave birth to a baby girl whom they named after his late mother – Yulia.

She was his baby girl. The apple of his eye. Every morning he walked her to school. He listened to her questions and answered where he could. As she grew into a charming young lady, Valentin eyed any potential boyfriends with suspicion. If you upset Yulia, you upset her father.

CHAPTER 2

2000 | June | The Moscow Affair

Krasnogorsk technology trade fair

Yulia sat at the rear of the room, listening to a conference speech. As the talk continued, it was not the speech that caught her imagination. It was the voice of the speaker. A handsome and well-built Englishman. She looked at her brochure. Jason Cooper from London. That city, she had yet to visit.

With her eyes fixed on his movements, gestures and his handsome face, she had a range of thoughts. Never did she feel so attracted to a man. Her feelings were wanton lust.

I bet he's fit in the bedroom. How much longer will he speak? I must meet this man. If I must wait, then I wait. Be patient, these people will soon go.

While presenting, he spotted her face amongst the others – her long blonde hair, pale skin and large blue eyes. The symmetry of her face captured him. Little did he guess she was keen to meet him. Yulia remained patient as he answered questions that seemed to go on forever.

We will meet. I can feel it. How long will this last?

Yulia bided her time. Until she presented herself and requested that he join her for dinner, she was going nowhere. Finally, he was free. Striding towards him with a hand extended, "Hello, my name is Yulia Lenevski."

"Hello."

"My papa is Valentin Lenevski. He will be much excitement in your security product."

From the way she spoke, he could sense an urgency, desperation even as he held her hand.

"For personal reasons, or to protect – say – company secrets?" he questioned with a smile, wondering who Valentin Lenevski might be.

"For family and business. Russia is not safe for adoring papas and daughters like me."

"How can I help YOU?" he inquired, keeping a hold of her delicate hand.

Yulia beamed and blushed with a modest giggle. "First we talk business, then afterwards we dine at a respectable restaurant in Moscow – yes?"

An evening out

To end the evening dining at a high-end Moscow restaurant with a fascinating woman was unpredictable but welcome. Like all pleasant evenings, the time passed quickly.

"Thank you for joining me, Jason."

"The pleasure was mine. Unexpected with delightful

company."

"My chauffeur will arrive to drive me home. My father worries."

"He cares for you as fathers do for their daughter."

"Too often. That is why I must migrate abroad. Where else can I be myself without my father looking over my shoulder and his?"

"Do you have someplace in mind?"

Yulia smiled and dropped her gaze. "Friends say London is interesting and safe; is that true?"

Before he could answer a black Mercedes drew up. From it stood the chauffeur, a man who looked capable and confident.

"That's for me," she whispered. Putting her arms around Jason, she drew him close in an intimate embrace and kissed his lips.

"Time to go."

He faltered then blurted a question. "Do you want to meet again?"

"I have your number. I will call you soon." She hastened towards the car, teetering on her stiletto heels. He observed and waited until the vehicle rounded a corner before undoing his tie.

Would they meet again?

The following morning his mobile shrilled as he packed his suitcase.

"Hello."

"Jason, Yulia here."

"Yes."

"I'm downstairs. Would you care to join me for breakfast?"

"I'll be there in five minutes."

Sheremetyevo International Airport Moscow

Three weeks later, Yulia waited in the Arrivals Hall, bearing an enormous smile. When she saw her man, she bounced into his arms and held him tight and close.

"Welcome back to Moscow, Mr Jason Cooper," she whispered, gripping his hand. "It is good to see you again. It's been a long time."

Her smile spoke volumes as she led him by the hand from the airport to the waiting car. Sitting in the back seats, she turned the conversation to the days ahead and the scheduled meetings.

"I have all your days prepared for peak performance."

"Go on."

"First, meet my father, who will meet you personally for fifteen minutes. I have explained what you do and my best to tell him you're an honourable man."

"And then?"

"The various meetings will take three or four days. During that period, you stay in a hotel. I stay with my father to show I'm a good daughter."

"No... distractions, for me, then?"

Yulia continued with an affirmative, "No

interruptions, once you have met the staff and confirmed a contract, then we leave. I have plans for us at my home."

"You own your own home?"

"Yes. Soon, you shall see it."

Small-talk with vodka

As Yulia predicted, it took four long days before the demonstration, the technical analysis and the tough negotiations were over, during which Valentin struck a hard bargain.

As if on cue, Yulia entered. "Are you finished with business?"

"Of course," replied Valentin.

"All is well, Papa?"

"Yes. We have been through all the necessities of this advanced security system. We have exchanged contracts. Go now. Have a good day. Both of you."

Yulia seized her man's hand.

Behind the locked doors of Yulia's flat, they exchanged kisses and hugs before Yulia grabbed her black tote bag. From it, she drew out a tin of royal Siberian caviar, black bread and a bottle of vodka. She cracked it open and poured the liquid into two tall glasses. Handing him the drink, she raised her glass. "Tva-jo zdarovye! To a lengthy relation."

"Tva-jo zdarovye! May the relation bear fruit."

The comment made her blush and chuckle before regaining her composure. Gesturing to the surroundings, she asked, "Do you like my home? It is of the Tsarist era, later government-owned and occupied by high-ranking apparatchik."

"Yes," he acknowledged with an accepting nod. "How long have you lived here?"

"Two, maybe three years."

"I like it very much."

"During the Soviet Union – if you do not belong to the party, you had nothing except what you work for. A pittance. Communist Party leaders accepted these for their duties and commitment to the USSR."

"History taught us the Soviet Union was all about equality." He took a sip of his vodka. "How did your father become so prosperous?"

"My father left the army when Soviet Union failed. The government sold state-controlled enterprises, he raised cash from investors to buy the company. He became wealthy and bought this place and dachas outside the capital."

"How old is your father now?"

"Sixty-six – and he has no intention to stop working."

"Was your father a devoted communist?"

"No, it was simpler to be a party representative and promote the state rather than conspire against it."

"I never knew that."

"Let us change the subject," suggested Yulia, puckering up for an intimate query. "Do you have a home in London?"

"I live in Belgravia and have another home in Dennenmiss, the Buckinghamshire countryside, that I must restore," he pondered before going on. "I must move certain artefacts to safety before the builders move in."

"Can builders not move artefacts?"

"No – they require careful handling!" *Do not elaborate further.*

Between them, the sexual tension stirred as they kissed. Seconds later, Yulia pulled aside to see her man's eyes. "Have you been with a Russian woman before?"

"What do Russian women have that English and American women do not?"

"Intensity – the craving to keep a man happy."

"Are you this, woman?"

Murder

Awaking with a thumping headache and a dry mouth, he heard what sounded like raised voices and a door closing. With no Yulia alongside, he called out.

Nauseous, he sat then gripped the bed as the room appeared to shimmer and shake. He lay down and swallowed to clear his mouth of a lingering stale taste. Crossing his arms to rub his biceps, he felt a twinge of pain. Stretching out his right arm, he stared at a deep blue bruise on his bicep.

I don't remember blacking out, and why do I feel so crap?

Leaning against the wall for the support, he

lurched into the hall where his clothes lay scattered over the floor. Falling to his knees, he crawled towards his clothes, trying to shake the fog clouding his thoughts. Outside on the stairwell in the corridors, came heavy footsteps.

Without warning, the front door crashed open followed by two men who glanced at him. He saw them separate left, and front, as Valentin Lenevski followed with two more burly escorts and marched straight towards him.

"I've picked up a distress signal from Yulia. You've been together here all afternoon – yes?"

"We have."

"Where is she?" demanded a tense Valentin.

"I've just woken up and haven't seen her."

A bodyguard called to Valentin. There were voices and more footsteps. Valentin emitted a despairing howl. Fearing the worst, he tried to stand. Instead, two guards thrust his arms behind his back and hauled him to the kitchen. Slumped in a chair was a dead Yulia.

"What's happened?" muttered a stunned Jason, unable to take his eyes off her pale, lifeless face. "I don't understand, what happened?"

"She's dead," snapped Valentin, "and you are the murderer."

"No... no... no... look at my arm; someone drugged me!"

"Who – who drugged you?" reacted Valentin with contempt. "Do not lie."

"They drugged me!" he yelled. "Look at my arm."

"Who is 'they'?" demanded Valentin, gripping Jason's arms to expose the bruise.

"Until you tell me who 'they' is – 'they' do not exist."

"I'm not guilty of this."

An emotional Valentin wiped his eyes and lowered his voice. "My men will take you to a secure place. I have matters that need attention. Be ready for my return because you are a dead man."

A struggle at revenge

He awoke lying on a thin mattress in a dimly lit jail. Nearby sat a bodyguard reading a newspaper and drinking coffee. The word 'vulnerable' came to mind.

What is Valentin planning? What will he do to me if he doesn't believe me? I need to manage and tread carefully. Stick to what you know.

The sight of Yulia occupied his mind. He visualised Yulia's face, the open eyes. Mouth open. What had happened? She looked like a porcelain doll, delicate, in need of comfort. He wanted to reach out and touch her, feel her soft skin and kiss her lips.

His chain of thought broke as Valentin entered the room with two bodyguards. Tucked under his arm were files. With obvious contempt and anger, Valentin sat at the desk with three armed bodyguards behind him. One guard stepped forward to unlock the cell door. Two pulled out their Grach pistols. Jason suspected that matters would not improve.

…Keep calm. Don't antagonise Valentin or his

bodyguards. Tell him what you know…

"Sit," ordered Valentin, pointing towards the chair opposite, "and keep your hands where we can see them. Try anything, my men will shoot to kill."

There was a silence as Valentin opened a file and removed three loose pages. "So, who are you?" questioned Valentin, brushing his hair back with a single stroke of his hand.

"Jason Cooper!"

"Tell me your name – your real name."

"Jason Cooper."

"No, that is not your name. My UK contacts dug deep to uncover information such as your name and business. They found men with similar names but not a business or personality to fit. I suggest you are someone else working in the shadows of society. A man of multiple identities to hide a past – a secret past. Either that or you are a British spy working for the UK government."

"I am Jason Cooper, who else could I be?"

"NO, you are not," replied Valentin with a shake of his head. "So, if you are not whom you say you are – this is my theory to you. Tell me when to stop?"

"Go ahead."

"I suspect the plan at the beginning was to meet Yulia, to learn about me for financial gain."

"No. Yulia approached me. I'm not after money," scoffed Jason. "I'd never heard your name until Yulia mentioned you."

"No – no – NO." Valentin visibly shook with

anger and hurt. "Tell the truth!"

"The truth is the killers are miles away enjoying large vodkas in some sleazy downtown Moscow club. To pass the time, they have hookers jumping up and down on their dicks, giving blowjobs between dances!"

"Then tell me who murdered Yulia. Please. Give your best guess. At all times, my security keep surveillance on the building where Yulia lives and no strangers entered the building. Who murdered my daughter?"

"I don't know," rebuffed Jason, eyeing the three bodyguards. "So, decide which version of your daughter's death to believe. The scum responsible for her murder is getting away because we are here wasting time."

Valentin followed Jason's gaze and turned to look at the three guards.

"Why do you stare at them?"

"Are you sure about their loyalty?"

"These are trustworthy men who served with me during my military service."

"I know many people who betrayed friends. It just takes the offer of cash. Money entices weak men with no conscience."

Valentin grunted with exasperation. *All I want is a confession. What will it take? More verbal threats or perhaps a direct threat to loosen his tongue… what about using a pistol?*

Valentin asked the third bodyguard for his Grach semi-automatic and turned to Jason, waving the weapon. "I will use this If I must."

"Then use it!"

"Tell me why you killed Yulia when she showed you kindness."

"I'm not responsible for her death!"

Valentin screamed in frustration and grabbed Jason by the hair. "Why remain so calm, Jason? Understand me; I will use this weapon; do you have no fear within you or no conscience?"

"Do it," countered Jason without a flicker of emotion. "When I'm gone, you'll be no nearer to the truth because I'm an innocent man."

"You – you," Valentin coughed several times, "are not innocent. You were there – only you were there. I want the truth."

"The truth is, I don't know what happened!"

Valentin rammed the Grach into Jason's mouth and whispered, "Death waits for you right here in this room. NO one will ever know your fate. There are plenty of places to dispose of your body."

Jason never moved as the barrel of the gun thumped against the back of his mouth.

Keep calm, don't flinch or move in case he pulls the trigger...

"Do you feel fear or relief? Tell me, and this will end." Valentin's trigger finger twitched. "What was Yulia thinking at this point?"

Who would blink first?

Careful, control yourself. Make one sudden or jerky movement, and he might accidentally pull the trigger. That for me will be game over.

Valentin's face turned crimson as beads of sweat broke over his forehead. The trigger finger continued to twitch. Nervous tension made his lips quiver, and eyelids flutter. Of more concern to Jason was Valentin's trigger finger placing pressure on the trigger.

Don't move, or speak. He's so nervous and undecided he could accidentally pull that trigger.

To Jason's relief, Valentin emitted a frustrated grunt and hoicked the gun from Jason's mouth. Turning away from Jason to face his bodyguards, he shouted in Russian. That was Jason's cue to act.

Three bodyguards, two have their Grach semi-automatics ready. What will happen if the guards are trigger-happy; how far would they go to protect their boss? Act now – or pay the price.

From his sitting position, he leapt up and placed Valentin into a chokehold. Ripping the gun from Valentin's hand, he stepped back against the wall to protect his rear.

The two armed guards, surprised by Jason's quick and unexpected move levelled their pistols at his head, but with Valentin in the way, would they risk a shot?

The third guard stepped forward with the palms of his hands held outwards ready to talk.

"Let him go; he's done nothing to you."

"What will you do?"

"We talk. Know the truth and nothing else?"

"I did not kill Yulia."

The guard turned to his colleagues who held their weapons steady, ready to fire. Tightening the chokehold on Valentin who was struggling to breathe, he weighed up an option or two.

What's my next move? If I release him, what will the guards do? Move to help him or shoot me? There is one way to find out!

Releasing the chokehold, Valentin dropped like a stone. As expected, the third guard rushed forward to help while the two armed guards made the mistake of lowering their aim.

Jason never hesitated and fired a volley of bullets into their chests while the third guard took a fatal shot to his head.

I gambled and won.

Jason crouched next to a cowering Valentin. "Out of respect for Yulia, a woman of beauty, you must use your time to seek the truth and leave me alone. I am NOT guilty; the real killers are long gone because you chose not to believe me."

Valentin rebuked himself for not killing Jason earlier. "You are a liar and revenge for this will come," he uttered. "Be warned, my men will hunt for you – there will be no hiding place and the day of judgement will come for you. One day an assassin will strike you with bullets made by me."

Without a backward glance, Jason walked away. Threats or no threats, if nothing else his life was exciting, but also dangerous.

CHAPTER 3

2014 | March | City of London

Heathland Properties plc | The archives

"What's down here?" asked a curious Vicky as her stiletto heels echoed off the narrow walls of the corridor.

Moira Paterson pointed to a door. "Before the computer age, the departments stored archived material. These days we have electronic systems to store valuable documents." Moira paused and pointed towards a door. "It must be fifteen years since I was down here. I bet it's in a mess."

Moira tapped her ID card against the reader to open the door. Vicky peered inside as strip lights flickered on casting a glare over a room full of boxes piled high.

"Unfortunately, as you see, they didn't bother to stack the boxes on the racks and left that for someone else. Much of this stuff needs shredding as the forms and documents contain personal data."

To prove her point, Moira weaved through a stack of boxes. Opening one box, she pulled out a stack of papers and glanced them over before commenting.

"Six-page application forms."

"Application forms!" exclaimed Vicky, rummaging through a bundle of papers in a wire desk-tray. "It's CVs these days. In my life, I don't think I've seen an application form."

"Back in our day, when a vacancy occurred, the personnel manager would review the application forms on file. If he found a suitable applicant on file, he'd call the applicant. If they were considering a new job, he'd invite the applicant in for an interview."

Vicky held up a sheet of paper. "Look here! It's a memo to you from a 'Jonathan Carrier'."

"Where did you see that name?" questioned Moira, begging Vicky not to read the contents.

"He wrote it on July 26th, 1992. 'I have offered Martin the chance to earn money by helping to clear out the basement. He will report to you at 09:30 on Monday to help tidy the storage rooms. I only hope he will be as helpful as he suggests'."

Moira frowned. Feeling emotional, she took a seat.

"Back in the nineties, Jonathan was once Chief Executive of Heathland. The directors sold off properties. Jonathan raised the cash and bought the properties. He formed a new company, Carrier Properties. Later, he resigned from the board of directors."

"Who was Martin?"

"That would be Jonathan's son." Moira's face turned down. "A dysfunctional boy with a dysfunctional mother. A family that had many problems."

"What happened to the family?" queried a curious Vicky who liked to hear a related story.

"Martin was hyperactive, noisy, curious and never slept. Pauline let him run wild. He ended up getting into all sorts of bother, but... Martin soaked up his surroundings. He was a quick learner...

"After problems at school, Jonathan hired a home tutor who had a calming effect on Martin. At fourteen, he passed 'A' Levels in Maths, Physics, Chemistry and Technology. It raised the potential of Martin going to Oxbridge. But, it came to nothing."

"What happened?"

"One day, Martin wandered off. Along the way, local lads beat him up in a bizarre gang ritual, not once, but two or three times. So, Jonathan hired a mentor who turned out to be a former Israeli special forces soldier. He taught Martin how to look after himself. Whatever he taught him was effective because he developed into a muscular young lad. When the same bullies were beaten up, the police questioned Martin with Jonathan in attendance. They found no evidence to implicate him and dropped their enquiries."

"You mentioned the mother, what did she do?"

"Pauline hosted adult-themed parties attended by gangsters and other people of low morals. The rumour was she supplied prostitutes, gigolos and even children to guests. However, when someone murdered a friend of hers who was a well-known gangster, she disappeared on a bender. She ended up in a mental health unit after a suicide attempt. Months later, when she returned home, there was an altercation with Martin. He tried to commit suicide and ironically was sectioned in a psychiatric hospital. It all started to go wrong for the family. A fire broke out at the hospital, and he died. A day later police found Pauline dead in her car – murdered. About two or three weeks later, Jonathan died of a heart attack; he was already dead for a week before the cleaner found him alone in a big empty flat."

"Let's stop for the day!" suggested Vicky, sensing the upset in Moira's voice. "We can do this another day!"

Eleven months would pass before they opened the cellar doors.

CHAPTER 4

2014 | April | An African Sunset

A herd of elephants silhouetted against the red African sunset called their clan together. At the onset of dusk, instinct told the elders of the herd it was essential to keep their young safe. They nudged the calves towards the watering hole for one last drink before nightfall. Antelope, zebras and giraffes joined them, all keeping an open eye for prowling creatures big and small waiting to strike and kill.

Nocturnal creatures scampered from their daytime dens to forage while reptiles took shelter from the chilling air. Insects disappeared down holes while birds took to the trees.

Leboo, a Masai guide, tugged at the red shuka draped over his shoulders to keep the chill at bay. Behind him was a tourist – a solitary man who spent every evening listening to the many sounds of the Masai.

The tourist followed the line of the setting sun and the deepening red horizon that disappeared into the earth – closing his eyes; he concentrated on the animal calls and the hypnotic swishing of the long red oat grass in the breeze. It was peaceful, serene and relaxing.

...The rustling gave way to a quicker, swishing sound. Out of curiosity, he turned just as a large black cat leapt toward him. Raising his forearms for defence, the cat bit deep, pushing him back under its full weight. Snarling and baring its teeth, its foul breath stung his eyes and struck the back of his throat. Huge claws raked at his chest, drawing blood and ripping flesh away. Massive fanged teeth ripped the skin apart, exposing the bone and unbearable pain. Baring its fangs, it lunged towards his neck. Gripping its big head, he pushed it back. His painful cries carried across the Masai as the claws of the predatory cat ripped his flesh away, exposing his beating heart...

Awaking with a jolt and gasping for breath, relief dawned. It was a dream. He was sitting safely in a Jeep.

A concerned Leboo approached. "You screamed as if in pain. Did you have a nightmare?"

"I dreamt a big cat attacked and ripped me apart."

Leboo replied knowingly. "To dream of a large cat attacking is a bad omen. It means enemies are nearby and will catch you soon." Leboo continued to nod. "You will die a most troubling death."

"My death lies on the horizon," he answered, directing towards the North West. "I expect a sudden violent death."

"Are you a bad man?"

"That will depend on your point of view." The quick pinch of chilly air on his bare arms made him shiver. He sided a puzzled Leboo.

"Tell me," queried Leboo, "do you have a story to tell?"

CHAPTER 5

1972 | London | It Began With

There was nothing Arthur liked better than sitting in his favourite chair reading the newspaper and a steaming mug of Rosie Lee, a cup of tea.

Molly, his wife, hurried by to open the door.

"Arthur," she called, "you've got a visitor."

In walked Dave Davis, one of his oldest friends.

"You awight, Arfur? How's it hanging?"

"What's up, Dave?"

"Mrs Watkins who lives at 93. Her son has taken all her pension. Poor old bird can't pay her gas and electric."

"I thought you had words with that scroat?"

"He's a lazy sod. Bit of a dole wallah."

Arthur leaned forward and pulled out his wallet. Drawing out £100, he handed it to Dave. "Go around there and give it to her with my blessing. An' tell her, any problems she tells me. I'll help her out."

The entire neighbourhood knew the Suggs family

and their connection to organised crime. For over three generations, the Suggs family engaged actively in fencing stolen gear, fraud, cigarettes, and smuggling before moving into extortion and supplying drugs. One role he relished playing was the judge and jury between two parties. For an upfront fee of 2,000 quid, he would listen and cast his verdict. Whatever he decided was gospel. If you disagreed, Arthur had men to help change your mind.

That was in sharp contrast to his late father George Archie Suggs who lacked the savvy instincts of his predecessors. He placed his trust in the wrong people who supplied duff information. It meant when he took on a job, he ended up behind bars when it failed, leaving the dreams of making millions to evaporate in a twinkle of an eye.

Somehow, George found a date to marry Kathy Bell, who was under no illusion her husband would spend forced time away from home. Therefore, it was a happy surprise when Arthur was born. Even after becoming a dad George never considered giving up the reckless lifestyle and attitude. The path he walked meant there was always trouble along the way.

George partook in high-stakes poker games, losing thousands. One evening his luck turned. He won more money than he thought possible. However, the disgruntled player who lost thousands on the turn of a card labelled George a cheat.

Angry name-calling and a slanging match followed before security ejected the disgruntled player. George collected his winnings and walked home. A delighted Kathy counted the cash. It was more than enough to clear their debts and take a week's break in Southend.

They travelled to Southend and stayed in a Bed and Breakfast for a week. During the day they walked hand-in-hand by the beachfront eating cockles and mussels and jellied eels. In the evening they enjoyed nights in the pub having a singsong and enjoyed a fish supper while walking back to the B&B. The good times had returned. George, to improve their lot, promised to mend his ways.

Four weeks after the card game, a gunman shot George in the head at close range. As the gunman never searched George who was carrying a small fortune after a rare win on the horses, his family and friends saw it as an arranged hit. Four days later a group of schoolkids saw the alleged killer lying dead on a railway track below a bridge.

Was he pushed, or did he jump?

His son, Arthur, twenty, stepped up ready to start a new era. As rivals soon discovered, he was to be a formidable force. Therefore, common sense told you – loyalty to Arthur and his family was your best friend.

Aged twenty-five years, he married Molly, a South Londoner. Their union merged two crime syndicates. That allowed Arthur to dip his fingers into the business of brothels. An area of business Molly hated for various well-founded reasons.

Arthur had needs, as did his close friends. Molly preferred to play three wise monkeys. He went to parties and always returned the next day stinking of cheap perfume and wearing an ear-to-ear grin. Molly arranged a day out shopping with her friends.

Divorce was not a solution. Molly viewed it as a quick dip rather than a steamy affair; something not to argue over while he treated her like a lady.

Unlike his father, Arthur avoided arrest. When the police came calling, he pulled on a coat and accompanied the police to the local nick and gave his usual no comment to the questions. It was in his interests to watch the police chase evidence that did not exist. With the rozzers tied up chasing their tails, his men could concentrate on other business. As a result, Arthur saw himself as invincible. No one he knew could stop him.

August | Illicit trades in women

Late one sunny evening, Arthur drove to North Watford with trusted associates to meet a Brighton-based gang who were selling prostitutes for hard cash.

The meeting place was a crumbling section of a former factory. Arthur peered at the surroundings before speaking to his driver Cyril, and his accountant Bart, a short, balding man who wore glasses with thick lenses. "This building is like the economy."

"Whaddya mean, boss?" asked Cyril.

"This country is going down the pan with inflation, striking miners, shipyard workers because of the pittance they get paid, and the high taxes government takes. Make your opportunities and find your life. Governments screw people every day."

"That's what you did eh, boss?" agreed Cyril while Bart remained silent, holding on to a briefcase.

"Yeah, like me," laughed Arthur as a Bedford van drove into view.

"This must be the geezers," suggested Arthur, sitting up to open his car door as a metallic blue 2.8 litre Ford Granada followed behind. Arthur leaned on the open car door as four men stepped from the Granada and slammed the doors closed. Arthur noticed one man, with flowing blond locks and wearing an expensive suit.

Who is he, dressed like a mannequin ripe for a piss-take?

As the 'mannequin' approached with an extended hand, he introduced himself.

"Saul Trench. I presume you're Arthur?"

"Yeah, nice to meet ya."

"And you," replied Trench. "I've heard many good stories."

"All good, I hope?"

"That's why we're here. Your reputation for fairness."

Arthur had a question. "So, why is ya sellin' the women?"

"We've got opportunities that need quick cash to buy information upfront and tools for the job."

"Information is never cheap, is it?" Arthur laughed. "Bleedin' 'eart liberals charge a fortune for gear and info." Arthur clapped his hands for attention. "Let's discuss business; yer've got girls to sell? Are they well trained? Because I hate disobedience from the ranks."

Trench signalled towards two men who opened the rear doors of the Bedford van and hustled ten girls of varying ages into a line. Arthur inspected each girl giving each either an approving nod or a grunt. When the tenth girl joined the line, his eyes became transfixed.

"Mark, how much is you after?"

"Bargain basement price of 100 pounds each."

"Do they speak English?"

"Not all of them, guvnor, but then they understand phrases like – Fuck and Blow-Job!"

"Do they give a good one?"

"Never tried but the boys have when the missus ain't home or shut up shop."

"If you ain't tried them," mumbled Arthur, "what makes you think they're any good?"

"The customers are drunks – pissheads who offer the cash without askin' questions. We take the money. Take them to the girl. If he can't get a hard-on, we chuck them out."

"That's harsh, mate, after you've taken their earnings. But business is business. If you pay for it and don't use it, then don't expect a refund."

"Yeah – well they can sue me," scoffed Trench. "The bastards ain't gonna run to the rozzers in case the missus finds out. I hear it's illegal to pay for sex."

"Touché," remarked Arthur, turning to his 'Accountant', who was muttering sinister approvals of the girls.

"Bart, open the case and let him see the loot," instructed Suggs, closing his eyes at the thought of that money going elsewhere except in his pockets. Trench smiled at the sight of so much money as he picked up a bundle to thumb through the notes.

"Give him the money. It's all there." Suggs walked to the end of the line and stopped to look at girl number ten. Grasping her chin, he held her face.

"I look the look of you, darlin'. When I see you, next, you'll look like a proper lady, you will. Do you speak English?"

"Yes," she replied, dropping her eyes.

"Good, I'll see ya later!"

Girl Number Ten

A week later, with girl number ten on his mind, Arthur drove out to discuss with his 'Accountant' the return on his investment and see his new acquisitions. He expected nothing less than a flash of class. In his eyes, he ran an establishment for the more discerning customer – not drunken perverts and yobs.

When he walked into the lounge, with his chest puffed out, they lined the girls up for his inspection. Behind him followed his 'Accountant'.

After a glance along the line, Arthur remarked, "That's better. Cleaner, fresher and no odd smells."

"They do, boss," replied his accountant, "and it confirms your theory, boss."

"What's that?"

"Women who wear the right clothes, with grooming and makeup, will look respectable."

"That's right."

Arthur glanced at Bart, noticing the leering look on his face.

I wonder if Bart has ever had sex.

"Bart, if you feel the need 'cos your better half ain't up to it, have a go. It should be quite an experience for ya."

"Could be, boss, I'm not married or have a girlfriend."

"Why doesn't that surprise me?" quipped Arthur, facing girl number ten. An attractive, slim blonde with ample cleavage and alluring, light brown eyes.

"What's your name?"

"Lynn Foster."

"I get the impression you might be big trouble. How old are you?"

"What age do you prefer your girl to be?"

"Just tell me your age?"

"Eighteen."

"Is Lynn your real name?"

"Do you have a name in mind?"

"I like your attitude," smirked Arthur, "'cos, I've something in mind for ya!"

"Tell me about your plans?"

"I don't see you getting too close to regular lowlife clients who don't recognise class when they see it. More so, I see you with my wealthy clientele, coordinating their needs. Clients like judges, politicians, business people who we can screw over if they get out of line."

"I'm aware of the type you mention," she replied with a civil smile. "I've met a few."

With a smirk, Suggs took one last glimpse at Lynn before wandering over to his men from where he pointed back. Seconds later, he drove off.

CHAPTER 6

The Family of Lynn

L ynn often reflected on the circumstances that had brought her to where she was. Three years earlier, she had been living with her mum and dad in a leafy Cheshire suburb. The problem was the father, a devoutly religious man who in times of worry, grabbed the bible to cite passages that were law within the family home.

Pauline, her older sister, was sexually active. Drank alcohol, used drugs and never took no for an answer. Father and daughter argued always. Hence when she moved out, peace followed. In the aftermath, Lynn found herself unable to go far without her father asking questions.

If she stepped out of line, her father took off his belt and used it across Lynn's back until her mother intervened and pulled him away. After that, full of shame and guilt, he fell to his knees to pray for guidance, citing the punishment was necessary to prevent the child from straying.

Her aunt and uncle offered short periods of respite. She loved to visit them on a country estate they managed. Her uncle taught her how to look after the

35

shotguns and rifles. She could shoot with unnerving accuracy. She also became a dab hand at recognising a vehicle by the sound of the engine. With so many vehicles in use, she soon learned basic mechanics.

The painful bruises her dad inflicted meant concentration during lessons was not a strong point. Her form teacher caught glimpses of bruising on her legs, which Lynn explained away as sporting injuries. When she collapsed, the sordid truth became known to the people who mattered.

The bruising and its extent became apparent when the school nurse examined the tops of her legs and her lower back. After a quick conversation with the headmistress, she alerted Social Services.

Two social workers named Jim and Chloe arrived at the Foster home with questions. Jim made his case clear.

"Mr Foster, we here to discuss Lynn and the bruising she carries? We need you to tell us how she got the bruising."

"Has my daughter said anything?"

"No."

"Tell me, are you, agents of the local council that serves the government, a NAZI body full of lies and deceit?"

"If you don't answer us, we will need to take Lynn into care to keep her safe from whoever is beating her."

"Beating her! Who told you that?" erupted her father while her mother broke down in tears. "You come in here, making threats and accusations. You must be devil's spawn. Go before I throw you out on your ears."

"Don't threaten us while doing our job; you'll only make matters worse," warned Chloe, feeling empowered.

Foster's face turned red with contempt and anger as he called upstairs, "Lynn, get down here this second and explain this charade."

When Lynn appeared, her father gripped her shoulders to face the social workers. "Now. Tell this devil spawn about the bruising and remember we do not tolerate sin. TELL them the TRUTH."

Lynn glimpsed at the gathered adults whose faces reflected their fears. *What should I say? My father beats me, but he expects me to say I hurt myself while my mother supports him. Does no one, my parents NOT accept their responsibilities towards me, to care for me and look after me? Adults should be our guardians, not make us a pawn in their stupid games.*

"Lynn, to end this visit," continued her father, "tell them the truth. If you don't, the government will take you away to a dark cellar to worship demon gods who penetrate children with evil."

"Mr Foster," interrupted Jim, "we are not a fascist state. Do not smear our profession with lies."

"You lie to a man of God," sneered Foster. "You must be one of those fascists, they always lie to get their way. A man who takes children away to torture them with abuse?"

"I am not a fascist. Neither is my colleague. We are caring humans out to protect the weak."

"More like spread your evil."

"Enough of the shouting!" screamed Lynn. "You're no better than each other fighting for control of my life." Then without care, she pulled up her skirt.

"Oh, my good god," muttered Chloe, agog at a mass of bruising and welt marks caused by the buckle of the belt. "What in Christ's name have you done to her?"

"What did you say?" queried Foster, his eyes agape. "You have committed blasphemy in my house," hollered Foster, grabbing his bible. "Leave my house, blasphemers. Leave my house now and take your sins from my door. Never again darken my door with your presence."

Lynn dashed upstairs and locked her bedroom door. Minutes later, her father hammered on the door with threats. By not responding, he would soon walk away and pray for forgiveness.

What was she going to do to save herself from the social workers taking her into care? Should she run away from home?

Not yet.

First, there were people to visit. Pauline refused outright. She wanted no family spoiling her fun. Her aunt and uncle were sympathetic, but her father might cause problems. They stopped short of offering her a home.

Back home, she sat on the bed to weigh up her options. The best idea was running away to a city where she could disappear. The best time to go was a Thursday evening when her parents attended the local bible class. They were always home by 10pm, then straight to bed. It gave her time to leave.

When her parents left, she grabbed her rucksack and a pile of cash her father had hidden in a (not so) secret place and caught the first train to London.

CHAPTER 7

Hello London

Despite finding London grimy and bigger, faster and busier than expected, Lynn's determination never wavered. Soon after her arrival at King's Cross, she found a hostel. By day three, she found work in an Italian ice cream parlour. By day five, her workmate offered her a room in a flatshare.

Within weeks, she met local boys eager to be friends. In her naïve way, she did not understand what it might involve and agreed to a night out, which ended when her date stuck his tongue into her mouth. When she bit it, his response was to slap her in annoyance. After that, she decided boys were to remain at arm's length.

Months later, she met Ashraf who kept his hands to himself and at no point did he try to stick his tongue down her throat. Instead, he wined and dined her at fancy restaurants. There she met his male friends and relatives. They offered her champagne, which she drank. Her companions avoided alcohol on religious grounds. Before she knew it, the men brutally forced her to have sex with them.

What was happening was beyond her understanding. Her intuition was to avoid Ashraf. However, his charm soon won her around. Within days she met his male relatives and found herself forced to have sex with more men.

They drove her miles to meet various men before locking her away in a room with no possibility of escape. Then one day they sold her to an English gang who used her until she was ill from exhaustion. Eleven months later, she became the property of Arthur Suggs.

CHAPTER 8

September 1972 | A Brutal

Demonstration of Power

Arthur stubbed out a cigar and stood from his leather desk chair as two juniors, Maurice and Herbert, led Lynn into his office. Puffing out his chest he placed one hand into his suit pocket and gestured to a seat. "Sit, please. As for you two, wait outside and don't come in until I call for ya."

Scratching his head and screwing up his eyes, he checked Lynn over. She exceeded his expectations. He saw her working for him and looking after his assets.

"Look," he began, screwing up his eyes with a frown, "I'm interested in you. Can you tell me how you ended here? What happened? Did you take advice from some kiddy fiddlers, or is it a career choice?"

"I ran away to London to escape my bible-thumping father."

"And your mother?"

"She did as her father told her or faced the consequences."

"So," interjected Arthur with a chortle, "we won't be visiting your parents soon, I take it?"

"When I got to London, I had one rule in mind. That was to avoid boys because they were trouble. I broke my rule and found myself involved with some Asian bloke who treated me like a princess, then turned me into a prossie after buying me presents and meals."

"Don't tell me the dirty bastards sodomised you in a chain?"

Lynn had no answer.

"What's your plan then?" probed Arthur, trying to meet her gaze. "No chance of a family reunion – for now? You got no money, no friends and nowhere to go 'cos I can tell from the way you talk you ain't from London. So, if you go now, without listening, you won't know my proposal."

"Tell me."

"OK, right – I'll tell ya! You'll be spreading your legs for a wrap while you service perverts and any nonce who wants to shag a kid – and fuck knows – I've met plenty of people like that."

Lynn listened while he spoke. His language did not differ from the other gangs. He sounded and looked like a typical London-born wide boy who told the funniest jokes, got things done but used violence to keep people in line.

Ask him a question and see how he answers.

"Do you fuck kids?"

Arthur briefly appeared confused by the question before scoffing, "Do you think I am, a bleedin' nonce? Well do, ya?"

"OK, so, what's your interest in me?" she demanded. "I can't be the first young woman who sparked your interest."

"You stand out. You talk and act like someone who has the ambition."

"Ambition. In what way?"

"You speak English for a start. Would you consider a job managing the other girls and make sure they take care of my customers?"

"How would I manage the girls?"

"However you see fit."

"OK... OK... Let me think. Stinky breath, how's that for starters, or when the perv thinks it's OK to beat the girl up? Can the girls refuse to give blowjobs to punters with stinky arses, balls and cocks 'cos they don't use soap, or can I force them to clean their little bits before they do their business?"

"Tell me more," urged Suggs.

Lynn closed her eyes, hoping for an end to the madness, the threats and dodgy offers. She had heard it, seen it and owned the T-shirt emblazoned with *'You paid for me; your wish is my command'*. It mattered not what Suggs had on offer, or even what he thought he could offer. Her mission was to find peace and make a stand.

"You're not offering me anything better than the rest. I've had enough, enough."

"Whaddaya mean?"

"You're trying to lull me in with kind words in the

hope I'll work for you. So, fuck off? I want nothing from you."

Is she deranged, why is she not jumping on this offer?

"I'm trying to help you return to some normality."

"Oh yeah, don't tell me – let me guess. You'll want me as your gangster's moll to take care of you when the wife isn't giving you enough blowjobs or ain't wankin' your cock. That's what men like you want."

"Relax, missus. No one is gonna hurt you or touch you. Neither will my wife. We understand each other!" A smirking Arthur lowered his head, finding her outburst showed spirit.

"Forgive me if I find that hard to believe," she scoffed, picking up a small but dense statue, which she flung at Arthur, striking his forehead with a crack. As he crashed to the floor, Herbert and Maurice dashed in, uncertain what to do. Lynn, sensing she might need a weapon, grabbed a stainless-steel letter opener from the desk and threatened both men.

Herbert rushed to help his boss while Maurice chased Lynn. He dodged the letter opener and encircled her arms and clumsily threw her across Arthur's desk and using his weight, pinned her down by her arms.

Humiliated and in pain, Arthur leaned on his desk for support before bawling into her face, "You had it in your hands, a way out of 'ere. You couldn't see it; you tossed it away by treating me like a piece of shit! Ya can sue me later when you're dead and buried!"

*****

When a sweating and breathless Arthur sat down,

45

Lynn was unconscious. He grabbed a bottle of brandy from his desk drawer, poured a generous measure and gulped it down before calling for Maurice and Herbert who were both skulking outside.

He pointed to the shelves. "Grab my Polaroid and take few pictures as she is, 'cos I will show her mates what happens if they don't listen. Now you two. Listen carefully. Take her away and drive her up the country. Bury her up the new M1 motorway where no one will find her until next century."

CHAPTER 9

A Police Chase

Keeping their eye ahead, Maurice and Herbert drove towards Watford and joined the M1 as heavy rains fell. On their minds was the task ahead. To get rid of the body.

Behind them an observant police officer driving an unmarked car recognised the Range Rover used in a recent attempted robbery.

"Where are we going to bury her?" inquired Herbert.

"Arfur said upcountry."

"That could mean Scotland. You got no idea 'ave you, mate?" jibed Herbert.

"No, and I bet you know naff all either. It's a first for us. I'm thinkin' get this right, and Arfur will see us right. There's got – to…"

Maurice's voice trailed off as blue lights appeared in his rear-view mirror. "We got rozzers behind us. Not just one but about three cars."

"What they after? It can't be us."

"It's this motor. It's the one Arthur used in that failed blag. It's not us they've seen."

Maurice glanced to his right as a police Rover V8 drew level. In the front, a police officer gestured to pull over. Herbert flicked a 'V' sign before turning to Herbert. "Fasten your seatbelt; this could get hairy."

Herbert buckled up as Maurice sped up and swerved towards the police Rover, forcing the police driver across two lanes.

"We must off get off the motorway else we'll never shake them," proposed Herbert as they passed a forty-foot articulated lorry that gave Maurice an instant but risky idea.

"I have a plan! Hold tight."

"What… What are you planning to do?" queried Herbert as Maurice pushed the Range Rover over 75mph.

"Hold on; this mightn't work," yelled Maurice as he pulled in front of the truck and slammed the brakes. From behind, the driver of the lorry blasted the horn and pushed the brakes hard. The cargo-laden trailer skidded across the motorway, hitting one police car and bringing the chasing police cars and traffic to a halt.

Herbert nervously gripped the dashboard as they sped up the exit ramp. Neither man spoke nor dared look behind as an anxious Maurice kept driving, turning this way and that for miles with no idea where they were.

Eventually Herbert broke the silence. "Any idea where we are?"

"Lost on a narrow road out in the sticks."

"Should we ring the boss and tell him what's

happened?" suggested Herbert – to which Maurice scoffed.

"Look at all the trees; we're miles from civilisation – electricity isn't here yet, never mind phone boxes. I haven't seen one yet. Have you?"

A distant sound ended their conversation, "Is that what I think it is?" asked Maurice.

"It's a rozzer's car," whispered Herbert. "They can't be after us, we're miles away."

"We've got to get off the road," proposed Maurice, pointing ahead. "That looks like an entrance into the woods coming up."

Maurice flicked on the full beam to get a better look ahead. He pulled slowly onto a dirt track between the trees. Killing the headlights, he followed a rough trail until he spotted a canopy of trees. Reversing under the canopy, he stopped the engine and slumped over the steering wheel. An apprehensive Herbert wound down his window and leaned out, taking deep breaths. At last, they could relax. It had been quite a chase, creating a rush of adrenaline.

"This gangster lark isn't easy. It's full of dangers," griped Maurice. "Why did we get mixed up with the Suggs family?"

"Job security! There ain't much work for working-class boys like us unless you wanna travel north and work the mines."

Herbert pointed to the trees. "We're up north now. Pretty, innit? Trees and all that. Fields, cows, sheep. We're safe here. I thought we'd cashed our chips back there. So close."

"Awight," murmured Maurice, "we've still got the job to do. We bury the body here then dump the Range Rover."

"Let's do it," enthused Herbert. "I'll be glad when we're home."

"And when we're done, we need to find a phone and call in. Arthur might send someone up here to collect us."

"I hope so 'cos it'll be a long walk," moaned Herbert, "and I'm fair whacked."

Hearing a noise from the boot, they glanced at each other. "The body's been tossed around," suggested Maurice.

"You checked she was dead before we left?" responded Herbert, rubbing his hands. "If she's alive, I don't fancy killing her!"

"I 'ope you're not squeamish, mate, because one day Arthur could order us to bump a nasty rival villain off and chop him up. We joined his gang because we're villains in the making. Bad fellas!"

On that exclamation, he opened the tailgate ready to bury Lynn Foster.

CHAPTER 10

1982 | Childhood Nightmares

Miss Taylor, the class teacher, hushed her class for their attention. The subject of that day's lesson was an essay on where they lived.

"How big are the fields?" she asked.

"Big," was the unanimous answer from the class.

Throwing up her arms, Miss Taylor asked, "How long will it take to walk across the fields?"

"Hours – days – months – years," came the noisy replies.

She gazed at her class with an element of pride. "When you are nine years old, the world is forever a big place, but, when you grow up, it won't look so big."

At home time, he strolled along a public path instead of the road that led to his family's farm. Miss Taylor's words lingered in his mind.

'When they were older, the objects and obstacles would be smaller and not so scary.'

"How big is the sky, the fields?" he whispered, stopping to gaze over the multicoloured fields. "Huge."

Ominous dark clouds in the distance caught his attention. He gazed, fascinated, as they consumed the blue sky and the sun. The gentle breeze became a gust of wind before the first flash of lightning ripped through the air. He stood motionless as a rolling boom of thunder crashed overhead trailed by a sudden wave of heavy rain.

The dark rumbling clouds grew darker while the trees that lined the nearby road swayed and rustled their leaves as the wind picked up and buffeted his body. Overhead there was a boom and a bright flash. He looked up, to see the power cables falling to the ground and like snapping dogs bucked their way towards him.

Instinctively, with panic driving his heart he ran toward the dry-stone wall and jumped the last few feet over a verge of rough grass onto the road as lightning struck again, pushing him to duck as thunder shook the earth.

With a fast road beneath his feet, he sprinted towards home, as large raindrops pinged off his head and into his eyes. As he stopped to wipe his eyes, something hit him.

...In a flare of white light, he stood in a long corridor along which voices echoed. From somewhere he heard crying. Cautiously walking along the hall, he opened the door to reveal a boy sitting on a bed looking lonely and lost.

"Hello. Why are you crying?"

"My mommy tells me no one loves me."

"Do you do naughty things?"

"Sometimes."

"Where are your mommy and daddy?"

"Mommy is here, but Daddy works away…"

Out in the corridor, a woman called.

"You must go now, that's my mommy. She doesn't like little boys."

"Why not?"

"Go," he replied, as the woman's voice grew louder and angrier, "before she gets here. Run – run away."

Running into the corridor, he found a wardrobe to hide in where he covered his ears to block out the crying boy. Much later, when it was quiet, he sneaked a*way*.

…Three days later, at home, his mother sat nearby knitting while reciting tales of the farmyard and the people who worked there. He remembered the storm, the darkening clouds and the heavy rain.

"I didn't like the storm when it came."

"You must never fear the storm; it's something to learn, my love."

"What's that, Mommy?"

"Don't let the storm frighten you."

CHAPTER 11

1989 | 30th May |

Death of a Gangster

"Archie, me boy, it's your birthday today, many happy ones."

"Thanks, Dad."

"No problem, son. I hope you're looking forward to your party tonight down the Nags Head. It will be a blast."

"I'm sixteen, not eighteen."

"Don't you worry my son," winked his father, tousling his hair. "Earl, the landlord, owes me a few favours. We got the function room. All your mates is coming."

"When you gonna be there, Dad? 'Cos you got the poker tournament going on."

"Yeah – yeah, I'll make sure everything is in running order, all pukka like. We have satisfied punters who are spending cash; I'll be home sharp. Then we go."

"So, Arthur," interrupted Molly, "don't be late home. I know this tournament is important, but so is your family."

"I keep my promise, darlin', to all and proper, and my word is my bond."

"You have never let us down, Arthur, and I appreciate that." Molly gazed at her husband. "I hope whatever's been bothering you over the last month has settled and won't raise its head today of all days?"

"Not at all, darlin'. It's all done and dusted. No geezer messes with Arthur Suggs."

Molly sighed. The recent events made her uneasy. "Might I suggest Arthur…"

"What's that, darlin'?"

"I thought it might be safer staying away from the tournament…"

Arthur hunched his shoulders. "If I call it off now, I lose tens of thousands of quid."

On that remark, Arthur left the house.

Molly knew he was lying. His demeanour. The way he spoke and lack of eye contact. Three weeks earlier a succession of events rocked their world, including a murder.

It was playing on Arthur's mind.

CHAPTER 12

Dave 'Diamond Geezer' Davis

Dave Davis (AKA Diamond Geezer Dave) returned home with his family after a weekend away. On entering the house, he stood in shock. Someone had broken into his house. On a bedroom wall, the intruder left a graffiti message that placed the fear of God into Dave. Gasping for breath, his entire body trembled. He must act and quickly before his wife came upstairs. She would ask questions. His wife was tenacious. Any problem deserved an answer.

Jumping down the stairs, he grabbed the telephone and called a local taxi company. With no explanation he sent his wife and children to her mother's before calling Arthur, who arrived post-haste looking concerned.

"Who did this?" hissed Arthur. "Whoever it was, better be ready. When I find out, I'll have his head on a platter."

Dave responded with a shrug and a hint of caution in his voice. "No idea, Arfur. Mebbe it's someone who attends a party regular like or knows something of them."

"That's what I was thinkin'…"

"Meanwhile, we need to be havin' a word with certain people. See what's new on the grapevine," suggested a nervous Dave.

"First things first," assured Arthur, "I'll call in some decorators to clean up this mess. I'll have the entire house revamped. New furniture to make sure your missus forgets this ever happened. Then I'll call my contacts. You've met them before; we ain't putting up with this shit."

*****

Three weeks later, Dave moved his family home. Arthur, true to his word, had the entire house transformed; modern furniture, a modern kitchen and bathroom, and redecorated throughout. He had to keep Dave's missus happy.

A bigger shock was coming. Dave did not turn up to an important meeting. Arthur repeatedly called before sending two men to find him. When no one answered the front door, they forced entry through the back door.

The first sight to meet their eyes was Dave's mutilated corpse lying in a pool of blood. They gagged and reached for the sink, avoiding the curiosity to look back at Dave. When they recovered enough to wander upstairs, his wife and children were hiding in a large wardrobe. With a shaking hand she handed them a handwritten note which read:

'Paedophiles are subject to Justice.'

When Arthur read the note, he shuddered. The graffiti artist knew damning secrets that could destroy his reputation, threaten his marriage and bring the Law crashing to his door.

The bad news continued only a day later with another telephone call.

"Arthur 'ere."

"Arthur, it's me, Billy Wallis – your North Watford warehouse is on fire."

"What you mean by the warehouse is on fire?"

"As I say, Arthur, I came out to pick up stuff for trade on the markets, and it's on fire."

"Is it a big fire?"

"Let's put it this way, Arthur, I 'ope you your insurance is up-to-date."

As Arthur threw a tantrum, Billy watched sections of the warehouse collapse.

"Listen, your place is collapsing, shouting won't help."

"How long you been there?" asked a hoarse Arthur.

"Five minutes ago. I called you right away."

"So, you saw nothing or anyone suspicious?"

"No one at all."

An exasperated Arthur thumped his desk – who was out to get him and why? Thinking was not Arthur's strong point. He preferred direct action. Who was doing this to him?

I gotta stop this shite before it takes over. Someone out there don't like me.

When the telephone rang ten minutes later, he

answered with hesitation.

"Hello. Arthur, here."

"I speak to you today to tell you in person, within twenty-four hours, you will be dead."

"Yeah - yeah," laughed Arthur, "what makes you think you'll succeed where others have failed?"

"I'm not a rival; I deal in death and little else. Keep an eye open, Arthur; I'm coming."

The colour drained from his face as Molly entered the room after overhearing the conversation.

Molly embraced her husband. "Then why do you look so pale? My little voice tells me the caller brings a warning. Either you stop to think, or will you rush like a fool into the unknown and risk your life. Mark my words Arthur. We must be careful."

"No one scares me, darlin'."

Molly scoffed and leaned closer to her husband. "Then why do you look so pale? My little voice tells me that ain't going to be any good outta that phone call. Mark my words."

CHAPTER 13

Arthur's Last Stand

After spending an hour chatting with guests, Arthur sided within his bodyguards to leave the tournament and return home for Archie's birthday party. The sudden emergence into the chilly night air made Arthur groan as the sudden urge for the toilet halted his tracks.

"I need the khazi, boys. Wait in the car for me."

"Shall we come with, boss?"

"Wait here," chuckled Arthur. "I can go on my own!"

*****

While Arthur relieved himself by the urinal, the door clattered open. He turned to see a young lad walk in pushing a large catering trolley full of bulging black bags. Staring at the young lad, he pointed to the doors. "The kitchen across the hallway. You're going the wrong way."

The young lad looked at Arthur before a hint of recognition lit up his face. "You're Arthur Suggs, ain't ya?"

"Yeah, I am. You know of me?"

"Not half. The proper legend you are. Can I shake your hand?"

Arthur held out his hand, which the young man gripped and gazed into Arthur's eyes while muttering, "I don't believe it – I've met Arthur Suggs."

Arthur chuckled at such recognition by a youngster and dropped his guard. Quickly and efficiently the kid struck Arthur's chin hard with the heel of his hand twice. Arthur stared cross-eyed trying to hold on before the kid struck again. The smirking kid guided Arthur's unconscious and limp body into the trolley and quickly covered him with the back bags. With no time to waste the kid walked through the kitchen to a van and drove off with Arthur in the back.

CHAPTER 14

A Tortured Conversation

Arthur awoke in a dimly lit and chilly environment to find himself naked and tied to the tubular frame of a stacking chair.

Where am I? Who is doing this? Archie, it's his birthday. By now, Molly will be going frantic.

Arthur kept his promises to friends, family and villains alike. Archie's birthday was not the time to find himself under threat.

"C'mon, c'mon out ya bastard, show ya face," he ranted. "Whoever you are – get me the fuck outta here, you nonce, before I kill ya with my bare hands! Who is ya? A man, or a mouse?"

"Arthur," hailed a voice, "I can hear you. As can the dead."

"Show yourself," retorted Arthur. "Who are you?" A lone figure appeared and lingered in the shadows before speaking.

"I can use clichés to describe me. Like I'm your worst nightmare… I'm your God. Put it this way – this evening I have plans for you."

The dark figure stood before Arthur. It took a few seconds before he recognised the lad from the gents.

"You're the kid I saw earlier! What is ya doing?" snapped Arthur. "Get me the fuck outta this shit!"

"I drove you here, in my van."

"You're not old enough to drive."

"You're right there – but unless I get stopped by the rozzers who cares?"

"Whaddya want with me?" grunted Arthur.

"Where do I start? Here's one for you. Does my face remind you of anyone?" asked the kid, framing his face with his hands. "Or perhaps someone you know or knew?"

"No, it doesn't," snapped Arthur, "and get me out of this shit!"

"When I ask a question, I expect a polite answer! Tell me – are – you – a – wealthy – man?"

"Fuck off; that's my business."

"Let me remind you," scowled the kid, "I've got you by the short and curlies. So, when I ask a polite question, I expect a polite answer!"

"Fuck you, kid. You should respect your elders."

"Respect! What are you saying? When DID YOU EVER show respect to the people you've had bumped off? The men you destroyed because they threatened your power?"

…Who the fuck is this kid? He's a fuckin' lunatic.

"What've I done? You're too young an' I've never met ya!"

"Stories, Arthur. I've heard lots of stories about your legendary help for the poor."

"Yeah, I'm an all-in-one welfare state. Help for the poor and unemployed."

"You is a diamond geezer, Archie. Also, I've seen you and your men selling drugs – trafficking kids and women. I see who you are, Arthur Suggs. Don't bollocks me with respect and welfare state rubbish."

…I'm gonna kick this kid's arse to hell and back.

"Who are ya?"

"It doesn't matter who I am." The kid winked. "We're talking about your associates and how they frighten the living hell out of people and what happens when they meet me."

"Whaddya mean?"

"Your best mate sang like a canary when I turned the tables… When I threatened to lop off his balls, he sang even higher. It made no difference 'cos he came to a sticky end as witnessed by his family."

"Did you do Dave?"

"Did I do Dave… did I?" scoffed the kid, mimicking Arthur's Cockney accent. "Dave was a kiddy fiddler, a nonce and a chancer who deserved death and you're the same, Arthur."

"Just who the FUCK IS YOU?"

"You and 'Diamond Geezer Dave' liked to indulge your dirty fantasies with children. I planned to subject Dave and his family to the pain – the unbearable pains you and others inflicted on vulnerable people."

"What a cunt, you murdered him and traumatised

his kids and wife!"

"No," answered the kid, waving his index finger. "The family – his children and missus were almost frightened to death when they saw Dave pissin' all over the floor with fear."

"What is you after, you evil cunt?"

"Me, an evil cunt! YOU call ME evil after your contribution to society. You socialise with useful idiots who take your word as gospel. This cunt wants you; so, let's make sure you understand. When I finish with you, which Suggs family member will I do next?"

"Touch my family. I'll do ya!"

The kid spoke with a mocking tone, "The problem is, Arthur – you'll be dead! Unless you can resurrect yourself, you'll be talking to worms."

"If you go anywhere near them, I'll kill ya!"

"Calm yourself, Arthur. Take it easy," countered the kid with a wide grin. "I have time on my side. You won't be here to see it, Arthur. My advice is to consider making your peace with your God before I move to the next phase of my long-term plans."

"Have you considered a different career?" suggested Arthur, wondering what the 'next phase' could be.

"A career. Like what?"

"Try something practical because violence and murder don't make good careers. I have experience." Arthur sniggered. "Find a job in the City and become a banker. Make some honest cash?"

"I see the fear in your eyes," scoffed the kid,

glancing at Arthur. "Could it be the fear of the unknown that haunts you? Or maybe I scare you because you see me as your Angel of Death?"

Watching the kid gather a thick rope with a bulbous knot at the end sent Arthur's anxiety levels sky-high. He knew what was coming as the kid dangled the rope.

Arthur broke into a cold sweat, shaking with nervous apprehension; if he could not convince the kid to change his mind – it was game over. In the background, the music stopped playing.

Arthur spoke. "What is this music you're playing because it ain't Chas and Dave?"

"Never heard of them. My dad, the sad bastard, listens to them!"

"You've never heard of Chas and Dave and a good Cockney knees-up down The Olde Cockney Pride Tavern in Piccadilly? You've no idea what you're missing, kid! Good times to be had down there." Arthur glanced at the kid. Was he listening, was he going to use the rope?

"People like YOU don't deserve a good life!" retorted the kid. "So, I will end it for you."

"People like me. Until now, I've never MET YOU. Why ME, WHY ME?"

The kid smiled and leaned closer to Arthur. "I've heard it whispered down draughty corridors you belong to a violent profession."

"You sound like a poet, kid."

"Perhaps I am. However, for now, I'm considering a career move."

"What's that then?"

"I'm considering a career in violence."

Arthur twitched keeping an eye on the rope which the kid turned and twisted.

...Is he going to use it?

"This profession of violence wouldn't be an application to join the rozzers' force... would it?" Arthur guffawed at his joke to lighten the growing tension. The kid stared at him, his eyes growing darker by the second.

"My first entry into that violent profession is to kill you."

A trembling Arthur offered advice. "You know what – killing a man ain't easy."

"I forgot to tell you, Arthur. I'm a hardened criminal. You're my first victim. I follow in the path of my ancestors. It's in the DNA."

The resonating sound of a tolling bell filled the room as the kid swung the rope over his head until it whistled. Once released, it wound around Arthur's neck, cutting into his flesh.

"Whoa, feel the choke, Arthur!" exclaimed an excited kid. "Feel the choke. It's no less than what you did to others. YOU – choked the life from people who could not fight back, making their lives hell, which is what I am doing to you now."

The kid unwound the rope from a gasping and red-faced Arthur. "Please don't do this," he begged. "There's no need for it."

"I've started so I'll finish."

"Don't, I beg you."

The kid continued until Arthur collapsed from the unbearable pain. As his body lost all tension, Arthur's last thoughts were on the kid:

Who is he? Why does he hate me so much?

CHAPTER 15

A Gangster's Wake

Following Arthur's funeral, Molly provided leadership and continuity. The Suggs legacy could not die. The first task on her growing list was to close the brothels and sell off the buildings. With the proceeds in hand, she sent the girls home and made sure they boarded their flights. She had the rest taken to wherever they had friends or relatives; she wanted them off her hands.

With her thoughts on finding Arthur's murderer, Molly offered hard cash to loosen lips or deliver any information on Arthur's death. Every month for over a year, Molly appealed for news. As Arthur's friends made clear, no one had any idea who the murderer could be. Even her contacts in the police could not help.

Five years after his death, the police consigned the file to a cold case status prompting Molly to give up seeking answers. Friends and colleagues suggested names far and wide, but all had good alibis. The police had no known suspects. Arthur's murderer was to remain a mystery for over twenty years.

CHAPTER 16

1993 | 23rd September |

Opposites Clash

02:30 – 03:15

Twenty-year-old Police Constable Stuart Grant ambled along the Watford high street when rain, which had threatened for so long, fell from the night sky. Cursing under his breath, he sheltered in the doorway of a furniture store as lightning struck. Seconds later, ground-shaking thunder rumbled.

To take his mind off the storm, he peered through the shop doors. The furniture reminded him that soon he would be a married man. Their house had no furniture. However, the price of the furniture inside the shop caused a frown; far too expensive. Not on his salary and Joan's.

He turned to continue this beat when a Ford Cortina pulled up with its engine idling and sidelights burning. When the driver switched on the interior light PC Grant approached and tapped on the window. The driver stared, unsure, before winding down the window.

"Good evening," greeted Grant, trying to sound jovial. "Are you lost, sir?"

"Thank God, Officer!" blurted the driver in a mild Scottish accent. "I'm on an emergency call, and can't find the address."

As the driver picked up a notebook from the passenger seat, Grant spotted the distinct shape of a Gladstone medical bag in the passenger footwell. "What's the address?"

"Queen Street."

"Drive straight for three blocks," pointed Grant, "then turn left. When you get to the traffic lights, turn right. That is Queen Street."

"Thank you," replied the doctor, gesturing towards the sky. "If I were you, I'd take cover because this is a serious rainstorm."

He waited until the car turned off before walking at pace until he stopped by a small estate of houses. Spotting a nearby bus shelter, he took cover from the lashing rain.

Where to go next? he thought, checking his watch. *Walk to the town or stay here?* Off to his left, he spotted light coming from an end of the terrace window. *Who would be up so early?*

Feeling a tinge of anxiety, Stuart clasped and unclasped his wet hands, feeling nervous.

Lightning lit the night sky. Thunder roared.

Through the haze of the heavy rain, he stepped closer to the window. What was he looking for? He did not need to wait long.

A woman's bloodied face slammed against the window. The hair on his neck stood on end when a figure dressed in black appeared holding a knife. Stuart stood frozen, shocked as the black figure dragged the woman by her hair away from the window.

What he was witnessing was unexpected. It was time to do his job. He hammered on the window, shouting, "Police. Move away. Leave her alone."

The black shape looked up, cocked its head and then darkness.

"Stop shouting; people are trying to sleep," came a man's voice from a nearby upstairs window.

"Someone is beating your neighbour to death."

"Yeah – yeah – it's called a domestic – they're always at it. If you knock on the door, he'll tell you to F off. Good luck." At that juncture, the neighbour closed his window.

With a pounding heart and dry mouth, Stuart pushed the door open and entered. To his right were two doors. The woman was in the first room.

Where is the black shape? What will it do?

His chest thumped as his heart rate increased. Panning the torch beam around all he could see was a kitchen straight ahead and stairs to his left.

...Deep breaths. Keep your nerve; keep your nerve. I've got to go in.

He peered around the door spotting bundle on the floor.

"Police," he announced, "I'm here to help you."

"I'm here," she panted. "Hurry, I have a knife in me."

He flicked the nearby light switch, only to trigger a bang from the fuse box.

No time to waste.

He knelt.

"I'm here. What's your name?"

"Jacquie Willis."

"Do you know where he's gone?"

"No," she groaned. "Get this knife out. I'm bleeding to death."

She curled her fingers around the hilt.

"Don't pull it out. It's keeping you alive."

"Hurry, please," she wept. "I don't want to die."

"Right, Jacquie, I'll get an ambulance to help."

Stuart stood, feeling something pushing into his back. He closed his eyes as if to pray.

What, or who is behind me?

His body trembled, and his head filled with a dozen scenarios. Slowly he turned to face the shape of a man, his height, but of a bigger build.

"You've interfered tonight. That is bad news for you. The good news for me is, you won't be alive to tell tales," warned the black shape, grabbing Grant by his collar and throwing him hard against the wall. "You'll be joining her tonight."

"Please," hissed Grant, "stop!"

It was a red rag to a bull. The black shape pounded

Grant with hard fists, targeting his face and chest until he slumped face down to the floor. Gasping for breath Grant tried to push himself up before the weight of hands pushed him down and leaned into his neck.

"Tell me, when you woke this morning did you expect to die? You're in the wrong place at the wrong time."

*****

The police quickly cordoned off the crime scene. The leading officer recognised the modus operandi; It was Zodiac, an active serial killer who had been active for the last twelve months had struck again. He had entered a victim's house with no sign of forced entry and murdered a woman with no clues to suggest who he could be. Or if he knew her.

The victim, Jacquie Willis was Zodiac's eleventh victim. He chose his female victims according to their astrological signs and struck close to their birthdays. Journalists and the police considered him to be an enigma, an invisible man. Someone who lived his life, gathering no attention or suspicion.

With PC Grant lying dead next to a Zodiac victim two senior officers considered the possibility that Zodiac was from their ranks. After all, a police officer would draw very little attention from the public.

If he was the killer, did the dead woman defend herself? Did she stab the officer? Or were they the victims of a violent domestic incident? Alternatively, did their constable stumble on the murder and in doing his job Zodiac killed him?

CHAPTER 17

2014 | Taurus | Apr 21 – May 20

Denenmiss | Bucks | May 15th – 06:00 Hrs

The driver of a Toyota Land Cruiser accelerated and turned up the volume of the Heavy Metal music filling the cabin. He headbanged to the music and sung at the top of his voice.

Ahead, was a sharp left turn. He touched the brake pedal and gripped the steering wheel as the tyres screeched on the tarmac and thumped the grass verges. His eyes widened as white van approached. He centred his Toyota in the road and held his hands aloft for the white van driver to see.

It was a game of chicken.

Who would blink first?

The white van driver wrenched his steering wheel left off the road.

"King of the Road!" he screamed above the music. "Get out of my way 'cos I'm here."

Winding down the side window, he relished the breeze that blew through his hair and cooled his face. Easing off the accelerator, he glanced at the scenery.

This all looks familiar. Am I where I think I am?

When a white building standing in a large field came into view between the trees, he stamped on the brakes bringing the Toyota to a halt in a plume of dust.

He slipped the clutch and manoeuvred the Toyota into a lay-by where he leaned on the steering wheel.

After so long away. Why here? Will this be where I die? On my home ground?

He had a strong urge to leave his Toyota and walk the path to the door. He could knock. Would anyone be home?

It's time to get some sleep.

Killing the engine, he took another look at the building. With tiredness overpowering him, he crawled over the folded down rear seats into the boot and settled on blankets. He covered his eyes to block out the light. Within seconds, he was asleep.

07:00 to 18:00 Hrs

First, it drizzled. Later, the sun broke through the clouds. A mobile cafeteria pulled into the lay-by; ten minutes later, the aroma of bacon, eggs, sausages, tea and coffee wafted under the noses of a queue of customers followed by more hungry truckers.

More dark clouds passed overhead with rain followed by gusts of wind.

Two police constables in a tuned-up Hyundai Interceptor pulled in for breakfast. When one officer spotted the Toyota, they played a best of three 'Scissors, Paper, Stone' to decide who should wander over. The loser strolled to the Toyota 4x4 and scribbled the registration in his notebook. He checked through the windows, spotting nothing of concern. Placing his hand on the driver's door to look inside, his colleague called and waved him back to the car.

Memories of home | 19:30 Hrs

When daylight faded, and the stream of cars dwindled, he awoke. He uncovered his face, blinked twice then sat up and rubbed his eyes, ending with a stretch of his limbs. He checked the time before peering through the windows. There was one undeniable fact amongst his travels. He was where he was. 'Home' was minutes away.

With his sports bag in hand that held everything needed, he fixed his eyes on the door.

Wait until Mom opens the door and tells Dad I'm home. Oh boy, will we be celebrating. Happy voices, a smiling family? Where have you been? Why not call, email, or something? Why?

Why indeed?

…The day was humid as the sun shone high in the sky. He opened the rickety wooden gate and walked along the tarmacked path skimming his hand off the top of the long grass. Wading into the long grass, he picked a spot and lay down to stare at the blue sky and white clouds.

The creaking of the large oak doors opening made him sit up. He watched his parents hug and kiss before his father drove off. During the week he lived in London, returning at the weekend.

He pulled on a blade of grass and placed it in his mouth as his mother closed the doors. A short time passed before a taxi arrived. His mother appeared carrying a small overnight bag. On Mondays, she met with friends in Oxford where they checked into a luxury spa. Later they would spend the day shopping, eating, drinking with plenty of gossip. IN the early hours they took to their hotel beds to sleep the alcohol off… OH, Mother – wow, you fooled the world with your lies.

The house looked shabby rather than chic. The white walls were greying. Plaster fell from the bricks. In his time away, he was surprised. 'The Tanners' still stood.

But there was a problem. "How am I going to get in?" he muttered, standing before the heavy weather-beaten oak doors held together with bolts and strips of steel.

"Let's start with the iron handles." He gripped and turned them both, hearing the latch slip without releasing the locking mechanism.

A sudden pain in his torso made him double over. The increasing pain was not easy to ignore as he briefly checked the wound. He hung on until the pain subsided before roaming around the house. On every window, the security grilles he had fitted twenty years earlier were still in place – doing the job of keeping intruders out.

At the rear of the house, he glanced up at a high redbrick wall that enclosed a courtyard. Before his father bought the building intending it to be the family home, it was a hotel. The kitchen staff used the yard to store the bins, take deliveries and have the odd smoke.

He pushed open the weathered wooden gate that squeaked and creaked. The small concrete courtyard now over grown with weeds breaking through the concrete. One plant he did not remember was a mulberry bush close to the kitchen door.

I don't remember that.

He pushed it carefully aside to reveal an open window. Below it lay the grille. Had it fallen out or was it removed by someone?

…Could there be someone inside?

He threw his bag through the window and grabbed the vertical frames to pull himself up to the ledge. Instantly he felt more pain and the flow of blood. He switched on his torch and stepped onto the wooden floorboards that creaked under his weight.

…Was there anyone inside?

If there was an intruder he had no time to think what he would do. As the pain intensified, he hurried through the reception hall toward the staircase taking two at a time. He walked straight past three open doors before entering the fourth room and closed the door. He was home in his former bedroom, safe and protected from the world outside.

The bedroom needed light. Facing the grille, he turned the central handle. The four bolts squealed from the metal frames and fell away. Heaving the bulky apparatus to the floor, he faced the twilight and the dark outline of the distant hills…

…He held his breath as someone on the other side pushed and tugged at the handle. They are not coming into my room

tonight; this is my place.' Downstairs he could hear his mother laughing with her guests. Was she drunk? It mattered not. Either way, she was a tyrant who ordered and bossed people around as they abused her father's house. 'How dare they?'

Outside, the voices grew louder.

Above the inbuilt wardrobes was a storage area. By opening a door, he could use the shelves to step up to the storage area, open a door, climb in and close the door. From there he could access the attic. It was a dark but a safe place from where he could watch the despicable people who desecrated his home...

The continuing pain in his torso needed attention. A slow trickle of blood was staining his clothes red. Dropping his kit bag, he removed a first-aid kit and a five-litre bottle of mineral water, two phials of morphine and a syringe.

Ripping off his T-shirt and denim, he threw them aside. He cleaned and bandaged the wound that ran from below his right ribs to his hip. Finally injecting himself with morphine, the pain relief kicked in.

He had a question.

Why had he come home, a place that held dark haunting memories that lingered deep in his mind?

Pinner | North West London

The previous evening had seen the tables against him almost turned. He waited for Paula Reed to return home. They had met two weeks earlier. As she was about to seduce him, he made an excuse and left, offering to return and make her birthday special. Nothing wrong with that, she thought, despite her need for sex. She would enjoy their meeting on her birthday. However, Paula had suspicions. When she thought about his charm, his smooth talk, knowing what to say and how to express himself, it all sounded too good to be true.

When she entered her front door, she threw her laptop case to one side. Minutes later, she sat down with a large glass of white wine. There she remained in silence before slipping to her bedroom. She returned, wearing her dressing gown and disappeared into her wet room.

He stripped off his clothing and snuck into the steam-filled room, ready with his weapon of choice – a knife. Standing under the open doorway prepared to strike, he felt a tap on his shoulder. As he turned, Paula hit him with a large metal tube that sent him stumbling back across the floor. She followed up with the metal tube and whacked him in the chest.

Before he could recover, she struck him twice in the face with balled fists then deftly kicked the knife from his grip. A painful kick to the groin doubled him over as Paula picked the blade up and faced him.

"My suspicions about you are correct. I told myself if you turned up tonight for my birthday, then you are who I suspect you are."

"Who am I?"

"You're that Zodiac killer fella. You murdered Theresa Baldwin, the mother of my best friend."

"I don't remember names!" he countered.

'I do. That's my secret.'

"She was thirty years old with a young child when you hacked her to bits in her home." Paula raised her fists. "C'mon, you coward, make my day. Fight a real woman."

In anger, he lashed out with his fists, forgetting the first

81

lesson his mentor taught him. When in a fight, control your punches and don't lash out. Make every punch count. Before he had the chance, Paula struck him, causing him to slip.

She stood naked over him, her muscular frame honed and streamlined. Her next move was to cause him agony and drain his strength. Armed with his own knife, she cut him diagonally from under his right ribs across to his left hip. Standing back to admire her work, she threw the knife to one side. It slid into the open drain handle first, leaving the blade exposed above the floor.

"Look at you," scoffed Paula as he struggled to his feet. "You're injured and bleeding. So, try me! You don't scare me." At that point, he could detect distinct sociopathic tendencies. That meant she would be fierce and unrelenting. It was either him or her!

She approached and struck him with a balled fist, not once, but twice. A third strike whipped his neck back where it was past painful. He had no time to recover as she punched him twice in his face, making his neck spasm. Dazed and surprised he squared up while blood flowed from his mouth and dripped from his nose.

"You're serious!" he snivelled.

"Either you deal with me or the police, 'tis up to you, Zodiac man."

'…A bold statement. She fancies herself…'

To strike back, he let all tension in his body go and dropped to the ground, grabbed her foot and pulled her to the wet floor. Her lightning reflex was a quick and painful heel kick to his head and then the shoulder. She rolled away and stood. Once again, her speed caught him when she moved forward and twice kicked him as he lay on the floor, leaving him stunned and in pain.

If he did not protect himself, she would kill him. He caught a look of pure contempt on her face as she dropped and kicked his feet away. As he crashed to the hard floor, taking more kicks, he thought it could be the end.

Paula grabbed a large towel from a hook and cracked it twice before gripping the ends and pulling it over his face. Using her considerable strength, she hauled him to his feet while keeping the towel tight over his face and neck.

Seconds later, they were back to back. Paula intended to choke the life from him as she bent over and pulled him onto her back. Feeling his feet leave the floor, it was time for a cool head.

'Keep calm, don't struggle else you do the job for her.'

The towel dug into his neck, constricting his airways. He tried to slip his fingers underneath the cloth to relieve the choking pressure on his neck only to feel Paula pull tighter.

His weight on her back, not helped by his flailing legs meant she was at risk of slipping on the wet floor. She needed to hang on. Letting go would mean a battle with a pissed off killer. 'You gotta keep going here, girl. Pull harder until he chokes to death and stops moving.'

He grunted, shifting his weight. Paula felt his weight shift. She gaped in disbelief as he stood before her. Caught on the hop, she was slow to strike as he grabbed her legs, picked her up, and carried her two steps. He dropped her over the drain onto the exposed blade.

The pained look on her face said it all as the blade entered between her shoulders. As she uttered, "Help me," through a blood-filled mouth, she caught his relieved gaze. Luck had kept him alive. He leaned against the wall and used the towel to cover his wound, aware that he was losing consciousness.

When he came to, cold water flowed from the showerhead.

He shivered from the pain and cold. Paula remained in place, eyes open, mouth agape. He crawled away from the splashing water and examined his wound. She had cut to the muscle. An expert cut meant to cause pain but not inflect damage.

On his way out, he stopped to look at her Mixed Martial Arts certificate hanging on a wall. She had been a lethal weapon. It was luck that saved him from a severe beating.

'Next time don't choose a victim that can fight.'

1990 | Sun, signs and victims

The Tanners – his childhood home was not always a place of security and safety. His stepmother held parties that attracted paedophiles. Those who abused prostitutes. If one stepped out of line – a sadistic line in torture followed.

Hidden away in dark spaces, he witnessed the cruelty and fighting regarding it as a natural act. It led to an obsession with death and a step up the ladder. He began torturing and killing any domestic or wild creature, that crossed his path.

He never regarded an animal he was about to kill as cute. His motive was to study its reaction to pain and see how long it would live as he cut it apart? It was a discovery, biology even. Days later signs would appear around the village, posted by owners searching for their missing pets. The entire experience was fun and an exercise in control and power.

At sixteen, he craved the experience to see first-hand how a person looked in their death throes.

From his hiding place, he listened to three men

discuss hook-up spots in Aylesbury, High Wycombe and Oxford; meeting points where men and women seeking sex could socialise in the open.

The hook-up spots were held in either pubs, selected houses or venues where entry was available to those in the loop.

So where were these houses and pubs?

After weeks of planning he followed the same men to a pub. Because of his height and size, he could buy a beer with no problem. However, it took three visits before a man who talked to everyone approached with an offer.

"If you're looking for some action, slip me a tenner, and I'll introduce you to the party."

"A tenner?"

"Yeah, but that buys you nothing, 'cos nothing is free once you're in there. Make sure you have cash as well. Without any, guests might think you're taking the piss and will kick you out."

Handing over a ten-pound note with a quick, "OK," it was as easy as that!

The parties were similar to his mother's; guests smoked weed and got naked. The difference was the guests were more interested in blowjobs, wanking, muff diving and getting laid.

One woman, named Celia, attracted his attention as she worked three men at the same time. She looked good with a slim body. But why was she there?

He found out later when she approached him.

"Are you a voyeur, mister?"

"What do you mean?"

"Was you getting a hard-on watching me blow those three geezers off?"

"I'm interested in you," was his hesitant reply, finding her approach provided a stimulus to his excitement.

"Why would you be interested in me?"

"Err," shrugging his shoulders, he stuttered before finding his words, "I'm interested."

"Are you interested in me blowing you – or do you have something more perverted in mind?"

"Whatever you do."

"I've seen you watching me getting banged." She looked him over. "I think you get off watching people. It gets you horny. Later, on your own, you have a jolly good wank. So, you wanna get naked with me and fuck?"

...*She's forthright.*

"Yes!" he replied, desperate to try this new experience.

...*Hurry, I can't wait much longer...*

"Would ya prefer a private party – you and me – or do you want to put a show on for the perverts? It's called dogging."

Dogging? he thought as her fingers gripped his hand and led him outside to the street. *What the hell is dogging?*

"Where are we going?"

"To my house."

"Where is that?"

She pointed to a door. "Before we go inside, keep your noise down as I don't want my kids woken."

"Do you have a babysitter?"

"Have you got money to pay for a babysitter? Or would you like the job? I then pay you in kind. I've got no money. So, everything is on the cheap."

"Who looks after the children?"

"I have a ten-year-old daughter who puts the young uns to bed and sings them a lullaby before she goes to bed!"

"OK."

"Have you got any more personal questions," she queried, looking him in the eye, "or do we do the business?"

Once inside she pointed to a dirty, worn-out armchair. "Sit there while I check the children," she ordered.

Minutes later, she returned with a wide smile.

"You're new to this, ain't ya?"

"Yes."

"How old are ya?"

"Old enough for you."

She smiled. It was not the first time she had entertained an underage teenager who had come into cash and decided to spend it on a sexual encounter.

"OK." She lifted her skirt. "Will you give me a good seeing to now or later? It's up to you."

"Now."

"Before we begin, I have rules." Holding out her hand, she continued. "Cash now, if you please. I don't give change for the odd fiver or give an extra gobble on yer cock. No kissing on the lips and don't expect me to cum. You cum. I stop. So, as you're new to this, put a cork in your cock or use two or three condoms to desensitise you. I don't want you complaining after thirty seconds you want another go. You got that?"

"Yes, I understand."

"Good. There's the bedroom behind you. Go in. Undress, put on the rubbers. I'll be with you soon."

Handing over the cash, he wandered into a dirty, smelly bedroom. He stripped and climbed onto the bed and pulled a sheet up to his chin. When Celia appeared and posed naked against the doorframe holding a whip, his mouth ran dry. She spoke in a husky voice, sending his excitement levels jumping tenfold.

"Right," she pouted. "My name is Madame Pain. Lesson number one is coming up, big boy. Pain is close to pleasure; I hope you enjoy it?"

*****

The first experience was enlightening and he wanted more. As a result, his presence around the hook-up spots was noticeable because he paid up front and asked no questions. As a reminder he was on a mission, he rotated his visits. Considering what he was planning, familiarity did not seem like a good idea.

He met Kylie Jenner, a single welfare dependant mother, who preferred to keep his visits a secret. Discretion, uppermost in her mind. A regular caller meant regular money – something her pimp, Matty Garrett did not tolerate. Like her friends, she worked the streets. Her welfare benefits did not stretch to life's little luxuries and a treat for the children.

In a naïve, immature way, she told fascinating tales of her clients – the desperate men with no life and smelly bodies because bathing or showering was not their thing.

One evening, she read her horoscope. It predicted a high end to the day. For a reason, the topic interested him.

"Tell me more," he urged, "I'd like to learn more about horoscopes."

"Well, for instance, I'm a Cancerian, the sign of the Crab, born on the 2nd of July. We're kind and caring towards people."

"When is your birthday?" she asked curious.

"I'm a Gemini. What does that mean?"

" Oh, Gemini is a twin, denoting a split personality, and you're self-centred apparently." Kylie grasped a small pair of scissors from the bedside table and jabbed the scissors around. "We may need to cut your evil twin away and leave the good twin."

"Does that mean I'm schizophrenic?" he queried as a sudden storm in his head fired mixed messages. His eyes rolled upwards as a mantra of voices screeched instructions, throwing his mind into a chaotic blur of thoughts.

Kylie frowned at her guest's sudden change in temperament. "That's a big word for a Saturday night. What does that mean?"

His mind darkened. She had a weapon.

Kylie jumped from the bed and glowered at him. "You're scaring me – you look evil."

In an absorbing trance, he stepped off the bed and swung a punch that knocked Kylie out cold. Wrenching the scissors from her fingers, he slashed at her body. In the doorway of the bedroom her daughter appeared.

'What are you doing?" she asked looking sleepy and confused at the noise.

"Go back to bed, my child. Your mother and I are playing a game. Don't come out until morning."

The daughter eyed him curiously and closed the door.

*****

In the aftermath, the police were speaking to suspects that included himself. He had a crucial alibi, his mother. Her boy was at home, where else would he be? Pauline did not want the police turning up when she was entertaining, or, anytime at all. Whatever Martin did she ignored. Whether she had seen him or not, she told the same story. He was at home doing whatever.

The police buzzed the area for a week before their presence dwindled. The only witness was her child who described her mother's killer as a man with a red face who spoke like the devil.

When the police shifted their enquiries elsewhere, he continued his quest in Oxford and met a prostitute named Melina who catered for his needs in return for supplying her with crack cocaine. One evening after a dissatisfying evening of sex, he refused her demands for drugs. Melina made the mistake of pulling a knife and holding it against his neck. He allowed her threats to continue until she removed the blade. His reaction was to beat her until she fell unconscious. However, before using his knife, he had a thought.

If I kill her, do I leave her here, or do I get rid of the body?

An idea came to mind. One house, four doors along, was derelict, used by junkies and the homeless. Behind the house, was a narrow path closed in by six-foot-high brick walls on one side and garages on the other – no one would see him because there were no streetlights.

Problem solved – yes!

Wrapping her body in a blanket, he carried her to the house. The pungent odour of the spliff and cheap cider filled the room. In the lounge, a fire roared away in the hearth. Nearby slept two men in dirty well-worn sleeping bags.

He nudged both men with his foot. Neither stirred nor raised a murmur. They were sleeping in a drunken stupor unaware of the trouble ahead.

A perfect situation!

He dropped her body between the two men and withdrew his knife and slashed at Celia. Shuffling away to admire his work, he visualised the two men explaining her death to the police when covered in her blood.

*****

In the early hours, he lay on his bed. His violent actions never registered on his conscience. Why should they? They meant nothing to him. Digging into his pockets, he found Kylie's Astrological pendant. While turning it through his fingers, an idea came to mind; to kill his victims while their star sign was in the ascendant. That would keep the police busy chasing their tails.

However, to target women by their star signs would not be easy. He could not go around asking because that would raise suspicions. So, the question was – how would he manage to find the lucky women? Also, what about the subject of Astrology. Should he learn about it? No! All he needed to know was the dates at which the various signs were on the horizon.

CHAPTER 18

1992 | Dealing With the Pimps

Money, the favourite topic of the pimps. They pushed their girls to the limit, the driving force behind it all being money, and plenty of it. Most of the women who worked the streets were forced into prostitution because of a debt they could not repay. To make ends meet they borrowed money from loan sharks. Due to the excessive interest charges many could not meet the payments.

The pimps, who worked with the loan sharks moved in like vultures taking control of the girls by acquiring their debt. When the pimps forced them to hand over their bank debit cards, and welfare books they had no option to do as they were told, else face the consequences. Many relied on Food Banks to feed their young families while the pimps raked in the cash.

After watching from the sidelines for weeks he identified two in particular. Matty Garrett a tall, surly, arrogant character from Oxford who had a thing for Kylie. He would pester her continuously; yet somehow, she kept him at arm's length. He had a loathsome personality who would show porn movies to his girls hoping they would find inspiration.

The second pimp went by his initials – JAG. If you wanted him the advice was to follow the trail of Marlboro cigarette smoke to the nearest pub. There you would find him enjoying a pint of extra cold Guinness.

Both men were bitter rivals and had come to blows in the street. Their confrontations were amusing, a comedy routine standing a metre apart in full view of everyone calling each other names with taunts about their mothers, and as for their granny, what a GILF. Matty kept promising to cave Jag's head in with an axe he kept at home. – two immature men with visions of grandeur.

What would happen if he brought both men together in private, away from prying eyes? Would Matty use an axe to attack Jag? To satisfy his curiosity he would plan ahead and see what would happen. It could be an interesting encounter.

*****

Garrett awoke with a raging headache and thirst after a heavy night on the tiles with his friends. Drinking with best buddies was fun, but the morning-after hangover meant in most cases, he lost a day's earnings.

Unable to stave off the call of nature, he shuffled to the bathroom aware of music coming from downstairs followed by voices. After relieving himself, he grabbed his dressing gown and hobbled down the stairs to the kitchen. Sitting at his table was JAG and a stranger who stood to introduce himself.

"Hello, I hope you don't mind. We've helped

ourselves to some breakfast."

"I recognise JAG, but who are you?"

"You invited us back last night. Don't you remember?"

"No, I don't." Garrett scratched his head, trying to remember meeting the stranger. "Where were we when we met?"

"At the 'Red Lion' on the high street."

"I don't remember being there." Garrett pointed to JAG, swaying from side to side.

"I do," coughed JAG. "You sat with us to discuss business and how to make more cash."

Matthew sat as the stranger switched on the kettle. "I remember nothing."

"The 'Red Lion', that's where we met," quipped the stranger, eyeing Matthew. JAG burst into a giggle drawing Matthew's contempt.

"Why are you still here?" queried Matthew towards JAG. "Go home."

"Because we didn't finish our business," responded JAG, "and I want in."

"How about an axe in your head?" retorted Matthew. "I'm not making deals with you, JAG; I can't stand the sight of you."

"Be polite, Matty, and ease up," interrupted the stranger. "We're here to discuss new opportunities over bacon sandwiches."

"Who are you again?" demanded Matthew, peering at the stranger with suspicion.

"Let's call me the facilitator as I brought you both together."

"What have you got to drink?" asked JAG. "Because I'd like a drink!"

"You're always drinking and smoking, JAG. It's a sport for you. The bad news, I have no Guinness."

The facilitator poured hot water into three cups, added milk and slid the cups to Matty and JAG who grabbed at the handles.

"You're soft in the head… fa – fa – whatever your name is!" scoffed Matty. "I ain't doing business with a geezer who's a crook and rips people off."

"He's soft in the head," responded JAG, nodding at the facilitator. "Why don't you soften his head 'cos he might listen to sense?"

"I tell you what," sneered Matty, "I'll soften JAG's head."

JAG pouted as he snapped a response. "I have a brother in the army who will do you for doing me."

"Where's your brother?" queried the facilitator. "He's not here. Have you told him where you are for your safety?"

"Yeah, he does."

The facilitator moved to the cooker and placed a frying pan over a heated hob. "Shall I make the bacon sandwiches?"

"I'd like kebab and chips with chilli sauce," suggested Matty. "I can't speak for him."

"You got no class, you miserable Banbury shithead," retorted JAG. "CHIPS, KEBAB and chilli sauce. Can't you eat anything else?"

"Ah," interrupted the facilitator, "I have a kebab with chilli sauce."

"Is it fresh? I could end up ill it's off."

"Yes. As of last night," answered the facilitator, placing a hot kebab on the table.

A hungry JAG tapped his fingers as Matty ate the kebab. "Can I have some?" asked JAG. "I'm hungry."

"No, it's mine!"

"How greedy are you?"

"In my house, I'll be as greedy as I like."

After demolishing the kebab and licking the chilli sauce from his fingers, Garrett grinned and rubbed his belly before emitting a loud belch.

"You're cheap, Matty," sneered JAG.

"Fuck you."

Matty stood and forcefully pushed his chair back. The facilitator placed an arm on JAG's shoulder as Matty stumbled through to the garage, returning with something behind his back. Pointing to JAG, he said, "I have a gift for you, my Welsh friend!"

JAG laughed at the suggestion. "What are you talking about?"

"Why are you in my house, JAG?" demanded Matty. "'Cos, I don't like you. I don't want you here."

JAG pointed at the facilitator. "This fella brought us here to talk business and deals." With a roll of his head, JAG stood to face Garrett.

"Stay where you are, JAG," warned Garrett.

"You've always got a sad tale or two up your sleeve of self-inflicted misfortunes or stories of an ex-girlfriend's woes. You attract women by making believe you care about other women. You know how to wind women around your finger. You're a predator. When you've shagged them and taken what you can – you shit all over them. You're a parasite who treats people like shit."

Noting Matthew's growing anger, the facilitator whispered, "Go on." Guessing what Matthew was holding he continued. "Do it, bury the axe in his skull. Then you'll be free to expand your harem of prossies who will make you loads of money," whispered the facilitator. "Go on, Matthew – do it!"

*****

Two police constables entered Matthew Garrett's house after a tip-off. The sight of a naked man with deep slash marks across his torso and legs with an axe in his head left them gagging for air.

After calling for support, they found Matty asleep on top of his bed covered in blood. Unable to wake him, the police called an ambulance. Twenty-four hours passed before doctors considered him fit for an interview.

After a full morning of questions, that Matty could not answer, the detective in charge produced photographs of JAG; Garrett's response was first to smile, then laugh. The smile disappeared when he recognised his kitchen. He denied everything. However, his fingerprints were all over the handle of the axe. JAG's blood was all over his clothes.

`Later, their SOCO colleagues found a blood-stained bank card and personal property belonging to Kylie Jenner stashed away in his draws.

When the magistrate read the charges against him, Matty repeated what he had told the police. He was a friend of Kylie Jenner but could not account for her murder or JAG's. His recollection of facts was a total failure.

What he remembered was a man called the fascinator who cooked a meal of kebab and chips.

*****

The significant presence of police in the area on a clean-up exercise ended his flirtation with the hook-up spots. His attempts to be discreet were time-consuming. He asked too many questions. Prostitutes and pimps were growing suspicious. Why did he want their personal details when the rule was discretion. That meant exchanging no personal information?

However, his dad offered him a job. When the job was explained, he could do nothing but smile. His plans were falling into place.

CHAPTER 19

2014 | Cancer | June 21 – July 22

July 2nd | Meeting the stranger | 23:55

Richard always welcomed quirks of fate that changed his life for the better. When friends invited him to a City of London charity function, he quickly accepted. One guest drew his attention. His demeanour, the cut of his hair, the tailored suit, the polished shoes suggested a pot of gold at the end of the rainbow. Wasting no time, he walked straight up to the stranger with a smile.

"I'm Richard. My job is retail!"

"I know your speciality!"

"You do?"

"You sell a commodity I buy."

"What commodity would that be?"

"Give me your card. When I decide to buy your commodity, I'll call twenty-four hours in advance. I'll tell you what I want. You give me the price."

*****

The stranger stuck to his word and called on a

semi-regular basis. When they met Richard showed the goods, and the stranger paid the price.

However, the stranger was sparking Richard's interest. Who was he? Where did he live and for whom did he buy the heroin? He wanted to meet at a personal level. Something told him it would be worth his while.

Richard had a rare night off and was entering his favourite restaurant when a taxi pulled up. From it stood the stranger who beckoned to him. "Get in. Please join two friends and me for dinner. It will be a good evening."

*****

The restaurant was one he had walked passed many times. It was expensive, belonging to TV celebrity chefs. The name of the chef mattered not. All he wanted was to eat. They headed towards a table where two attractive ladies were sitting holding tall glasses filled with champagne.

"Ladies, may I introduce Richard. He'll be joining us. Introduce yourselves."

The woman nearest to him looked up with startling green eyes and patted the seat next to her. "I'm Davina, that's my bestest friend Helen."

"And I'm Jack Kruger."

"Pleased to meet you all," responded Richard, shuffling closer to Davina.

"Now you know my name; please take the opportunity to expand your social circle and start with these delightful ladies. I've earmarked this as an evening of fun," reaching for the champagne. "We'll finish this, have more, have a meal, then we're off to an exclusive club up West for an evening of dance!"

"Will we get in?" queried Richard to Jack.

"My influence knows no bounds!"

23:45 | Belgravia

Stumbling out of the taxi, Helen and Davina waited while Jack paid the driver. Inside Richard marvelled at the size of the lounge and the furnishings. Never had he seen such opulence and wealth on display. He had well and truly hit the jackpot.

Davina and Helen kicked off their killer heels and settled themselves cross-legged next to the coffee table. Their eyes widened when Jack placed a silver bowl on the table.

Davina winked at Richard as she removed the lid. Inside was the heroin Jack had bought the previous day from Richard. Davina tipped the white powder onto the table and used her credit card to cut the heroin into lines.

Davina rolled a twenty-pound note and snorted two lines before rolling over as Helen went through the same routine. Jack said nothing. He never touched the stuff. Neither did Richard. People made their choices and lived by them.

It had been a long day, and Jack could no longer hide the fact he was tired.

"There's beer in the fridge and snacks should you want them. Sleep where you like. We'll speak in the morning."

July 3rd | 01:10 Hrs

Moonlight filtered through the windows as he sat up to check on his three guests. All were asleep. Creeping upstairs, he undressed and pulled on dark clothing before leaving the house.

Rickmansworth | Mddx | 02:00 Hrs

Sara Raye returned home and poured a large glass of white wine. He birthday bash was fun-packed and the celebrations passed all too soon. Laughter, mirth and girly chat. What more could she want.

Sinking on the sofa, she opened her handbag and removed a ready-rolled spliff, lit it, and took a long drag. She switched on the television and channel hopped until she found a music program. As the spliff and wine slowed her senses, she mimed the lyrics trying to imagine herself as a pop star when she recognised a man whom she met only weeks earlier standing in her kitchen.

"What are you doing here?" she asked as her mouth ran dry.

"Hello, you invited me over to wish you many happy returns. How was your birthday night out?" He approached to stand feet away.

"Where did you come from?" she snapped. "Did you knock?"

"My apologies. We're here to have fun," he answered with a glint.

"HOW DID YOU GET IN?"

"The door was open."

"Don't you knock like other people? I want you to leave NOW!"

"From the moment I met you, I knew that you'd break my heart," he feigned looking at her contorted face.

"Go away," she retorted, pushing him in the chest. "Please leave. I'm tired."

"I will then leave."

"Get out!"

She waited until he had left before jumping up to lock and chain the door.

The cheek of the man. How dare he? What a creep. I can't even remember his name.

Shaking and breathing deeply, she shuffled towards the kitchen. A movement to her left caught her attention.

It was nothing.

With a shrug, she stepped into the kitchen and grabbed a small bottle of mineral water from the fridge. A sound behind made her turn.

"Hello, who's there?"

Her eyes widened, and the hairs on the nape of her neck bristled. A gaggle of goose pimples covered her skin. Her mouth ran dry.

"Who's there? Stop this. You're scaring me."

Her heart leapt when a tall, dark outline moved close and whispered, "Many happy returns, Sara."

Conversations with the Past

All day the unearthly voices that taunted him faded. As daylight gave way to a moonlit sky, he pushed away from his chair, untied his robe and removed his aviator-style sunglasses.

Stopping before a full-length mirror, he spent an egotistical minute gazing at his 'six-pack' and his overall taut physique. Patting his abdomen, he strolled to the bathroom as a familiar voice called to him.

"You have killed again?"

"Mother – can you not see I'm about to bathe?"

"You have nothing I haven't seen before!"

Her dark eyes and pale skin shimmered into being as she circled like a vulture waiting to feed on the remnants of carrion.

She thrust out her arms, leaned forward to release a rush of sound that filled his head with voices. Crumpling to the tiled floor with his ears covered, a sickening stench filled the surrounding space. He gagged as her pale skin split while a grey glaze formed over her eyes that turned black. They dissolved to reveal a myriad of worms inside the recess of her skull.

Hearing a thump, he retched as a putrid decayed body with a cracked skull landed beside him, got to its decaying feet and limped away. A despairing scream ripped through the air before another three, four, five, up to ten bodies dropped through thin air.

Their hollow black eyes focussed on his presence as they either walked or limped away while their bodies fell apart. They formed two lines through which a woman appeared wearing a red chiffon robe. She stopped to glare down at him with back soulless eyes.

"I'm here, my son, to keep you company."

He spoke and stared with utter contempt. "For a dead woman, you seem intent on harassing me with your army of the dead. What is it you want, Mother?"

"Your life."

"You're predictable. Try another story; else fade away and leave me alone."

"You told lies to your father about the company I kept. I kept telling you they existed only in your imagination."

"They were real, Mother. Unlike you."

"No. They were not real. You have never spoken to living people."

"Leave me be and return to your cold grave and lead your creatures away."

His mother shimmied and wailed like a banshee beckoning her followers to her. "Let me warn you, my son. You cannot avoid your death. It stalks and walks closer every day."

CHAPTER 20

2014 | Leo | July 23 – August 22

July 25th

In Bushey, police responded to a call from a woman who had not seen her neighbour, Jeanette Brown, for over a week. When they entered her property, they found her corpse. Looped through her fingers was a pendant depicting the astrological sign of Leo.

August 17th | A disturbing discovery

Walking through the fields was a daily routine for Tricia Strong and her two Irish red setters. In recent days they had shown more than a passing interest in 'The Tanners'. Until recently, they ignored the building; now they stopped to howl in its direction before descending into a barking frenzy.

After watching their unusual behaviour, she gave in to curiosity. Clipping the dogs to their leads, she allowed them to drag her to the house into the courtyard. They stopped close to the broken rear window where they sniffed and yelped at the window.

A touch of apprehension settled as the dogs barked ever louder; she peered through the window into the darkness. When she took a deep breath, a pungent smell caught her throat, making her gag. Tense, she stepped back, gripping her mobile; she pressed Emergency and retreated to a safe distance while the dogs continued snarling at the window before fleeing with their tails down.

Forty-five minutes later, the same police officers who six weeks earlier stopped in the lay-by to buy refreshments turned up. As Tricia Young calmed her dogs the two police constables, Young and Henry, played a best of three game of 'Paper, Scissors, Stone' to decide who would go inside to look. The loser, PC Young, tied a handkerchief over his nose and mouth before Henry helped him through the window where he disappeared into the darkness.

Minutes later, from inside, a frantic PC Young was banging on the inside of the oak doors; as his calls became more desperate, PC Henry pushed and pulled at the doors.

Moments later a bewildered and horrified PC Young hauled open the doors and collapsed on the tiled patio looking deathly pale. PC Henry stared inside as an audible low humming sound emanated from the darkness. Pulling the doors closed, he dropped to his knees before vomiting.

*****

Police erected an incident tent against the doors of 'The Tanners'. Four SOCO members dressed in white overalls and wearing eye protection entered. As the individual officers showed their readiness to proceed, two pushed open the oak doors. Spotlights were activated, lighting up the large reception hall. From within came a humming sound drawing closer and louder.

Seconds later, a humming pall of darkness swooped down over the SOCO members as millions of flies turned the interior of the tent black.

There was more to come. Rats in various sizes scampered into the tent weaving in between and over each other, seeking a way out. The SOCO team flapped their arms around and kicked away at the rats, colliding and stumbling as they did.

The police officers outside the tent gaped in astonishment as the tent collapsed. Four SOCO members scrambled to their feet as a swarm of flies dispersed while the rats scampered away in different directions.

Along the boundaries of the field, curious onlookers used their mobiles to record the scene. What were the police looking for? The place was abandoned. Anyone with sense stayed clear of the building. Never mind going inside.

When a whisper amongst the crowd mentioned the missing teenagers, the onlookers switched off their cameras and dialled their friends to spread the word.

Within thirty minutes, the anxious parents of all the teenagers had gathered demanding answers while others continued recording the scenes with their smartphones.

*****

The overpowering pungent smell of rotting flesh

met the SOCOs and technicians rigging the lighting equipment.

When a police dog handler arrived, his springer spaniel headed straight to a small gap between the staircase and the wooden floor and sat down. The dog handler lay on the ground catching the smell full on. Jumping to his feet, he examined the panelling on the side of the staircase.

"What are you doing?" asked a police constable.

"I have an idea this staircase is hiding a secret entrance."

"Can we break it down?" suggested the PC.

"If we do, we could destroy evidence," scoffed the dog handler.

"Quite right," boomed the voice of a uniformed Police Inspector Nathan Scott who entered the hall. "We can't afford to destroy evidence."

"What do you suggest, Inspector?" queried a detective. "Can you find a way under? Because I can't see one."

"There's a door behind the stairs. Before you ask how I know – I don't – but, as a lad growing up nearby, we heard the rumours of a secret tunnel running from the village to this place. That staircase could be the entrance. On that staircase is a hidden switch that will move the stairs."

Two officers tapped, pushed, and twisted anything that would prove the inspector's theory correct. More by luck, the dog handler touched the right anomaly.

A click followed as the staircase moved away from the wall to reveal as the inspector suggested, a hidden door. A SOCO member stood forward and opened the door. They recoiled when a dead naked male body splashed to the floor, releasing further the pungent odour of rotting flesh.

*****

Ryan Norton, a rookie in matters of Crime Scenes, stood over the trapdoor in the reception hall. Gripping the handle, he pulled it up, then let it fall over with a bang. Everyone stopped what they were doing wondering what they had heard as the vibrations rippled throughout the house. He apologised to three police officers standing nearby who approached to take a curious look as Ryan stepped into the circular stairwell.

Would he find anything?

He panned the torch around, as a shiver ran along his spine, unsettled at the shadows created by his flashlight. On the way to the house, two of his colleagues recited tales of the house and its violent history. For no logical reason, he expected to see a body torn apart. Maybe a group of flesh-eating zombies.

My colleagues don't half talk a load of bull.

Above his head were thick cobwebs hanging from the ceiling. It reminded him of the Ghost Train, a funfair ride. In the light of his torch, the fibres looked like old net curtains that over time, had fallen apart. The strands hung onerous with grey dust touching to the ground.

Another shiver ran along his spine, making him hunch his shoulders as he stopped by the refrigerator.

It's spooky down here. Why do I feel so nervous?

Gripping the handle, he tugged three times, hearing a crack as the stem snapped and a hiss of air followed as the door opened enough to swing it open. He pointed the torch beam inside the dark, square-shaped room.

Five objects lay on a four-tiered storage shelf unit. He touched both ends of the nearest object – at a guess, it was over five feet, as were the rest.

What were they?

Using his torch to peer at the lowest object, he looked closer and closer, uncertain of what was behind the cellophane. He swept away a thin layer of dust before placing the torch on the polystyrene.

Is that a face? Surely not.

He moved to the next object. Blowing away the dust, he looked closer.

Tempted to run as he was, he checked the remaining four objects. Certain about what was under the polystyrene he backed out of the refrigerator and dashed upstairs.

Inspector Scott, hearing the rushing sound of footsteps watched as Ryan, in distinct part distress and part excitement struggled to get his words out.

"Easy, easy lad. What have you seen?"

"I counted five bodies in an old refrigerator. They look like they've mummified."

Events ramped up when an hour later his two SOCO colleagues found the six teenagers lying together in the 'dead zone' along with more bodies.

What they found was beyond imagination.

The uninvited

The noisy opening and closing of the oak doors was followed by loud voices echoing throughout the building. He watched from his bedroom as lanterns were used to light the hall to the delight of two teenage boys. He felt some relief it was not a full-scale biker bash, a police raid, or something worse. However, they were intruders. Uninvited guests who were having a conversation.

"You checked this place out last week?"

"My old man tells me no one has lived here for like, mega years, man."

"Hey, dude, a lunatic lived here once. A right maniac who beat boys up."

Am I that lunatic? Interesting!

"The last owners had far-out druggie parties with like gangsters, and other like, cool dudes!"

"Yeah, well I heard the loony who lived here went 'loop-the-loop' and beat people up."

They high fived.

"A homeless dude told me that if I broke into an abandoned house and lived in it for twelve years and made it a permanent home – it would be mine."

Not on your life. No way. Get your own house.

"Yo, man! How rad. You'd own the mansion, dude. You could party every night! So, hey, dude, you gotta key?"

"At the rear, there's a broken window. I found the key on a hook."

How could I forget that?

"Do your parents know where you are?"

"Hey, dude, you gotta be kiddin' me – like, they'd be doing one if they thought I was here!"

"Like, I told mine I'm dossin' over at Pete's house 'cos his parents are away. We're pulling a late-nighter."

"Have you got any gear?"

"YUP, I got the skunk to get hiiiigh."

When a third teenager arrived with three teenage girls, the group hugged.

Upstairs, keeping out of sight, he considered leaving.

…No, I'm not going!

Why should I go?

It's my house!

When the music started, he stepped onto the landing hoping to catch sight of the intruders drinking their beer and smoking their skunk.

I'll introduce myself later and what fun we will have!

Dealing with intruders

Much to his disgust two teenagers entered his room carrying a camping lantern and bedded down. Their noisy shagging was driving him to distraction, but for the time being he let them continue. Why spoil their fun at the moment? When the music and voices from downstairs came to a sudden stop Daisy and Paul continued.

Why were they desecrating his house? These

trespassers had no right to enter without his permission and use it as their pleasure palace, disturbing his need for space and tranquillity.

The uninvited would see no mercy.

How to play this? Kill two birds with one knife, or pull them apart and run them through individually?

Their noises stopped. Paul stood.

"Where are you going?" asked Daisy.

"I need a piss."

"The toilet is down the landing."

"I'll piss in the corner; no one will know."

"No, you won't," reprimanded Daisy. "Go to the toilet."

Muttering under his breath, Paul grabbed a torch and wandered off down the landing while Daisy rolled over.

*****

Daisy sighed when Paul slipped under the sleeping bag, "Where have you been? I'm cold; warm me up."

She cooed at the touch of his warm body, positioning himself against her.

"I wonder what they're doing downstairs?" queried Daisy, touching Paul's leg. "They're quiet down there; I was expecting more – em – more… noise."

She giggled as she caressed Paul's buttocks then stopped. Something was not right as she moved her hand further along Paul's legs. The smoothness of the skin and the lack of body hair unnerved her.

Who is lying next to me?

Grasping the lantern, she held it up.

A strange shadowy face appeared, "Hello, Daisy, I left Paul sitting in the toilet."

*****

"Don't kill me, please! My name is Dennis." He pointed at his friends. "They talked me into this. I'm doing well at school. It will upset my parents if they find out what I'm doing. Please don't kill me! I so want to see them again!"

His three friends, all tied together, sat in petrified silence as the naked bogeyman dragged their friend Dennis by his hair to stand before them.

"See what happens when you run from the bogeyman. He chases you, brings you back and then demands you get into line and behave."

"Please..." pleaded Dennis. "Please don't hurt me."

"So, Dennis, my advice is not to listen to your friends and follow like a lamb to the slaughter. Follow your lead. Do not be a sheep!"

"I will only listen to you."

"Tell me, Dennis, how sorry are you?" scoffed the bogeyman, slapping him across the head.

"I'm sorry. I didn't mean to come into your house or run away."

"Why did you run?" asked the bogeyman, sitting cross-legged in front of a petrified Dennis who kept glancing at his friends. "We were about to have some fun. Now you're filthy because you ran across the field through the mud and into a barbed-wire fence."

"Why are you doing this to us?" pleaded Dennis.

"Shut the fuck up and don't be so impatient. I haven't decided on your fate. I might leave you and your friends here in the dark with no food or water and the company of vermin."

"If you let me go," cried Dennis, "I won't tell anyone what happened here tonight… I promise!"

"My, my, my, Dennis, how will you explain their death to the police and their parents?" questioned the bogeyman, fluttering his fingers.

With tears rolling over his cheeks, Dennis responded, "I'll tell them I was far away."

"You will. The police might think you were the murderer and lock you away in a psychiatric hospital and subject you to assessments while you continue to plead innocence. It's a strange world when no one listens to what you have to say, even when you're innocent. The need to shout is overwhelming."

Dennis trembled as the bogeyman shuffled behind him and placed his neck in a chokehold.

"No, please don't," pleaded Dennis, flinching as the bogeyman's arm tightened around his neck.

"Dennis, I am putting you to sleep, to spare you the sight of death."

Dennis could see the terrified stares of his friends as they faded from his sight.

August 18th | A family farewell

In the Bucks village of Chalton, a sudden rain shower

swept in by a north wind caught the gathering of mourners by surprise as they listened to the eulogy read by the vicar for their friend Joan Grant. Standing with his head down between his two sons was her husband. Occasionally he looked up and acknowledged the familiar faces.

He drew in a deep breath with his arms around his boys. In the distance, a figure dressed in black walking by the boundary of the graveyard stopped, faced the congregation and waved.

Almost riveted to the spot, he whispered, "Of all the days to show yourself, twenty years later, you show up on the worst day of my life."

"Dad... Dad!"

"What?"

"The coffin!"

"Earth to earth, ashes to ashes, dust to dust..."

Dropping his gaze to whisper to his second son, he threw earth on the coffin, fighting to hold his tears.

Lifting his eyes to peer at the wall, all he could see were two pedestrians.

23.15 Hrs

That night in bed, he tossed and turned as lucid dreams of long corridors with no exit kept him in a state of anxiety. He would awaken, turn over, whereby the vision continued until he found himself trapped by a looming black shape.

"What are you?"

"Wherever you go, I go. Escape is impossible; there is no escape from your deeds."

"What deeds? I did nothing wrong!"

"Why do you run?"

"You killed me."

"But you're alive."

Finding a burst of energy, he leapt at the black shape ready to trade blows only to awaken with a deep intake of breath. He threw the duvet aside and crept downstairs where he flopped onto the sofa and placed his feet on the footstool. It had become routine; fall asleep, awaken, toss and turn, drop asleep or get up and go downstairs.

Picking up the TV remote, he spotted a half-filled tumbler of whiskey; reaching over, he sunk it in one gulp. He 'surfed' through the channels and stopped when he found a film to watch; an old tearjerker he and Joan had seen on their first date. He only saw a minute before falling into a restless and haunted sleep.

August 19th | 07:30 Hrs

Stuart Grant stood near the kitchen window sipping tea from his favourite mug while listening to the news on BBC Radio 4. From upstairs, he could hear the footsteps of his youngest son, who appeared looking breezy.

"Yo, Dad, how is you?" inquired Harry, pouring a bowl of cornflakes then drenching them in milk.

"Yo, I'm OK," responded his dad. "Where did the word 'yo' come from?"

"You were asleep in the armchair when I came down this morning."

"What time was that?"

"Four-ish… I think."

"Did I wake you up?"

"Oh yes, because you were talking in your sleep. I thought you had a late-night visitor, or someone was hanging around after the wake."

Talking in my sleep is a new one, he thought. It was accusations of snoring, screaming out when he had a nightmare – but, as for talking in his sleep – that was new.

"What was I saying?"

"You weren't so much talking as wheezing as you do after you get home from a run. Are you training for a marathon in your sleep?"

"Very unlikely."

"Are you off to work today to catch bad boys?"

"Yes, but remember, we're going on holiday soon."

"The holiday is yours to enjoy because I can't go, and Ross wants to hang with his mates."

Harry ate more cornflakes before continuing the conversation. "Tell me, how are you? I ask because that's one question you haven't answered."

"I'm good thanks."

"How about you?"

"I'm working today. Gotta catch up with progress at work; see what's new."

"Before you go, apart from hanging with his mates has Ross mentioned any plans before university starts?"

Harry shrugged. "Ask him, not me."

"I'll speak to Ross later."

"Yeah, smart idea, Dad. Make sure you and he have the talk."

"Talk? About what?"

"Meeting girls. He's scared of them. So, talk to your eldest and reassure him. He'll be all right or miss a significant opportunity."

"And what will that be?"

Grinning, Harry punched the air. "Having his cherry popped!"

"Nothing to do with his degree?" scoffed his father.

"Ross worries too much. I've told him when he gets to uni, he needs to slurp loads of beer then find a fit bird gagging for it."

"With that attitude, he could end up in trouble, so, I hope he uses common sense."

Harry looked his father over. "He's a lot like you, isn't he? All common sense and sensibility wrote into the DNA."

"I hope we passed those genes on to you," Stuart paused, "and you're too young to drink!"

"Yeah, but... but... we're not talking about me. We're talking about my brother."

"So, Harry, where do you drink?"

"I never said I did." Harry grinned. "Oh, I see,

what you are up to."

"Tell me."

"You're playing the concerned cop. In my defence, I have no comment to make before I fall foul of the law – that being you, Dad – the long arm of the law!"

Stuart remembered them as children. Ross spent hours reading books, authoring short stories, and writing poetry. His friends took their turns to visit one another to listen to music and do whatever they did.

Aged sixteen Harry left school to start an electrician's apprenticeship with a local company. Unlike his brother, he was not academic. After work, he spent more time out than in, playing either rugby or football. Like his dad, he was tall and good looking.

Upstairs Stuart found Ross sitting cross-legged on the carpet staring at a crate full of books bought by his mother.

"I'm sure when you start your studies, you'll have enough books to line your shelves without all those. Are they on your uni reading list?"

"No," sighed Ross.

"So, are you looking forward to starting uni?"

Ross dropped his head, which Stuart recognised as his way of saying, 'I need to think about this.'

"I'm leaving my friends and family behind. I'll be starting all over again."

"We'll still be here. We're not going anywhere. What are your friends doing?"

"A mixture of travelling, jobs, nothing. The rest are off to uni."

"If you're still wondering about travelling or taking a year out, it isn't too late."

Ross looked at the bare bookshelves before replying, "No. I'll do my degree. Then I'll decide what to do."

DS Truman & Archie Suggs | 13:00

Bill Percy, a criminal solicitor, placed his hand on his client's shoulder while giving DS Truman the hard stare.

"Tell me, Mr Truman, why exactly is my client Mr Suggs here? He's a pillar of the community; he gives to community causes. An upstanding citizen."

"Marine police found his best mate Mickey North floating naked face-down in the Thames. All the signs indicate he'd taken a severe beating."

Bill and Archie glanced at each other. "Is this why my client is here?"

"Yes," replied Truman. "We're following up on Mr North." Truman gauged the reaction on their faces. Both thought it was for something serious.

"I don't expect a confession unless you have one."

One day, he might sing, and do jail time. Eyeing Suggs' face prompted another question. Where did he get all those scars? Could the rumours I've been hearing about be correct?

"I've heard a few stories about you, Archie," suggested a grinning Truman.

"Once Upon a Time fairy stories?" snorted Suggs.

"The story goes, you and Tricky Mickey had ideas about muscling in on turf south of the river. For your trouble, you both received a good beating."

"News to me, Mr Truman."

"A contact of mine suggested Mickey – your best mate – was bludgeoned by a baseball bat. You took a beating. Later you were dumped in a construction site."

"No comment," simpered Suggs as Truman tapped the desk.

"Mickey had a problem – he was a fantasist and believed he was a hard man, a violent gangster. When faced with violence because of his health, he had to act all humble and friendly."

"You're disrespectful to my best pal."

"He trusted you to look after him, Archie. Where were you?"

Archie smirked and tilted his head back. *Be careful what you say else I'll be here all day.*

"So, what happened to Mickey?"

Archie scoffed.

"Come on, Archie," coaxed Truman. "What happened? His mother wants to see him."

"I can't help you," sneered Suggs, wanting the 'charade' to stop. "Are you gonna charge me or what?" he retorted, banging his right fist on the table in frustration. "Because you have nowt on me!"

"You're free to go Archie," announced Truman, "but we'll talk again."

"Has no one ever told you, I'm like that Tony Blair geezer coated in Teflon? It avoids the shit sticking. Punters will never grass me up. They'll say it wasn't Archie; it was Mr Blobby over there!"

"You and Blair have something in common, Archie."

"What's that?"

"You're both liars with useful idiots for friends."

It was the same old story. Suggs had it all worked out and always told a fascinating tale. Despite that, Truman held a grudging respect for Suggs. Crime in his manor was almost non-existent. Anyone stepping out of line would stand before Suggs and pay the price.

Archie Suggs

Archie's passion for health and fitness was well-known. For at least two hours a day, he worked out in his private, custom-built gym, pushing various weights and running on treadmills. To finish, he swam ten lengths of his indoor swimming pool – his body was his temple. When he stood before you, he was a formidable figure.

After a shower, Archie splashed his body with expensive colognes that made him, in his view, attractive to women. Despite having no noticeable hair loss, he shaved his head because it better served his 'hard man' image.

When Archie took over the business from his mother there was a simple rule for members to follow – they were a family who looked out for one another, to offer backup, friendship and alibis where necessary.

However, that did not stop the occasional 'family' member from trying to escape with cash in their care. Only two members had disappeared. For those who never got past the start line, they faced Mel Greene who had spent his best years fighting in unlicensed boxing matches and bare-knuckle brawls. His role was to soften the runner up before Archie did his bit. The result was a bloody mess and Archie's warped sense of justice satisfied.

*****

It was a Saturday evening. There was the usual business to be done up West London. Archie stood before a wall mirror to check and admire his appearance.

In the lounge, his mother Molly joked and flirted with his associates. They all loved her style, humour, and she received due respect. Her long association with the business meant she understood the risks involved.

The business was in her blood. She brought order to chaos and sense to stupidity. Without Molly, the Suggs organisation would fail.

Eventually, making his entrance, Molly grabbed her son's hands.

"Archie," smiled his mum, "how like your father you are."

"So, you keep saying," he countered as his mother removed specks of fluff from his jacket.

"Listen up – make sure Archie comes home in one piece; else I'll play merry hell."

With a wagging finger, she turned to face Mickey, Archie's oldest friend with a stare he recognised. Dropping the tone of her voice, she spoke. "Mickey, no shenanigans tonight; you're a bad influence on Archie!"

"No worries," reacted an embarrassed Archie, kissing his mother, "we've got loadsa business doing tonight, and we're making money. Let's not forget that."

Molly hovered, planting a peck on the cheek of those she liked best. She shuddered as Mickey and Archie jumped into a car and drove off knowing the evening would bring bad news.

Mickey had always been bad news. But Archie never let friends down.

Saved by a Samaritan

Mickey and Archie turned off in a different direction and headed into South London. When they arrived at an address, two men opened a large wooden gate and directed them into a yard. Once parked, four men wrenched them from the car and dragged them inside a small empty building.

Two burly men pinned Archie to a wall while more stripped a hollering and crying Mickey. They flung him to the floor and forced Archie to watch while three men beat Mickey to death with baseball bats. As attention turned to Archie, he bellowed out a warning as two men knocked him clean out.

*****

Archie ached. Lying on the hard surface of the van

hurt him more. Next to him lay Mickey.

Who are these guys? What's Mickey done? They killed him, the bastards. He must've crossed a line. Or a set up to lure me. But there was no warning me off. They said nothing.

The driver called out before swinging the van left, screeching to a halt. Seconds later, the side door crashed open. Two men dumped both him and Mickey on the hard dusty ground. When the van pulled away Suggs glanced around. He shuddered when a young man appeared. "Don't worry, mister," assured the stranger, "I can help you."

Who are you?" asked an apprehensive Suggs.

"I stopped for a piss. When the van pulled in, I saw them throw you out with your mate."

Suggs looked at Mickey's lifeless body. "That's Mickey, my best mate. The bastards killed him. I hope you're friendly?" whispered Suggs. "'Cos I need help fast, like. What's your name?"

"Richard."

"Richard, can you call a number for me?"

"No problem. Glad to help. What's the number?"

Richard Deayton | The mean streets

Richard Deayton, twenty-nine, was born in Maryhill, Glasgow. His aims in life were to make big money, buy a Scottish castle and live like a laird.

He was no stranger to poverty and hardship. Over 90% of the people on his estate were unemployed suffering from long-term illnesses, alcoholism and drug dependency. The crime was an industry; drug addiction was rife. Alcohol stoked the violence. Stabbings were frequent.

From the age of eleven, he pondered his future, and what it might bring. To get ahead, he needed a purpose. An education he told himself was necessary. Also, while in school his mind was occupied and it kept him out of trouble.

His parents offered nothing except the same daily routine. From waking to bedtime, his mother sat glued to the television while smoking weed and drinking vodka mixed with Irn-Bru. When needs must, she took to the streets to offer backstreet blowjobs for a tenner. With money in her hands – she headed directly to the shops to buy more vodka and baccy.

His stepfather spent his days in the pubs with his cronies. They talked nothing but shite, putting the world to rights while their brains grew more addled and soaked in alcohol. In the mid-afternoon, he would stagger home and crash on the floor to sleep while the television flickered away.

One day a friend of his mother came to visit who had seen better days. When his mother fell asleep, her friend pushed a naive Richard into a sexual encounter. The quick fumble was memorable but soon faded. Two weeks later he received treatment for an STI at his local hospital. The experience changed his ideas concerning women – the next woman would be someone who took care of herself.

Every day he observed the junkies and homeless congregate to pass their days chatting with like-minded lost souls. The majority lived in a never-ending circle of collecting their welfare benefits and using it to buy alcohol and drugs. When their cash ran out, they trawled between friends looking for handouts and resorted to begging in the street. Those who kept that element of hope wandered the streets seeking the chance, for a lifetime break.

Gangs protected their territories by whatever means necessary. The odd stabbing or shooting was a warning to stay away.

His pals at school bragged about meeting men who offered - a 'glamourous lifestyle' by selling drugs. However, the glamour was more dangerous than anticipated. He could count on two hands former classmates and friends who had died chasing that dream. The big players kept tight control of the supply and price of hard drugs within the locality. Should you wander into their hood it was best to run, else suffer the consequences.

In recent years the police adopted a zero-tolerance attitude towards gang crimes. The crime rate dropped, with word of betrayal rife amongst the members. Richard kept a low profile. He kept gang membership at a distance. He was his own man.

The police action left him as the sole supplier of hard drugs in his neighbourhood. As the top dog, he had ready customers to buy gear. After they cashed their welfare cheques, they appeared regular as clockwork. If they came into money by other means, he saw them more often.

At no time did his conscience trouble him. It was their choice to live the life they did and was not his problem.

When the odd do-gooder questioned his motives, his answer was straight. If it were not him selling drugs, then someone else, more ruthless would – that being Giuseppe Scaffardi.

The Scaffardis

Giuseppe 'Papa' Scaffardi – the patriarch of the Scaffardi family – owned high-end restaurants, small hotels, a chain of coffee and ice cream parlours. After his wife died, he became a recluse. In doing so, the rumours were his weight had ballooned. People reported a team of carers entering the house from the rear. He needed help.

Papa had a son named Guido, who preferred to use the name Francis. He was a pathological bully. You made no deals with him unless you were desperate and could honour the agreement.

Richard for business reasons wanted to meet the Scaffardi's. He saw his daughter Rosemarie, who frequented Clubs in and around Glasgow. He would watch her dance with her friends smiling and joking. If he could say hello, maybe…maybe he would meet her father Papa. However, the opportunity to meet Papa came unexpectedly and by surprise.

One morning as he headed to his favourite café for his morning latte a BMW pulled up. A tall slim stranger stepped out. Looking at Richard he asked, "Are you Richard Deayton?"

"I may be. Who's asking?"

"Mr Scaffardi Senior."

Am I hearing this right? Papa Scaffardi? What's he want with me?

"What's he want?"

"My name is Alan and I'm his security advisor. Don't worry. Nothing serious but something to your benefit."

Richard jumped into the back seat and sat in silence during the fifteen-minute drive to the Scaffardi home. As they pulled up at the doors Richard knew his luck was about to change.

Alan ushered him through several rooms to a sun-filled conservatory. Sitting by a window in a reinforced custom-built armchair was a corpulent Papa. He smiled and raised a hand to beckon his guest closer.

At least the rumours about Papa's weight are true. Here goes. You wanted this meeting, let's see what happens.

"Please, sit close. These days I'm a little deaf. My late wife screamed too much, as did the children. Would you like a drink?" asked Papa.

"I haven't had my morning latte. Your man turned up before I got to my local café."

"Alan, if you please. Ask Rosemarie to bring our guest a latte," requested Papa, turning to Richard. "So, why are you here?" prompted Papa, eyeing Richard carefully. "The Bruce Brothers owe me money but have fallen on hard times. Under duress they handed over a large quantity of cocaine – I believe you have done business with them?"

"Not on a direct or personal level. But the word is the brothers have been having financial and supply problems."

"So, we need a trusted face to sell cocaine for the best price. I don't trust the brothers."

"Their reputation for deceit and lies goes before them," confirmed Richard. "I don't blame you for looking elsewhere. I can help you. I have contacts."

"If you can sell this consignment, your cut will be 15%."

Richard tried not to show any excitement. But he had a vital question. "What about your son Guido, can't he do that for you?"

Papa suppressed a laugh. "Guido-Guido-Guido. His reputation goes before him. No one trusts him to do a deal. People don't like the way he manages a business. He's too ready with his fists. So, I asked for referrals, and your name came up."

"And Guido doesn't mind?"

"He knows nothing about this." Papa nodded vigorously. "It's between me, you, Alan and the wall over there."

"OK." Richard felt assured that Papa was ruling Guido out. "I'll do that for you."

"Good. Then I will arrange to have the product delivered by Alan to a discreet venue of your choice. Keep this to yourself as loose talk gets about. I don't want Guido hearing about my arrangement."

Papa, held out a hand, which Richard shook.

The sound of stiletto heels on the wooden floor made him turn. Unconsciously his eyes lit up at her presence, and a smile lit his face. Rosemarie Scaffardi.

She looks more beautiful close-up.

"My daughter," confirmed Papa, looking proud. "She needs a man. When she goes to Glasgow for a night out, the men keep their distance when they hear her surname."

Papa noticed Richard's approving look and smile as Rosemarie left the room. Papa waved his right hand ever so majestically and slightly. "I see a look of approval. I'll send her your compliments when you leave."

*****

A week later Richard stepped from a train carrying a rucksack. He walked along the platform of Glasgow Central while making a mobile call. Thirty minutes later Alan picked him up on the corner of Glasgow's Argyll and Union Street.

Waiting at the door of the Scaffardi residence was Rosemarie wearing a stylish red dress. It suited her slender figure, her long dark hair and shapely legs. Seeing her made him smile. Should he ask her out on a date – later – maybe?

Rosemarie turned to Alan. "Thank you. I'll accompany Richard to my father."

"How are you?" inquired Richard as they entered the reception hall.

"I'm OK, and you?" she smiled.

"Are you going out somewhere? You look nice. Your red dress suits you."

"Thank you, kind sir. I have a loose arrangement to meet with friends much later." They entered Papa's lounge where he was watching football on a 52-inch television.

"Ah, Richard. How are you?"

"Good, and you?"

"No complaints. I trust all went as expected?"

"Yes. Place the rucksack on the table next to the banknote counter. Rosemarie will count the money."

Rosemarie opened the bag and tipped out the banknotes watched by her father.

"You have done well. Resolute, trustworthy."

"I have contacts and an idea of how much they would buy and pay."

"That's a lot of money." Papa glanced at Richard. "How much is there?"

"Yes, bang on 300k pounds."

"The Bruce Brothers told me it would be worth much less than you sold it for."

"Don't trust the Bruce Brothers. A pair of con merchants and thieves."

"300k," confirmed Rosemarie.

The figure pleased Papa. "That is £50,000 to you as promised."

They shook hands as Papa asked, "Are you hungry?"

"I am."

"Then, stay for dinner as my beautiful daughter has cooked an excellent meal. Tonight, you are my guest."

*****

Pushing his empty plate aside, he thanked Rosemarie. "Thank you. That was delicious."

"Have a Scotch," offered Papa, grabbing the bottle.

"I've had enough thanks. I haven't had a meal this good for ages."

"What are your plans now?" asked Papa, looking concerned.

"I will walk the delicious meal off and clear my head of the alcohol. I'll be safe. Don't worry."

"Alan has gone home and can't give you a lift," remarked Papa. "That's a lot to be carrying. I'll call you a cab."

Thirty minutes later, after another Scotch, Rosemarie walked Richard out.

"I'm always in Glasgow with friends. You can catch me at Bannisters. You can ask me for a dance."

At the end of the drive, a taxi flashed its headlights.

"When I see you, I'll come straight over."

Rosemarie smiled in return. "I'll hold you to that."

*****

The taxi driver pulled up on the boundaries of his estate. "That's it. I'm not going any further for any amount of money."

Richard pulled out a twenty-pound note and handed it over.

"Cheers, I'll walk from here."

Stepping from the taxi, he spotted a small gathering of NEDs; instantly recognisable by their clothing. In their hands, they held bottles of vodka and Buckfast. A staple diet. For years he had avoided such groups for two reasons. Their accent was impossible to understand and NEDS had a reputation for violence.

Such gatherings meant something big might be about to happen. Avoiding eye contact with the group, he strode away. It was never a good idea to show an interest in their gathering. That could provoke a response to regret – usually a beating and an ear-bashing. Their verbal abuse contained more 'f' and 'c' words than ordinary people uttered in a lifetime.

Against his own better advice, he chose to walk home along a dead-end road flanked on both sides by high stone walls known to be a notorious area for muggings. When a familiar voice called to him from the opposite side of the road he stopped. Matt Duncan, an old school pal appeared and leapt down to the pavement. Richard spotted a bloody gash on his forehead.

"What happened, Matt?" whispered Richard. "Tell me."

"Our old enemy Jim Stone. I looked at him the wrong way. So, he hit me."

"You should know not to cross paths with him."

"It wasn't intentional. I was near your house and bumped into him. He sees me and walks over and battered me twice because I look like a wee Jessy."

"What an arsehole!"

"There's a rumour you've come into a lot of cash. Jim Stone is waiting for you with Marley Tunnock. Watch your step."

"Why are you telling me?"

"You've helped me many times. I'm repaying you for all the favours you've done for me." Matt paused,

"Do you know what?"

"Tell me."

"This place would be a lot safer without Stone."

Richard sighed and gazed down the road. "What do you suggest? The man's a menace and I agree. But, unless someone takes him out he'll be a pain in the arse for a long time yet."

Matt turned to go. "Be careful on your way home. Don't let the Stone catch you."

Stone ran a loan shark scheme, and protection racket backed up by organised crime. He had heard rumours Jim Stone and Francis Scaffardi were friends; although there was no confirmed sighting of the men together in public.

Those with sense avoided both men. Getting tangled in their murky world was a risk to your well-being. Even a stray glance in their direction could trigger a violent reaction. People who did business with either man risked dire hardship owing more money than they received in annual welfare payments.

To avoid Stone and Tunnock; he avoided the open paths that crisscrossed the estate. Instead, he followed a path that ended behind a row of garages. He was minutes from home when a distinctive guffawing laugh boomed out.

That was Jim Stone.

When the laughter boomed out again, Richard crept around the garages. Sure enough, between the rows of garages was Stone leaning on his Subaru Impreza talking on his mobile. Tunnock wandered back and forth, smoking a joint. Less than fifty metres away was his front door.

Bastards. Stone can only be here because someone's tipped him off that I've got cash. OK, so, I need to wander around the back and avoid these two.

As he walked, he formed a plan.

Enter through the back door. Once inside, don't switch on any lights. Pack what little I have into my rucksack. What next? Think. Turn on the gas and switch on the toaster… stuff paper into the toaster slots. Open the back door. Next – switch on the lounge light briefly to attract Stone's attention. Let him see me. When he and Tunnock charge over, I'll leave by the back door.

When Stone and Tunnock saw the lounge light flicker on, giving them a glimpse of Richard, they charged at the door. The door rebounded off the wall and slammed shut. Stone called out, "Deayton my friend – come out – come out wherever you are and bring me a bag of money… Come out, Deayton, and face me, ye wee Jessy. I won't hurt you – but I don't make any promises."

Stone primed himself ready to knock Deayton into the next century while Tunnock sniffed the air.

"Can you smell gas?" asked Tunnock.

"No, I can't," rebuked Stone. "It's all in your imagination caused by that weed you smoke. It's done your head in. It's probably a Deayton fart polluting the air."

Stone laughed at his joke. He wanted Deayton before him carrying a large bag full of cash. The more, the better.

Tunnock's eyes darted to every corner. "That is

gas, no' a fart."

Stone retorted with his usual wee Jessy taunt. "Are you frightened o' a wee smell o' gas?"

When the toaster began to smoke, both men exchanged knowing glances. It was too late. Rooted to the spot, a blue flame leapt between the toaster and the gas fire. An explosion brought the house down. Months later he heard from a good friend that two gangs, the Merchants and Glasgow South Siders had placed a bounty on his head. They wanted him to answer for the death of Jim Stone and Marley Tunnock. It meant a return to Scotland would not be possible.

A discussion on murders

Alan Truman was busy skimming reports when DCI Stuart Grant appeared in his office.

"The boss told me you were interviewing Archie Suggs earlier?"

Truman smiled and gestured to a chair.

"Are you busy or still sweating over the fact Archie remains beyond your grasp?"

"Nice to see you," laughed Alan, shaking Stuart's hand. "I wasn't aware you were back at work."

"Joan's gone, I can't sit at home and mope. I need to work."

Truman caught a whiff of alcohol on Grant's breath.

"Sorry, I couldn't make the funeral. I was giving evidence. How are Ross and Harry?"

"They're OK, they'll adjust. So, what's Suggs done now?"

"Tricky Mickey, AKA Michael North – marine police dragged his body out of the Thames. Witnesses said he looked like he'd been in a fight with a pit-bull terrier. Suggs denies all knowledge despite looking like he suffered a similar fate."

"Like revenge," suggested Grant.

"And to top it all, they were the bestest buddies," concluded Truman.

"Does he still do extortion?"

"Archie's into most things," replied Truman, smacking his lips.

"I've said this once, and say again," began Grant, "when I see Suggs, I sense I know him. I've no idea why."

"OK, so, will you tell me why you're here?"

"OK." Grant paused in thought. "Brace yourself. During the funeral, I saw the Man in Black watching us. Zodiac. He's back. I'm in no doubt about that," whispered Grant.

"Zodiac?" queried Truman, narrowing his eyes, not believing what his friend had said. "Hey, he disappeared something like twenty years ago. Really… we don't want our hands tied by the search for a serial killer. We're talking months of work at a huge cost."

"I agree. No argument there," remarked Grant, pulling out a sheet of paper, "I have the names of three murdered women. The first was Paula Reed on May 14th in her wet room at her bungalow in Pinner. Sara Raye on July 3rd in Rickmansworth, and Jeanette

Brown at home in Bushey on July 25th – are you aware of them?"

"Come on. Every day we have gangs shooting and stabbing people. In answer to your question, those murders don't stand out!"

"Check them out for any connections."

"Can't you do it?"

"No I can't. Because I'm off on holiday tomorrow."

August 21st

Alan Truman was sifting through paperwork when Chief Superintendent Hobbes knocked on his office door and sat without a word. First, he gazed out of the window at the gathering rain clouds then sighed with a look of concern.

"Let's get going on this. Your queries about the three murdered women have proved correct. There is a connection. So, I've considered your points to suggest we set up a task force to track this killer down."

"It was DCI's hunch – not mine."

"First. As the killer has crossed police boundaries, we're joining forces with Thames Valley. The good news for you is you'll be on TVP territory in your HQ close to Beckersfield."

"That's handy. The DCI and I live that way."

"Thought you'd like that. Not far to drive in the morning. DCI Grant will be the SIO. There's news for you… I'm promoting you temporarily to Acting Detective Inspector with the possibility of making it permanent."

"Oh," reacted a surprised Truman. "That's unexpected, but thank you."

"We have a Detective Sergeant Bruce Franklin transferring over tomorrow. His senior officer told me he's a focussed officer, an asset. Also, a DC out of training who's made of stern stuff, DC Janine Johnson. I believe she lives in Northwood."

So far, so good. But is Stuart up to this?

Despite admiration for his friend, he had doubts. Those doubts were weighing on his mind. "Can I make you aware of my thoughts regarding the DCI?"

"Go ahead," gestured Hobbes. "Say your piece. You appear quite anxious to do so."

"No matter what he tells you, he's still haunted by the Zodiac incident. Mentally I don't think he's ready."

Hobbes stood back. *Truman could be right. Could this investigation push Grant into the unknown – out of the comfort zone?*

"The DCI is a master of his art. Overlooking him could be a mistake. Also, Grant has more reason than others to get a result."

"I know that."

"Did you know the Chief Constable kept Stuart's identity secret at the murder scene to prevent press intrusion and speculation?"

" Yes, I did. But the cynic in me suggests the Chief Constable had ideas to end the Zodiac case by accusing Stuart. I think the top brass were on the verge of arresting Stuart and accusing him of being

Zodiac. But there were too many holes in their case, and he had reliable alibis including his commanding officer at Hendon. Am I right, or am I wrong?" Truman met Hobbes' eyes. "The investigation took place while he was in hospital. Sneaky."

"I am aware of all that. I know there were rumours everywhere and I believe Stuart heard them. He became a man driven by duty. There was no stopping him and he trusted his instincts on various cases. That's why he's heading this investigation."

"Ok, I'll run with it. Who am I to object to Stuart and his methods."

"Touché." Hobbes clasped his hands, bearing an edgy look. "This return of a serial killer who disappeared twenty years ago concerns me. It could overwhelm us without careful management. We can expect questions and press intrusion and distraught relatives who lost loved ones and who've never seen justice."

"I'm with you there."

"How's he coping with the death of his wife?"

"He's lost weight, looks gaunt," suggested Truman. "But then I haven't seen a close relative suffer for years with cancer or lost anyone close. How you feel afterwards is a mystery to me. I've dealt with delivering bad news and witnessed personal reactions. It's difficult to watch when you deliver bad news to parents about their child. I don't know how some officers remain detached."

"I needn't remind you the DCI is an excellent police officer. He didn't achieve his current rank because he waited for things to happen. He went out and did his job."

Hobbes stood to leave. "Before I go. The Home Office has insisted we use Dr Harry Pitcher who's a renowned FBI profiler to help us search for Zodiac. The top ranks want this wrapped up by Christmas."

"Christmas?" scoffed Truman. "Do they know how difficult it can be to track these killers?"

"Nevertheless, can your team afford him the courtesy he needs to do his job?"

"He's actual FBI?"

"I'm told he's attached to the FBI's Behavioural Analysis Unit."

"What is that?"

"They develop research and training to understand criminals."

"What's their interest?"

"Their own Zodiac slipped their surveillance many years ago. There is a chance he landed on British soil."

"Are you suggesting Zodiac's American?"

"That's what he'd like to discuss when he arrives on the 29th."

Hobbes turned to leave but stopped, "I hope this time we get an answer to the question that plagued the last Zodiac team."

"What was the question?" asked Truman.

"Why did Zodiac stop at victim number eleven and not complete the cycle and murder a twelfth victim."

23rd Sept 1993

Zodiac had stalked his prey for twelve months. The discussion point on TV, radio and in women's magazines was how he accessed what was personal information. Police interviewed postmen, government workers, anyone who could access personal information. However, it was a job too far. Police questioned an entire gamut of people trying to find a suspect. The police found nothing in common to link the women.

Jacquie Willis became the last official Zodiac victim. Alongside her, lay a police constable. Both displayed signs of a brutal beating and stab wounds. An attending doctor declared them dead at the scene.

A local undertaker dispatched two attendants to collect the bodies. They drove the corpses to the local mortuary and placed them into coolers.

Three hours later, a mortuary attendant heard screams coming from the cold room. Nervously he opened the drawer from where the screams were coming. When he unzipped the bag, he stared aghast as a bloodied and frantic man with his arms flailing screamed for release from a black hell.

Four days later, Stuart awoke alone in intensive care. He was unaware of the three operations he underwent to fix his shoulder and jaw. He could hear beeping machines, and people with distorted and ghostly voices. Dark depressive moments followed with vivid memories and images. He could feel the punches and see the man in black taunting him. Ahead he could see the light. But to gauge his plan, he remained in darkness.

Nurses and staff could hear him muttering and gesturing to unseen entities. It was a typical process witnessed by nursing staff as a patient neared death. As the nurses prepared his parents, siblings and Joan to expect the end, there was a sudden change. He awoke from the dark and thrived.

Joan spent what time she could by the side of Stuart, talking to him – holding his hands. With her help and calming words, he recovered with a glint in his eye. The promise to himself was to exercise patience. One day he would catch the man in black – Zodiac, a serial killer who was wrecking the lives of innocents.

Three months later an eager Stuart returned to work to make right that personal promise. In the meantime, he and Joan married.

News Flash, Local Newspaper Report

December 1993

To date, Zodiac has murdered eleven victims, all from the London area. He selects victims according to their Sun Signs. Mary Cox, the first official victim, lived with her husband, Marcus. Together they had a daughter who is now looked after by her maternal grandparents; such is the distress of the husband. Despite making a public appeal for witnesses, no one came forward. Zodiac continued to strike one woman every month from November 1992 through to September 1993.

Here we include a list of his victims:

Name	Sun Sign	Age	Status
Mary Cox	Scorpio	30	Married
Josephine Elliott	Sagittarius	21	Single
Natasha Platt	Capricorn	28	Engaged
Julia Singer	Aquarius	18	Single
Freda Lowe	Pisces	21	Single
Patricia Hugo	Aries	24	Engaged
Theresa Baldwin	Taurus	30	Divorced
Jennifer Cryer	Gemini	22	Single
Michelle Forget	Cancer	27	Married
Harriet Adams	Leo	29	Single
Jaqueline Willis	Virgo	29	Married
Name	Libra	Age	Status

The question is, how did he choose his victims?

June 1994. Who is Zodiac? Where is he? Has Zodiac died, or left the country? There's a possibility he was jailed for another crime: questions but no answers.

September 1996 Could Zodiac be dead? A police spokesperson confirmed there had been no more killings bearing his trademark signatures. The case remains open. However, in recent months police numbers have been cut and reassigned detectives to other cases.

A dirty, smelly fellow | 18:30

By force of habit, when Truman arrived home, he always checked his telephone for voice messages; that evening, there was only one from Carol Schaefer, his long-term girlfriend, telling him what time to expect her.

By force of habit, when he arrived home, he always checked his telephone for voice messages; that evening, there was only one from Carol Schaefer, his long-term girlfriend, telling him what time to expect her.

*****

After setting the table, Alan watched the news. Carol was unusually late. When the regional news at 7:00pm ended, he picked up his mobile to check for messages.

Nothing.

Then to his relief, she walked in, looking upset. "I'm sure someone followed me again."

"Who followed you?"

"A dirty and smelly man – I first noticed him on the tube a few weeks ago. He kept smiling at me. Since then, I've seen him twice."

"Has he said anything to you?"

"No, he's never spoken, but he's come close enough to catch a whiff of his odour."

"You've not mentioned this before?"

"Because it wasn't important until now. Can we eat? Because I'm overworked, tired and hungry."

August 29th | The Profiler | 11:00

Dr Harry Pitcher's arrival at ZHQ shattered Truman's mental image. He was shorter, rounder with a greying goatee beard and wild hair. His wire-framed glasses looked small and on the brink of snapping at the bridge.

In the briefing room, he placed his files on the table and glanced over the assembled Zodiac team. He took sips of water before facing his audience.

"Hello, I specialise in profiling serial killers. I'm here to assist you with the serial killer known as Zodiac. In the USA, we had a serial killer with a similar MO. I've read a summary of the first set of killings. I have written up notes…"

Truman had a question to ask that reflected his impatience. "Does Zodiac have a name?"

"Yes, several in fact. The first name we have for Zodiac is Raymond McCoy. But before you tap your laptop keys, let me share my information. First off, our McCoy is not on social media. Far too cautious for that public display. We know McCoy arrived in the United States in September 1994 to study at MIT a year after the killings ended here in the UK with the 11th victim.

"Go on?" responded Truman, leaning forward, his interest raised.

"McCoy came to our attention in 1997 because he frequented an area once known as 'The Combat Zone', a former red-light district full of clubs with dancing girls and well-known for its prostitution. The murder of a local prostitute brought him to police attention. The police called on her boyfriend. In his apartment, they found the knife used to kill the victim and blood-splattered clothes. He denied the charges but told a convincing story to the cops about an Englishman setting him up. As a result, the FBI watched McCoy…

While at MIT he befriended Francis Brooklyn Harris. These men were Engineering geniuses who collaborated on the design of hardware and software. A tech company called NetEye heard what they were up to and approached.

"What is NetEye?"

"A hi-tech engineering company. Harris and McCoy were invited in to demo their ideas. In the aftermath the board made offers."

Truman raised a hand. "What's so special about this technology?"

"A potential military application. It caused a fallout. Harris walked away while. McCoy stayed and left many months later. We suspect his growing relationship with a Maria Dominguez hit turbulence. She provided discreet services to men with peculiar sexual requirements. She was found murdered."

"And McCoy?"

Morris withdrew an A4-sized photograph from his briefcase.

"A few days after we took those photos he disappeared."

"You don't know where he went?" remarked Truman, looking perplexed.

"Nope, no idea at all."

CHAPTER 21

2014 | Virgo | Aug 23 – Sept 22

Sept 3rd | 09:00

After a holiday, a return to work meant a return to routine. During Joan's illness, time was precious. Now, he needed a daily routine. Drag yourself to the shower, or bath... whatever... decide if your hair needs washing. Clean your teeth and finally get dressed.

Breakfast. Yes or No? You can't go to work without breakfast inside you, Joan would remind him. He could almost hear her voice. Eat up, go to the car, drive to the railway station in Amersham. And catch the Met line to Wembley. But not this morning. He was driving to Beckersfield, a quaint town he had rarely visited.

Stuart stood outside the entrance to the temporary accommodation. There was no hint of what it was or who was working inside. He entered ZHQ drawn by DI Truman's voice to a gathering of the team discussing their updates on Zodiac. When the officers dispersed, he declared his arrival.

"You're leading Alan. I always said you could do it! So, c'mon, tell me what's happening. Could it be Zodiac is due for imminent arrest!"

"You wish. But guess what — we have the FBI to help with information."

"FBI?" queried Stuart.

"Long story — it's more like a compare notes thing. Show me yours, and I'll show you mine."

"Why?"

"You'll find out soon enough! Follow me to your office."

"Can I meet the team first?"

"No! Tomorrow after you've read the files and note any questions you have."

"This is your office."

Grant glanced at the walls and desk. "Nothing like my office." With a nod, he continued. "Thanks, it'll do for now." As Grant sat, the desk telephone rang.

"There you go," reacted Truman, "you're not back five minutes, and already your phone is ringing. You're in demand!"

He answered the phone with a gruff hello. A classical tune played before a calm voice spoke.

"Such solemn music, so perfect for death. 'The Death March' by Tchaikovsky. It captures the whole experience of death and its sorrow, Tchaikovsky had much in the way of perception."

Stuart beckoned Truman to stay as he asked, "Is this who I think it is?"

"Yes, do you find this thrilling?"

"I wish I could say it was a defining moment in my career!"

" Unlike other men you survived me Stuart."

"Men?" responded Stuart, activating the loudspeaker. "I thought your target was defenceless women?"

"Got you going now, haven't I?"

"Can you answer a simple question?"

" I'm Zodiac, what I am depends on your belief! But, understand this," chuckled Zodiac, "and anyone else who hears my voice. The Headshrinkers will tell you, *to catch me – you must BECOME me, see the world through my eyes and make a choice.* Can you do that, Stuart, can you BECOME me?"

"I could never be you. My conscience remains intact!"

"I find talking to you therapeutic. It lets me unburden my inner self. You're listening as a brother does. Shall I tell you why I do what I do?"

"Tell me," asked Grant. "It all helps us understand who you are."

Zodiac whispered down the phone, "It's a sport."

"When you and I speak, choose your words carefully. I detest name-calling. It's cheap and unnecessary. I kill for thrills. Unfortunately, the victims were on my birthday list. Nothing more, nothing less!"

"You're a grade one lunatic. What created a monster like you?"

"Grade one lunatic – such a choice of words. Fate chose me to clean up society; you never appeared on my list. But you came close."

"Close to what!"

"Death, Stuart, you survived me, but, let's change the subject. Stuart – what will you do if you catch me in the act again on a dark rainy night? Listen. Wherever you go, I go. Then fate will decide our last moments. We are closer than you know, Stuart Grant."

"In what ways are we close?"

"Temperament, stature, outlook. It can be one of your attributes, which one would you like? How shall I compliment you?"

"Drop the bullshit! Surrender yourself. I'll wait by the door to arrest you!"

"Here we are two characters trying to outwit one another, coming together in a final scene, in which good and evil fight for notoriety and fame – are you in my play?"

"Only one will win – and it won't be you."

"Oh, Hark! The call of the victor! You're so sure about the result you forget something important."

"What?"

"The advantage is mine. I know where you live with your boys. You'll see yourself before you see me. My hands will encircle your throat while I hold my knife to your neck, Stuart. Goodbye."

Stuart shuddered at the thought.

Zodiac must be caught.

September 4th | Northwood | Middx

In the West London suburb of Hanwell, he sat in a comfortable lounge watching a broadcast on the BBC 24-Hour News Channel, entitled: 'Zodiac: Copycat or the Original?'

As the documentary ran, he shouted at the screen, "You know NOTHING, about ME!"

Bored with what he was watching, he strolled to the bedroom and pulled back the duvet uncovering his latest victim – Anjna Singh. He leaned over her face to gaze into her eyes. "I see the lights have gone. Such a shame. I'm sure you had plans, ambitions. NO more for you. Ever."

CHAPTER 22

2014 | Libra | Sept 23 – Oct 22

5th Oct | 07:30

Voices drifting from the radio in the kitchen awoke Stuart. Swinging out of bed, he leaned over the dressing table to focus on his dishevelled reflection. For the first time, he noticed his leaner figure.

During the last few weeks of Joan's illness, she was taken into hospital. He had grabbed food on the go. Occasionally, he cooked a proper meal for him and the boys. Most evenings on his return home, he'd have a whisky to relax, then another, followed by too many. Without seeing it, or having Joan nearby to comment, he had no reason to stop.

Gazing at the items on the dressing table, he picked up a perfume bottle and sprayed the liquid into the air. Breathing in the scent, he saw a movement. In the mirror, he could see Joan sleeping with her hair swept back, showing the contours of her face he remembered so well.

The death of a wife

When doctors first diagnosed Joan with cancer, she took life in her stride. There was much to do. Through the years, she achieved what she wanted with help from family, friends, and the kindness of strangers.

Five years later, as the battle closed in and her strength began to wane, she found herself bedridden. During her last week, Ross read her stories or sat with her as she listened to her favourite radio programs.

When she cried out in pain, Stuart administered morphine to relieve it. At times she lay so still that visiting family thought she had passed.

In a rare moment of prolonged sleep, Joan awoke to see Stuart sleeping in the chair next to the bed. Pushing back the duvet, she shuffled towards the window, gripping what she could for support. One final look outside. As she leaned on the window, sill Stuart's arms wrapped around her. She sighed.

"What are you doing?" he whispered.

"I'm taking a final look."

Stuart held her tight and close stifling his tears.

Outside a mixture of dark and white clouds drifted by allowing the sun and blue sky to peek through. Overhead a Red Kite circled looking for food; wings outstretched using its tail to change direction. Two squirrels chased each other across the lawn. Sitting in the corner of their garden next to the shed was the neighbours' elderly cat Tigger. Joan tapped on the window to draw his attention. Raising his head, he blinked his eyes and meowed.

"I hope that is not thunder in the distance."

Not today Joan. It will be filled with sunshine and gentle rain. Do you remember our first kiss in the rain, that moment when we had discovered mad crazy love? The water soaked through our clothes."

"I remember it clearly."

"And our two boys. We made them."

"Yes, we did. They are your responsibility now Stuart." Facing Stuart, she kissed his lips and held him before taking one last look outside.

"I've seen what I need to see," she murmured, "Back to bed please."

Stuart helped Joan make herself comfortable. As he did she gazed at his face. He knew she had something to say and sat on the edge of the bed.

"When the sun lowers in the sky and casts its golden shadows across the bedroom wall, I know it will be my time."

Stuart gazed lovingly into her face.

"Please listen to me."

Stuart tried to hold back his palpable grief.

"Dying from cancer has been a lonely path despite the constant attention from family and friends. As my time draws closer, I thought of the days I have here with you. It isn't the thought of dying that makes me weep; it is the emotional thought of leaving my young family behind. When I fall into eternal sleep, I hope to have said my goodbyes. But I will look down from the corner of the room while my family, friends and relations gather and whisper their farewells. They will neither see me nor feel me, but I will hear their last words.

"My affairs are in order. You, my husband and our boys, will have a family and friends to ensure you use your time with wisdom. My regret is not seeing my boys grow to be men in the image of their good father. I trust you will give a guiding hand to help them achieve what they want from life.

"While you nap and it's quiet, I have wandered outside to feel the air on my face to remind myself, for now, I'm alive. My time has come, whereby I accept my allocation of life. To go when called…

"…I no longer ask, 'Why me?' and I have stopped shouting at God and have accepted time is short. No longer do I fear my destination. I now accept and embrace death as must we all. So, before I go, I will embrace the people who have graced my life and kissed their lips one final time. So, my message to them is I am ready. My dear, dear friends, please accept my death."

Turning to face her husband, she asked him, "Do you love me, Stuart?"

"Yes."

"Good. I need you to feed me that bottle on the bedside cabinet because the pain is too much to bear. I hope to die in peace and with dignity before the pain kills me. Your last memories of me will be peaceful and not of constant pain."

She spotted a look of concern on Stuart's face.

"Will you do that for me?"

Her request caught him by surprise. It was the last

thing he expected. But, sitting there looking at her face and the increasing pain she bore, her request sounded modest.

"Will you do it?"

"Yes."

"Please get the boys so I can speak to them," she asked. "I'll make sure they live to the max. Time is precious and passes by quickly."

With Joan's request foremost in his mind, he called their sons to the bedroom. With their heads bowed fighting to hold back their tears, they sat next to their mother who looked frail, tired and a shadow of her former self.

When Harry and Ross returned downstairs to sit with their grandparents, Stuart sat on the bed and waited until Joan opened her eyes. With no words between them, they gazed at each other. Then as if on request beams of sunlight light cast a golden hue against the wall.

With a smile, Joan propped her frail body against her husband for one last cuddle and spoken farewell. Blinking her eyes twice, he lifted the bottle to her lips. When she coughed, she took deep breaths, which slowly faded as she drifted into a peaceful and painless sleep.

The empty nest | 18:05

During the journey to Bristol, Harry kept winding his brother up by pointing out other cars where a teenager sat crushed next to a pile of luggage while in the front sat anxious-looking parents.

Ross never understood Harry nor his sense of humour. He did his best to ignore his brother by concentrating on his iPad and the occasional glimpse at the Satnav to see what time they might arrive.

The sooner, the better.

Stuart sighed with relief when they arrived at the campus. The boys had avoided a full-blown argument. Without a word, Ross left his brother and father and followed the various signs to the Admin block to register and receive his keys to his room.

When they pulled up outside the accommodation, Stuart looked up three landings as he grabbed three small boxes followed by Harry, who seemed more interested in the surroundings.

An exhausted Stuart eventually took a seat while Ross collected the last box. Harry meanwhile was doing his best to chat up his brother's fellow female students. Ross returned and dropped his box; looking at his father, then brother, he made a sudden and unexpected announcement. "I want you both to go now."

"Is it something we've said?" asked his father, looking bemused at his son's sudden change in attitude.

"No, leave me to sort my room."

"Are you sure?" asked a cautious Stuart.

"Yes. Both of you go now."

"Hang on," wailed Harry, "I could have a few dates here."

Ross sighed and pointed towards the exit. "Please. Just go now."

"Move!" scowled Stuart, pushing Harry.

"Hey, I'm only saying goodbye!"

"You've said goodbye."

"No, I haven't!"

"Yes, you have!"

Spliff debts and teenage know-it-all

During the return journey, Harry was uncharacteristically quiet, leaving Stuart to start a discussion on the long-debated issue of Ross's bigger bedroom.

"If you're planning to move into Ross's bedroom, forget it."

Harry stared at his father in disbelief before adopting his ultimate teenage stroppy brashness.

"I never said anything about his room."

"I know what you're thinking. The answer is no – for now."

"What's the problem? He'll be home for Christmas and Easter, Dad," Harry pouted, "but after that, he won't come home during summer, I guarantee it."

"Is that so?"

"Charles's told me. His brother and sister went to university, and neither returned home during the summer because they found jobs to pay off their spliff debts."

"Spliff debts?" A concerned Stuart wondered where the conversation was going.

"Yeah. Spliff debts. You're a nark, Dad. You understand perfectly."

"No! You explain it to me. What DO YOU mean?"

"There are loads of stories about cash-struck students getting into debt because they spend their money on beer and ciggies."

"OK! Tell me about the spliff debts?"

"University towns have well-known local drug dealers. They visit the campus and give the students credit to buy their spliff and other stuff."

"Like what?"

"Crack, hash, methadone."

"Methadone?"

"Yeah… metha—"

"Where do you hear such things?"

"Common knowledge. You should know, you're a copper."

"First off, methadone is only available via chemists to treat addicts. Second, if dealers were selling crack cocaine to students, I'm sure the local force uses intelligence to keep track of these dealers."

"Intelligence!" queried Harry.

Here it comes. Showing off again. Running down the police.

"Would that be individual intelligence or group intelligence?"

"Intelligence gathered from various sources that help a local force target criminal."

"If you say so, Dad. You are the big brain."

"And – err, returning to what started this conversation – what happens if the student doesn't pay their debts?"

I've got Dad worried here. Stir that pot.

"The heavies threaten them until they pay for it or work the debt off in some shitty job."

"Such as?"

"Scrubbing out the peep-hole cubicles used by perverts to watch live strippers on the wrong side of town."

"Oh, OK." *What is he talking about?*

"But…" Harry trailed off, noticing a distinct look on his dad's face, which suggested he had said too much.

Is Dad taking me seriously? Be careful because Ross could receive a stern lecture by phone when we get home.

"That isn't Ross's deal. He's a good brother."

"You have a vivid imagination," remarked Stuart, glancing at Harry.

"I have a vivid imagination about what, Dad?"

"Scrubbing cubicles."

"Who said it was vivid?"

Stuart stared at his son. *Is he for real, or is this a wind-up?*

"Anyway. When Ross recites the love poetry he writes, the birds will be gagging for him. He'll love it," snorted Harry, clapping his hands. "He'll have a permanent stiffy because he'll be forever shagging. Wow, what sort of education that will be for him?"

Stuart pulled himself closer to the steering wheel while squinting at Harry, wanting to clip his ear. However, there was more to come.

"Charles's brother, you know him, Dad?"

"Vaguely."

"He was always at it when at uni, so he claimed."

"He was at always at what?" interrupted his dad.

"Having sex with women!"

"I made the same claims at his age, but it was all bull."

"Fair play. But you've never met Charles's sister. She's fit!"

"Mmmm. Let me get this straight; you've changed the subject to the sister of Charles. Correct?"

"You should see her."

"Why?"

"Some sister, believe me – huge bosomers and thighs that could crush a man's hea— do some damage!"

"Your head wouldn't be crushed… would it? Just asking. Considering the conversation we're having."

"Err… Not yet."

"I can tell the world of political correctness passed you by."

"I say, as I see, and see as I say."

"Be careful. I don't want angry fathers calling and telling me their daughter is pregnant, and you're the father."

"Chance be a fine thing!" muttered Harry as he grasped his buzzing smartphone. When his friends were active through their preferred media apps, it became pure silence and an end to any discussions.

*****

When Stuart pulled into his driveway, Harry ran inside to answer the call of nature. When his mobile rang, displaying Truman's name Stuart sighed wondering when the day would end.

Rickmansworth | Herts | 19:00

Stuart pulled up on a long driveway. He stared at the house, lit up in every window. He turned to see Truman tapping on his side window.

"What's the story here?"

"Potential Zodiac victim."

"What are you up to?"

"Talking to the neighbours."

Grant slipped into white cotton overalls before venturing upstairs to the bedroom. The distinct smell of human decay and acetone made his nose twitch. During his twenty-plus years as a police officer, he had seen many visually unsettling crime scenes. He expected no less here.

From his position outside the bedroom, he saw a blood-stained white sheet under which lay the distinctive shape of a body. In the bedroom overseeing the collection of evidence was Doctor Ron Tyler, a Home Office pathologist.

"Who is she?" asked Grant.

"Her name is Hillary Berger. She's been dead for at least two to three days; a clean cut through her neck."

"Can you add to that?" asked Grant.

"The killer left a pendant. Your Zodiac has struck again."

A breakfast conversation

"Do you like your boss?"

"If I don't show loyalty, he could make life difficult."

"So, tell me," requested Jack, "are you showing him the loyalty – the commitment he wants? Bringing home the bacon to increase his wealth?"

"I'm doing what he wants."

"Does he piss you off with his bragging, his lust for dirty, ill-gotten cash, cheap whores, his workouts? The daily swim followed up by dousing his body with expensive Eau de Colognes because his idea of human perfection is himself?"

How does Jack know about Archie's morning routines? Does he have a mole inside Archie's gang?

"I could snap his back like a twig," pronounced Jack, his eyes turning black while making a fitting gesture with his hands. "The man is worth nothing, and soon, he'll be worth even less."

Jack stared at Richard with a personal question in mind. "Truth or dare, Richard. Have you taken a life? Everyone has a story to tell about a ruthless deed to protect ourselves. What is your story?"

Sold out

It was time to visit Paddy Mac. They had met eight years ago in Manchester during a pool tournament. On a personal level, they had much in common. Paddy taught Richard the art of picking pockets. How to con people; sell on credit and debit cards, watches, cameras and jewellery.

Arriving at Paddy's flat in Milton Keynes, his face dropped when Tina Brooks, his on-off girlfriend, answered the door with a huge smile.

"What are you doing here? I thought the law sent you down?"

"I'm a free bird." Throwing her arms around him, he continued, "I'm out on a license and must report to the probation office."

Paddy appeared and beckoned him in. His face suggested he was not happy at Tina's presence.

"Paddy, how are you doing fella?"

"Great, sit and have a beer," suggested Paddy, holding up three cans of semi-cold lager.

"Thank you; I will."

Paddy looked over his shoulder to see where Tina was before leaning towards Richard. "What's she doing here?"

"Six weeks ago, a judge sentenced her to eighteen months for assault and possession of Class-A drugs."

"I read about it."

"When did she arrive?"

"Yesterday, she said you were on your way."

"How did she know that?" quizzed Richard, looking puzzled. "I haven't seen her since her sentencing."

"That's what she said, but hey – why are you letting her hang with you? She's unpredictable. Her behaviour will drop you in the shit big time, my friend."

"She's like the proverbial penny," scowled Richard, knowing Paddy was right.

"Yeah, she's lurking, sniffing, listening to my mobile conversations. She's up to something. When she thinks I'm not listening, she's making phone calls else receiving them. It's making me suspicious. You, my friend, needs to find out what she's up to before it's too late."

"I'll work on it."

"All right," rapped Paddy, "tonight you can stay here and think about it while I go across town to visit my girlfriend. But tomorrow, be gone. I don't want no shit landing on my doorstep."

*****

Early the following morning, the police mounted a raid. Dragged from their bed and restrained while police searched the premises. A police dog handler appeared with a sniffer dog.

Little did the police know Paddy received a tip-off of an imminent police raid. He cleared the flat of any drugs and paraphernalia.

Two hours later the police placed them in separate

interviews rooms and questioned them at length. Richard had nothing to say. He knew nothing. But what was Tina saying? It came as a surprise to him when twelve hours later, they walked away without charges.

Richard's suspicions about Tina were mounting, stacking up high enough to block any view. When the raid happened, she remained calm. There were no offensive outbursts. She was polite and suspiciously helpful. She had a rap sheet that contained severe charges. Her change in attitude was like watching someone who was not Tina.

They walked straight to a café where before they had ordered drinks, Tina made a sudden suggestion. "Let's go to the Highlands."

What was she planning?

"I can't go to Scotland; I'd be a dead man!"

"Oh, come on," scoffed Tina, rolling her eyes. "Are you sure?"

"Two gangs are offering a reward for information on my whereabouts and capture. If I crossed into Scotland, it could be game over."

Rolling her eyes, Tina responded, "You've never told me what they want you for, or who these gangs are. Listen," encouraged Tina before he could answer. "Think about it for a while; it might make more sense than you think. I don't doubt what you're saying about the gangs. But think about this. I'm not suggesting we stay in Glasgow or Edinburgh. We go further north to the Highlands. Would they think to look for you up there?"

"Probably not," he agreed with a nod.

"You'd be hiding in plain sight."

"You've got this worked out, haven't you?"

"My idea is we go somewhere quiet. Recuperate and decide where we go and what we do next. That's my plan."

"I thought you didn't like peace. You like the noise of a big town or a city. Pubs, clubs and all that?"

Tina fixed him with a stare, "I'm attempting to change my lifestyle for good. Try something different … for a change."

That statement from Tina sent shivers along his spine. He had known her long enough to know she had a motive behind the suggestions. Whatever it was, for the time being, he would go along with her plans. The reason was his return to Scottish soil. But as always, he would keep an eye on her behaviour.

*****

Renting a crofter's cottage through a web-based holiday home service, they drove to Loch Torridon cutting through the centre of Scotland to avoid Glasgow before heading due west.

Richard was more than happy to be home on Scottish soil with its wide-open spaces, fresh air that invigorated his outlook and where he could relax and enjoy the scenery and quiet.

After two days he was enjoying the scenery so much he bought a pair of walking boots. Every day he walked further and further afield under skies that stretched forever. The landscape of the Scottish Highlands was breath-taking; he was home and amongst locals with whom he could share wee drams of Scottish water in local pubs.

The one disappointment was Tina. Every day she was stoned or drunk. It was becoming a challenge to handle Tina. She threw a regular tantrum and refused his offer to go out and meet people. Her behaviour was more than a concern.

During a tantrum, he would walk to the loch. Moored at a small dock was a rowing boat. He would let it float under open skies to enjoy the silence.

It gave him time to think. Remembering Paddy Mac's advice, he had to find out what she was up to. Her mobile that never left her side would no doubt provide the answers.

Outside, as the heavens opened, he watched Tina go through her daily routine of snorting cocaine followed by a bottle of white wine. She either switched on the TV or her music. Her attempt to converse was babble. What little food she ate was from a tin or a jar. When she could neither walk nor talk, she slept.

That was his opportunity to check her mobile. He scrolled through her list of 'Recent' mobile calls, read her text messages, emails and listened to her voicemail messages; his blood ran cold. She had been in regular contact with a police officer and the head of the Merchants family who had placed a bounty on his head.

As he saw it – Tina had engineered a situation to use him as bait to entice the Merchants out of their environment to collect him, then tell the police where the handover was happening.

How did Tina become involved with such plans? To whom had she spoken? He had never mentioned the Merchants, or Glasgow South Siders by title or mentioned any names associated with either gang. He referred to them only as gangs. The reason behind that was the fact he had never trusted Tina.

Tina was volatile and had threatened on many occasions to drop him in it. When he occasionally refused her drugs, alcohol, or money, she made it clear he needed a lesson. She would storm out of the house and return hours later. So, from where did she get the information about the Merchants family?

He shuddered; meeting either gang or been spotted by one of their many associates would have consequences. He would face certain hospitalization or be buried alive in a field in the middle of nowhere

He could visualise the scene – the police clashing with armed criminals. Watching from the sidelines was Tina, who had played both sides off against each other, with him as bait.

In haste, he packed his bags; unaware Tina was awake. When she spotted him in the bedroom, with her mobile, she grabbed a poker from the fireplace. Screaming like a banshee, she ran into the bedroom. Richard raised his arms in defence, as Tina struck him twice. Ignoring the pain, he grabbed her poker arm and knocked her flat out.

The lake

When she awoke, restrained by ropes, Richard glared at her from the settee eating an apple.

"Why did you attack me?"

"You were going to leave," she answered with a chuckle, "and if you did, I'd lose my bounty."

"Bounty? Are you saying you've sold me out?"

"Yes."

"Who knows I'm here?"

"The Merchants want you because you killed their mate Jim Stone."

"I've never mentioned the Merchants. How do you know about them?"

Tina shrugged her shoulders, "When they get you, they'll pay me a crisp ten grand in notes to disappear."

"You stupid bitch!" he retorted, wanting to smash the ceiling. "They'll kill you before handing over any cash."

"THEY WON'T! They promised me the money."

"You have no fucking idea, do you? You've signed your death warrant. They won't waste their money on an addict like you no matter how many blowjobs you offer. Why do you think I never mentioned their names to you?" He banged his fist off the arm of the chair. "To stop you from going off and talking when you're on a bender. How many times have you dropped us in it because you're pissed or stoned? Where are they now?" he snapped, dashing to the window to look outside. The last thing he wanted to see was two or three cars driving towards the croft. That meant they were coming heavy handed ready to take him out – and Tina. "And did you have an arrangement with the police?"

"Yes, but they aren't interested in you. My orders were to use you to lure the Merchants out into the open. I did as they told me. They wanted the Merchants behind bars and then use you as a witness."

"A witness to what? I ripped them off. I wasn't part of their activities."

"That's not how the cops see you. They want you for being part of the gang. The reason you weren't picked up sooner was you disappeared."

His patience snapped. For years, her demands, her wants and needs led him to cross personal boundaries. She had betrayed him to a gang who would kill as a warning to others. Finally, her contact with the Police. What was she thinking?

"I guessed there was a reason why the law released you so soon."

"And now you know," she mocked him. "Poor little boy growing up on the wild side and finds the big bad world of drug dealing too tough. I got what I needed from you – free drugs – and now I'm handing you over to real men."

Unable to contain his resentment any longer, he grabbed her throat and crushed the life from her. Tina's dependant drug habit and behaviour had proved to be a liability. The fact she was talking to people who wanted him dead was one step too far. Her betrayal after years together was the final straw.

He left her dead in the bedroom and took shelter in the small shed outside from where he could see the road leading to the croft. For all, he knew the Merchants might have lookouts watching the croft waiting for Tina's signal to move in. Tucking a thick blanket around for warmth, he dropped in and out of sleep. As the hours ticked away and morning broke, he breathed sighs of relief when the odd car drove by.

At sunrise, it was time to dump the body. Richard placed Tina's body in coal sacks weighted with large rocks before rowing out into the vast open water. There he heaved her weighted body overboard into the dull, peaty depths.

Only her parents might consider where she might be.

Time to leave Scotland and move to London; not the best of places, but it would, he hoped, give him the space he needed.

In Central London, he rented a service flat and set out to do business. However, finding people with whom to do business was a time-consuming business. Fate was about to change his life when he stopped for a piss behind a hoarding board on derelict land.

A vehicle pulled into the entrance and screeched to a stop a short distance away. Richard gasped in disbelief when the driver and his mate appeared and hauled another two men from the cargo area onto the dusty ground before leaving. From where he was standing, it was clear that only one man was alive.

As his curiosity took over, he offered his help. He got the needed break with none other than Archie Suggs.

A breakfast conversation – continued

"I have a proposal for you."

"Go on."

"Let's play a game titled – kill the gangster." Jack locked his fingers. "You want Archie dead, don't you?"

Is this a joke? thought Richard. "Is this a joint enterprise or an individual effort?"

"You're close to him most of the week."

"He's never alone," groaned Richard. "And if I moved on him, I'd be dead."

"That's the challenge. So, let's see which of us can kill our favourite gangster."

"Are you serious?" questioned Richard, unsure if it was a joke.

"I'm always serious. The name of the game is 'Kill the Gangsta'."

"What's the prize?"

"A dead Archie."

Jack left the table grinning from ear to ear.

Why did Jack want Archie Suggs dead? Do they know each other?

CHAPTER 23

2014 | Scorpio | Oct 23 – Nov 22

Oct 24th | 02:30 Hrs

Once again, after drinking too much alcohol, the settee became his bed. Through the haze of restless sleep, a shrilling telephone awoke him. Slipping off the sofa, he picked up the receiver and croaked a Hello.

"I'm just phoning to play a game with you, titled 'mock the copper'."

"Show yourself, coward!"

"Ah, you've been hitting the bottle," laughed the caller, "finding comfort way down in glasses of Scotch."

"Where are you?"

"I am here. You're my obsession, my muse, my speck of fun. I'm otherwise a man of leisure, a man who enjoys the good life who haunts you for a laugh. When I get bored, I'll kill you."

"What am I to you?"

"I'm the man whose shape has haunted your life. When you see me again, you will fear me or do what I did to those women. We're playing cat and mouse – run, play, hide-and-seek. You run – I play, you hide – I seek, or shall we do it the other way around?"

"Bullshit!"

"Will you be ready for our confrontation?"

"I'll be ready."

"Just like your wife!"

"Don't disturb the memory of my wife, you evil bastard."

"Your wife – an attractive, a charming woman."

"You never met her… never!" gasped Grant.

"She was so fresh, so alive when I touched her – believe me – that woman did not shudder at my touch – she loved my touch."

Rage swelled in Stuart. *Did Joan meet Zodiac?*

"An attractive, approachable woman, oh how I'm sure you miss her touch, how she looked after you on those long, cold, winter nights."

"You're a sick bastard. Tell me something. If you had met Joan, then you would know she had a distinctive mark. Where is it?"

Moments later, the lounge door swung open. A dark shape appeared with a familiar voice.

"I've dropped by tonight to let you meet your nemesis – me – Zodiac!"

Stuart was slow to react and was caught flat footed. Before he could move he took two blows to his face painfully wrenching back his neck. The shape pulled Stuart to his feet and held him, punching his face and chest. Stuart tried to defend his head and lashed out randomly trying to land a decisive blow, only to strike air. As the shape held him in place Stuart spoke.

"Why are you keeping me alive? demanded Stuart, "why don't you kill me, get it over and done with. You have won, I lost. Go – on – you have me at your mercy – end it for me, come on!"

"Not yet, not just yet," replied Zodiac. "If I killed you there goes my amusement. No doubt, once you recover from tonight's meeting, we'll speak soon."

Lying back, he struggled with the pain and agony of the thrashing. It was the past coming to life in the present as the man in black repeated his actions. Through a blur of movement, he saw a light and a familiar distorted voice.

"Dad, what's happened?"

"Harry, call the police," he grunted, "he's here!"

"Who's here?" asked Harry, glancing around the lounge expecting someone to appear. "Who's here, Dad? There's no one here."

Gawping at his father's bloodied face, his eyes darted back and forth, spotting an empty bottle of Scotch next to the armchair.

"Have you had a bad dream and smashed your face in, Dad!" snapped Harry, grabbing the bottle. "That bottle was new today. You're drinking too much?" Harry watched in disbelief as his dad collapsed in a heap against the settee.

04:30 Hrs

Truman sat next to a depressed-looking Harry sitting alone in the Hospital family room, vulnerable and alone.

"What happened?"

"A noise from downstairs awoke me. Shouting and that. When I opened the lounge door, there was my dad on the floor, his face covered in blood. He said someone was there and told me to ring the police."

"What do you think?"

"He fought with a battle with Scotch and lost; he's always losing to drink."

"Has he been drinking a lot?"

Harry stared at Truman in disbelief. "Are you telling me you can't smell it when he arrives at work? Most mornings he reeks of booze. My dad's getting a sugar rush every day on all the mints he eats to hide his smelly breath."

"I can smell it. No one else has mentioned it to me."

"Then don't ask stupid questions."

"OK, message received. I've learnt my lesson. Last night was a result of drinking. But as of now, you can't stay at home until we know what happened. Your home is now an official crime scene."

"I'll call my Uncle Stan and stay there."

Truman walked to the A&E where a nurse pointed towards a cubicle. Stuart lay semi-conscious hooked to various machines that buzzed and beeped. Next to him was a doctor reading a chart.

"What's the damage to my friend here?" queried Truman, checking Stuart over.

The doctor glanced up, tired and in need of rest. When he spoke, his voice sounded dry. "Severe concussion and we suspect a fractured eye socket, a fractured jaw and several broken ribs."

"That bad?"

"It could be worse, What I've told you is a preliminary diagnosis."

A nurse threw back the curtain. "There's a call for Mr Truman at the reception desk."

*****

"Detective Inspector Truman."

"Ah, yes, how is Stuart?"

"Why should I speak to you?" snarled Truman, "You're a wanted murderer who should be behind bars."

"I reasserted my superior ability to move unhindered and inflict pain where necessary. I had to teach Stuart a lesson for arguing with me."

Truman scoffed. "Someone disagrees with you, so you go and beat him up?"

"He should listen to me and stop arguing."

"We are coming for you. Make no mistake."

"I have advice for you, Alan Truman. Keep watching over your shoulder – you're next."

Nov 1st | 20:00 Hrs

Archie Suggs was enjoying the delights of a porno mag in his man-cave when his landline rang.

"Am I talking to Archie Suggs?" asked the caller.

"Yes, mate."

"I have called to give you a piece of advice."

"What ya talkin' about, geezer?"

"Advising you to plan for a funeral."

"Who for?"

"You!"

"Fuck off, mate! Who the hell are you?"

"Your executioner."

" Enjoy your last day because, in twenty-four hours, you'll be history."

"Who are ya?" raged Suggs

"Who I am doesn't matter. I'm on a mission to kill you. I just thought I'd give you fair warning."

"You think so, geezer," rasped an apprehensive Archie, "You won't get near me. I have protection.

"Yeah. You're Archie Suggs. Do you have another name?"

"Seeing as you know my name, then you know what I can have done to ya."

"Heed my words. I will come for you, Archie. You won't see me coming."

Archie called three men known for their no-nonsense approach to dealing with like-minded criminals. Their task was to visit well-known rivals and ask questions to determine who the caller was, and then deal with him. They returned many hours later with no information of value meaning Archie was none the wiser.

Nov 3rd | 03:00 Hrs

After the caller's twenty-four-hour deadline passed with no names in the hat, a relived Archie pressed on with his plans to meet business contacts. He dismissed the threat as another hoax; more hot air from an unknown crank, it was a way of life in his profession.

Archie decided that travelling alone might not be a good idea, he called in Higgins, his driver, and six men, including Richard. He wanted reliable protection in case the caller decided to act.

When two cars arrived, Archie jumped into the back seat of the first car. Three men joined him. Richard sat in the second car with two colleagues wishing the evening was over.

In the nightclub, Archie finished the new business within thirty minutes; he had no patience for long, tedious meetings. The right price meant business. If not, go elsewhere. After that, the alcohol flowed while the girls danced and offered private dances.

Archie, using his unique brand of chat-up lines, persuaded one hostess to go home with him. However, he wanted privacy to get the hostess warmed up, ready to do as he wished when he got her home. The planned foreplay meant all the men were to follow in the second car.

Richard found himself crushed against the door listening to his colleagues chatter about football, a topic in which he had no interest apart from making money to buy his Scottish castle. He was close to sleep when a clunking noise under the car raised moans from the driver. Seconds later, the engine cut out. Richard perked up and gripped the door handle.

Richard pushed the door open and rolled away just as an explosion filled the interior, blowing out the windows and the doors. The driver and passenger screamed in abject horror as flames engulfed their entire bodies. Seconds later, the whole car blew up.

Two passers-by dashed towards Richard, grabbed him and dragged him away. He stared in disbelief at the burning car. What was Jack thinking? That bomb could have killed him. As he pressed up against a wall, a crowd of people gathered capturing the moments on their smartphones. With attention on the car, he walked away before the police arrived.

Archie ordered Higgins out to see what had happened while the hostess shrunk down behind the seats wondering what sort of people she had met.

With attention on the fire, no one noticed the lone figure dressed in black who slipped into Archie's car and drive off at breakneck speed. Many hours later police found the hostess dumped dead by the side of a quiet road.

A sorry end for a gangster

Turning off the A413 down a narrow lane, he turned

onto a dirt track. He killed the headlights and coasted to the doors of a large barn. The land belonged to his father, but you never knew who you might meet.

Collecting a trolley from the barn, he wheeled a heavy Archie inside where he stripped off his clothes then used a pulley rope to haul Archie into a standing position.

Ten minutes later, he reclined on a bale of hay to wait for Archie to come to and react as expected.

"Hoi you, I can see you, ya cunt – why am I here and why am I naked?"

"Who are you talking to?" asked Jack, strolling towards his captive.

"You," beckoned Archie, "come and tell me why I'm here and let me see ya!"

"Archie – Archie, you are mine. I will do with you as I please. If that frightens you. It oughta."

"I'll start again," snapped Archie. "Are you a shirt lifter – a cunt!"

"You're feisty, much like your dad who you take after in so many ways."

"What's he got to do with you?" seethed Archie. "No one talks about my dad."

"Oh. The mystery of your dad's death is out. What a shocker for you to hear. I killed him!"

"Who are ya? You couldn't have killed my old man, you're about my age, what ya talking about, YOU killed my father – who is ya kiddin'?"

"On your sixteenth birthday, he prioritised a poker tournament over your birthday. A day or two later police found him dead."

"That's how the newspapers reported it," retorted Archie. "So tells me something the newspapers didn't say."

"He had ligature marks around his neck, wrists and feet and rope fibres in his arse?"

Archie's face dropped as his eyes narrowed. "You ruined my sixteenth birthday and destroyed my mother! What was my old man to you?"

"Let's call it personal. It's called therapy. A retrospective treatment for my soul."

"You know what?" sneered Archie.

"Yes, I do. I told your father I was considering a professional career in violence. His answer, 'Anything but that!'"

"He was wise, my dad," whispered Archie. "If you will kill me, tell me who are you? I have a right to know."

Jack framed his face with his hands. "Look; who do you see?"

"What am I supposed to see?"

"Your dad couldn't see it. Neither will you, but I'll tell you a secret."

Jack held his index finger to his lips before whispering into Archie's ear. As the stranger moved away, Archie looked at him in bewilderment.

"I don't believe you!"

"Why not, Archie?" chuckled the stranger as he grasped a rope with a knotted end. "Now you know the devastating secret it's time for you to go."

As Archie's eyes settled on the rope and the way the stranger ran it through his hands, it was enough to make him shudder. Like a dark foreboding cloud, death stared down. It was too late for concluding this encounter was not a warning but a callous disregard for his life. There was no probable about the situation; he was dead. His jaw dropped to emit a silent scream.

"WHAT YA GONNA DO WIV THAT, NOW?" bellowed Archie.

"Swingball, Archie!"

A shade of pale crept over Archie as he pleaded.

"You can't do this, I deserve—"

"You DESERVE nothing, Archie. I'm a man forged in a world of self-indulgence. Where violent men cheapened the right-to-life by using murder as a weapon to silence those who thought of grassing, it created a profession for me. I am a professional whose commodity is death. You, Archie, are my next victim."

Nov 4th | 11:30 Hrs

Rob Lloyd, a member of the forensics team, paced the floor examining a burnt-out car as Alan Truman glanced over four charred bodies still in their seats.

"Did you find any ID to say who they are?" queried Truman, stepping up to the car.

"Are you kidding?" scoffed Rob. "That's charred flesh, you see there."

Truman checked each corpse before commenting, "Archie Suggs isn't one of these bodies."

"Do you have a close a personal relationship with him?" asked Floyd, wondering how Truman could tell. "If you know the names tell me."

"Archie is over six foot six and weighs at least seventeen stones. These men are nowhere near that height or size."

"Did you know Suggs was in a separate car? No one saw what happened."

"I didn't know," replied Truman, looking around the yard. "Any news on that?"

"That's your area of expertise, is it not? But since you ask the kidnapper dumped the woman dead in the road. Before you ask, that's all I know."

"Thanks, but it's a CID job, I'm on Zodiac watch. That's my brief."

"Before you go, how's the DCI? I hear an intruder beat him."

"Yeah, he's on the mend. He looked like he tangled with juggernaut and came off third best."

"That bad?"

"Far worse."

"Anyone in the frame?"

"We're working on it."

"Give him my best. We've enjoyed a few nights out with him in the past."

"I'll catch up with him today, not that he can talk much with a broken jaw."

Truman strode off towards ZHQ. A dead Archie was a loss to his community. His influence and presence kept order amongst the various crime syndicates. What would happen now he was dead? Would Molly keep order in the neighbourhood?

Nov 6th | 11:00 Hrs

The previous evening brought the news Truman hoped not to hear. A pedestrian had found Archie Suggs dead down an alley.

Truman tapped his fingers on the desk just as his landline chirped.

"Truman."

"Hello Alan, Ron Tyler here. Before I talk about Archie, it's worth mentioning his father."

"Arthur."

"Yes – Arthur Suggs, before your time, I know."

"Tell me."

"The injuries to Arthur and Archie are almost identical. They were both tortured to death with something heavy designed for maximum effect; we think it may have been a rope. Archie died of multiple haematomas, from multiple bruises, what we call Critical Level Bruises that led to his death."

"Why is that dangerous?"

"Internal bleeding is dangerous for two reasons; the excess blood can compress organs and cause their failure. So, when the bleeding doesn't stop, losing blood will cause haemorrhagic shock, which can lead to brain damage and death. And that's what I'm suggesting for Archie although I haven't done a full-scale autopsy on him yet."

"Much appreciated, this belongs to CID."

"Also, just to shake it up." Tyler paused. "Wasn't one of Suggs' men tortured to death earlier that year in his own home, but not in the same way?"

"I'm not sure I like the suggestion."

"Yes," chuckled Tyler. "You may have another serial killer doing gangsters."

Watford | Kings Langley | 22:30 Hrs

Desiree Scorer stumbled into her lounge after an early evening out with her friends. After checking the fridge for snacks and wine, she sat down and gazed at the blank television.

"Where the hell are you?" she whispered. "Why didn't you turn up as promised? Men, I can't live with them, can't live without them."

During her birthday soiree, she kept checking her mobile for messages – nothing. He became a no-show. That meant her evening was ending sooner than expected. As it was a work night, her friends left early. The silence after the laughter in the restaurant was unbearable.

"Where are you?" she snapped, thinking back to four weeks earlier when she had met a man who she could not get out of her mind – a smart, smooth man who spoke eloquently and treated her like a lady. As the evening wore on, she visualised ripping off his clothes. Jump on him, be spontaneous.

To her considerable surprise, he suggested they wait.

Come morning, does he think I won't respect him, or the other way around? What am I thinking?

Unusual but she respected his decision. When they hugged, she could feel his muscles rippling under his clothes. It did not help her growing lust.

I may carry a bit of weight, but I'm an attractive woman. My curves are all in the right places, pretty face. Mean kissing lips that no man could ignore, wherever I place them! What is wrong with him?

Oh, my god, she thought. *Is he gay? – At this rate, I'll be a shrivelled prune. All dried up.*

With a sigh, she wandered to her bedroom. Flicking the light switch, the bulb lit up then popped, leaving her bedroom in darkness. That was all she needed.

Gripping the curtains, she looked outside at the streetlights and houses across the road. With a deep sigh, she drew the curtains, undressed and fell into the bed to snuggle under the duvet.

Fifteen minutes later, hot and restless, she threw off the duvet and stretched out. As she rolled over, she touched something warm and firm. Her heart leapt. Someone was lying next to her. Who was it?

Shaking with anxiety and indecision, she threw the duvet aside to expose the dark outline of someone in her bed.

"I said I'd be here for your birthday!"

She freaked as she leapt up and threw open the curtains.

"Where did you come from? Creeping up on me like that?"

"Happy birthday, Desiree."

"Jesus, who do you think you are scaring me like that? What's up with you?"

"I came to surprise you!"

"SURPRISE ME? You're giving me a heart attack. Why can't you do the usual thing and call me up or text me and ask me if you can visit?"

He frowned, curled his lips and gave a small, "Oops."

"Get out of my house now," she demanded.

"You are so – so, ungrateful," he reacted with a tilt of his head. "You've wanted to fuck me for weeks."

"Get out!" she screamed. "Get out, why don't you? I didn't invite you, weirdo."

"Happy birthday, Desiree!"

CHAPTER 24

2014 | Sagittarius | Nov 22 – Dec 21

December 11th

Stuart looked at the calendar as a wave of haunting depression dropped his mood. It was too easy to sit and stare into space, trying to fight an invisible demon.

That day, he needed a chink of light and a clear head. Ross had finished his first term and was coming home for Christmas. Bristol was a long drive. During the journey, he occupied his mind with trivia and lively music. Zodiac. A certain subject.

From the moment Ross jumped into the car, he could see changes. He looked different, spoke differently. It was non-stop chatter about his new friends. His degree and all the essays for submission before the semester end. University was working out. Stuart could relax until Ross mentioned money.

"Oh, thanks for the hundred pounds."

Bemused, Grant glanced at Ross. "Sorry, what do you mean?"

"The hundred pounds you transferred into my account on Wednesday."

Grant smiled. "Oh yes, an early Christmas present."

"You've forgotten about it? Nobody transfers a hundred quid and forgets about it."

"A senior moment. I do something and forget." His father bore a look of confusion. "It's called a senior moment."

"Obviously!" remarked Ross. "But don't let that stop you making more contributions to student finances."

"Of course… of course," flustered Stuart.

"Are we going to France for Christmas or have you forgotten?"

"Yes, we're going to France."

December 12th | 10:30

With his mood staying in a dark place, he thought about taking a walk to update his knowledge on hacking. The best place was the local internet café. There he researched online fraud and the more he learned, the more concerned he became.

His only choice was to call his brother-in-law – Doctor Tom Jeffery, a cybersecurity expert – who he knew would ask awkward questions. What other options were available to him – none.

*****

"OK," responded Tom, opening his kit bag. "I'll sweep your house and see what my equipment detects."

"Is that what you call your James Bond kit bag?"

quizzed Stuart, glancing at the various bits and pieces.

"This equipment is real and more sophisticated than James Bond Q Branch inventions," suggested Tom, holding up a small device. "This is a bug detector. It will find any electronic devices hidden in the house and disable them. Might I suggest you wait here until I'm done."

*****

Tom placed three small items on the dining table, along with Stuart's laptop and mobile phone.

"First, these three items are listening devices."

"Where were they?"

"In your bedroom, meaning he's been listening to you for some time."

Stuart's face dropped as Tom continued.

"Your mobile phone contains a personalised tracking device. The bad news is he knew where you were and heard your conversations," remarked Tom, watching Stuart's face for his reaction – which was a huge sigh.

"Every movement," repeated Tom.

"So, he's been tracking and listening to my conversation?"

"I suggest 'sweeping' the entire house," placing a hand on the laptop he continued, "but first, let's check this laptop," suggested Tom, inserting a Memory Stick to start the boot sequence. As more information appeared Tom traced his finger on the screen with a look of suspicion on his face.

"It's infected with multiple Trojan Horses that

have recorded your online activity."

Tom's eyebrows raised as the list grew. Giving an audible lament, he said, "I'll take your laptop home to examine in my lab. I'll return later with the results."

Stuart watched Tom depart feeling a dark mood settle. The only way it could end was to neutralise Zodiac or kill him if the opportunity arose. His mood lightened?

18:30 Hrs

When Tom returned, Stuart guessed whatever he had learned would not be good news.

"I called a friend who's an expert on covert technology. He asked where I got this RAT. I told him, for now, I can't say." Tom met Stuart's gaze. "So, given the fact you're working on the Zodiac case, there's something you ought to know."

A tense moment absorbed Stuart. "More! OK. Go on."

"No one knows who Zodiac is – right?"

"Correct."

"For years, security communities worldwide have been trying to track a certain hacker. So, why am I thinking hacker and Zodiac? Rogue states use these Remote Access Trackers – RATs – found on your laptops to collect sensitive commercial information. Our hacker uses these as spyware to steal sensitive information from competitors. That intel sells on for millions. I've attended conferences sponsored by banks. Once these RATs are embedded, they can cost businesses millions of pounds from cyber threats. However, there are rumours that the RAT, like the one I found on your laptop, can adapt to remain undetectable."

"Right, so we're looking for a serial killer who is a technological wizard."

"More than that. I suspect you're looking for an engineer with some remarkable skills."

An earlier discussion with Alan Truman came to mind.

"...the FBI has suggested Zodiac, Raymond McCoy, is a talented engineer, a technological genius..."

Shall I tell him we know that? No. It's confidential information.

"OK, so you think your hacker and my Zodiac are the same men?"

"It's possible."

"How close has he been?"

"Let's go outside," suggested Tom, grabbing his laptop, "and I'll show you how easy it is to access a wireless network."

Outside, Tom pointed to a list of Wi-Fi networks. "Here is yours at full five-bar strength, the rest belong to your neighbours. Let's see what happens when we walk along the street!"

They ventured along the street where the list of Wi-Fi connections expanded. Tom stopped walking.

"Until two to three yards back, it was detecting your wireless network at full strength. We're thirty yards from your house – as you can see – the signal is down to one bar."

"Let's walk back," suggested Tom, pointing to Stuart's Wi-Fi name that resumed its five-bar strength.

"What does that bolt-shaped icon mean?"

"That means they have a unique key to prevent an outsider from accessing their network – but—"

"Don't tell me," interrupted Stuart, "anyone with the skills could hack the key."

December 15th | 11.00 Hrs

Leaving his Bank Manager to reflect upon their discussion, an exasperated Grant stared skywards. He shivered as drops of rain and a frigid wind whistled through the Town Centre of Cheston.

The dull skies hanging over the town did not help his darkening mood. Zodiac was pushing him to the limits of sanity; pushing all his buttons. He needed it all to stop. How much more could he take? The pressure and stress.

In the pocket of his trousers, his mobile phone vibrated. Swiping the screen, he answered with a brisk, "Hello?"

"Stuart. So glad you answered. It's your favourite killer!"

"You've been in my house, what gives you the right?"

"Rights? What are those." Zodiac laughed, "I like sneaking around in strange houses. Yet these days yours isn't so strange."

"Don't fuck with me. What am I to you?"

"Language, Stuart. I like you – I like you a lot!"

"Yeah, sending me and the boys spyware by email and using it to skim keystroke information – what do you want from us?"

"Your brother-in-law knows his stuff, so much so he took all my toys to have a closer look."

"Will his analysis tell us who you are or are you beyond being exposed, hiding behind a barrier of smart technology?"

"I'm smart. That's why I'm alive today and not dead."

"Show yourself. Are you scared to show your face?"

"You're not brave enough to meet me face to face to fight me."

The line went dead, leaving a fuming Stuart to scream, to vent his anger. Instead, he crossed the road heading towards a homeless man holding a sign, which read: 'Homeless and hungry'.

Grant opened his wallet and placed a ten-pound note in the hands of the homeless man.

"Thank you, sir."

"You're welcome." Grant walked off into a café where he ordered a large latte and a millionaire shortbread and sat close to the window to watch the people passing by. After eating the last morsel of the shortbread, he read his emails. While he did, his head slowly nodded forward.

…Holding a photo of himself and Joan, he traced the outline of her face. Checking his reflection in the mirror, he

jumped as a man in black reached through the mirror and grabbed his throat…

"…Sir – sir, are you OK?" He awoke to find a barista standing next to him. "You fell asleep. It sounded like you were choking."

December 16th | 08:30 Hrs

Truman was sitting at a desk going through reports, when Grant entered the office. "What are you doing here? I didn't expect you back until the New Year."

"Got bored and need action. Zodiac is getting up close and personal, and it's going to stop soon. Very soon."

"What's he done now?"

"Zodiac's been in my home planting bugs."

"He's determined to wind you up. Any idea when it was?"

"No."

"The thought of a serial killer mooching around your house planting devices is a total invasion of privacy."

Grant glanced at Truman. "I'm up for this return to work in case you're wondering."

Truman caught a whiff of alcohol as Grant fell into his chair, opened a bottle of water and took a massive swig before grabbing at the papers on his desk. Moments later, his mobile shrilled.

"How you are?" asked Zodiac.

"Are you taking the piss?" questioned Stuart, "Go

away. Leave me be."

Zodiac clicked his tongue several times, "Recently I've been close enough to see you walk a lonely path to the shops. I can almost hear the arguments that rage and absorb you."

"Is that your usual MO, to sneak into homes?"

"Yes. It's fun. Twice I had you. But I didn't kill you. Why? Because I like you, Stuart."

"That's encouraging. Give yourself up?"

"Why would I do that?"

"Because it's the right move."

"Let me finish," chuckled Zodiac. "What is pure misery for others, I consider fun. When I spared you, little did I know you'd be the head honcho trying to lock me up. The press sees me as a bad boy because I'm famous in all but my given name. Their review of your performance is journalistic integrity at its best!"

"I haven't read that article yet."

"Oh, you soon will. The Guardian journalist who wrote the article is an ardent feminist and considers male coppers to be useless and suggests women would run the police force better."

"If she does, then she's welcome to join the team and share her experience of policing."

"No, she won't do that…"

"Have you met her?"

"Oops, I slipped up."

"Have you met her?"

"Ask her. Be careful, she's all mouth and trousers

and writes a good game, but I doubt she'd even know where to look. Very much like yourselves."

"Is she going to be a victim?"

"After this conversation? No chance."

"Get to the point!"

"Today is December 20th with Capricorn in the ascendant. It's a long time since we spoke, Stuart; I'm calling to wish you a Merry Christmas. I like to be sure family, friends and enemies alike are not suffering undue seasonal distress in their work."

"Who is she?"

"Check your email, Stuart? – I've sent you some homemade entertainment."

Death on film

Attached to the email was a MPEG film file, which Grant, with the help of the tech department streamed through to a larger screen. The team sat in silence as a camera wound its way past hanging jangling chains, blood-soaked shower curtains and mannequins hanging from their necks. A strip light came into focus while in the background, there were indistinguishable murmurings.

The camera brushed past a set of shower curtains and floated over a young woman. She was gagged and strapped to the frame of a physician's couch. Her eyes widened as the camera pulled back to show a man approaching from behind the curtains. The camera swung to the rear of his head, obscured by the lack of light.

Inclining over the woman, who thrashed about, he asked, "Are you comfortable, can I get you anything?"

To his right, was a stainless-steel tray holding an assortment of medical tools.

"As you will not answer, we need to continue. Shall we begin?"

Her expression changed to fear as he chose a scalpel and held it up to the light.

"Let me tell you about me – the visionary. I don't care what people think. The way I talk, think, does have its moments. But it works for me. I know how to live. My fellow humans cannot match me for intellect. I'm a saviour, a transgressional. My acts are that of mercy. I give people the gift of death and leave behind the horror of daily existence."

He moved the scalpel back and forward slowly. The blade cut fine lines into the skin – a precision blade.

"Tell me. How would you feel if I held an object you desired? But you can't have it. You decode nothing will stop you from owning it. From deep inside – instinct – drives you forward. But should you get it, will you be able to keep it? What could that object be? An item, cash to live beyond your dreams or an intangible desire such as peace."

The camera pulled out as he replaced the scalpel and turned his back on the woman while speaking in a rich, hypnotic tone, devoid of threat, of violence, but with a distinct edge of finality.

"As a child, they corrupted my eyes and mind creating deep flaws in my world, blackening and tarnishing my mind. The excess of others. I feel neither pain nor sympathy. My conscience is non-existent. My parents died lonely deaths without loved ones. Death can be lonely if loved ones do not attend your dying moments. I have no faith. My fractious mind creates my truth influenced by sodomites and parasites."

The camera focused on the medical tray as he selected a knife.

"Your search is over. I'm here to fix you."

The camera moved to the knife which he held aloft. In a blur of movement, a wrenching scream cut right through the audience as the victim's blood spattered the curtains. The camera moved above the dead woman as a man in a black mask came into focus.

"Death becomes you, dear," he whispered, placing a silver water carrier charm around her neck. "Let me deliver a message to you, the police searching for me. What do I care about morality? It has different meanings for different people. My deeds give society a platform to debate how men judge guys like me. If you read books, you can read the nonsense written by academics and libertarians who look to make excuses for the immoral deeds of others – the man I am – the man whom law-abiding citizens want so they may wallow in the glory. I have you in my grasp. When I kill, I do so because I can."

CHAPTER 25

2014 | Capricorn | Dec 22 – Jan 21

December 23ʳᵈ | 02:50 Hrs

His dreams kept repeating the video the team named the Zodiac file. The images and the build-up to the final scene remained etched in his memory. It was not a fictitious Hollywood death, but a real murder of a real person.

There were consequences. He slept little, and drank too much. As usual in those depressing times, his thoughts turned to Joan, visualising her presence. The prevalent silence since her death hung like dark clouds around his head. Where was Joan with her comfort and her love now when he needed her?

The moment of her death ushered in a dark time where all their conversations ended. The silence erupted. He wanted to walk with Joan to that unknown place; hold her, talk to her and touch her.

He had grieved internally and shown little of his grief to friends or his sons. It was biting away at him. In a moment of rare clarity, he grabbed a coat and left the house. The night was chilly, misty, damp. He entered the graveyard where he sat on a bench opposite a headstone unaware of his actions.

'Here lies Joan Grant. Beloved wife and mother...'

The long-awaited grief numbed by alcohol spilt over. Since Joan's death, he gave the pretence that he would cope; her death left a larger hole then he could ever imagine.

Gone was the pretence as he visualised her within an aura of light standing only feet away watching him. Around him a swirling mist and cold wind closed in. Ignoring it as best as he could he pulled up the collar on his coat to stop the shivering. Lifting his legs onto the bench, he stretched out and yawned as again a cold wind bit at his face.

08:15 Hrs

When their alarms blared, the Grant brothers showered and dressed. There was no time to waste. They were spending Christmas with their aunt in France; travelling by Eurostar before catching a connection to Normandy.

Before they sat for breakfast, Harry dashed upstairs and barged into his father's bedroom. He glanced at an empty bed, an empty suitcase and plugged into a charger on the chest of drawers was his father's mobile.

A graveyard, a church and a vicar

Wearing a black cape that reached her ankles, the Reverend Josephine Hooper entered the cemetery under the lychgate and followed a path covered by a ghostly white mist.

The mist reminded her of horror films she and friends watched as teenagers only to scare themselves and cling to each other for comfort as Dracula sunk his fangs into the neck of a victim. Despite her spiritual beliefs, she had niggling doubts about ghosts and evil spirits.

As the path turned, and the mist reached her knees, there came a call for help. She stopped and listened. It was not unusual for the homeless to sleep within the precincts of the church, or the odd drunk who lost their way going home from a local pub.

"Who's there? Are you a lost sheep?"

"I'm not lost. I'm frozen."

"Oh dear, did you sleep out here?" she asked, spotting movement through the mist.

"I don't know."

Josephine cautiously approached the ghostly figure and leaned over to get a closer look at the face. "Ahh, Mr Grant. It's a little early to be visiting the grave of your wife."

Looking sheepish and embarrassed all at once, he croaked a reply. "I wasn't aware that I had. I don't remember leaving the house."

As she caught the whiff of alcohol, she remarked, "More than one spirit was at work last night. You're a lucky man, Mr Grant; it was cold out here last night, it's a wonder you didn't freeze to death."

Stuart gazed up, swallowing hard, trying to rid his dry throat of the lingering taste of Scotch.

"Can I invite you inside into a warm lounge and let me make you a hot drink and maybe something to eat?"

Stuart's joints ached with the cold as he followed the reverend as they traversed the narrow pathways leading to the porch of the vicarage where they entered the reception hall. Josephine threw off her cape and ushered Stuart through to a chair in the lounge warmed by a log fire. Tired, cold and confused, he slumped into the chair battling to remain awake.

Tea with the vicar

Eight hours later, he awoke just as Josephine appeared clad in her robes. Noting his wide-eyed stare and confusion, she offered comfort.

"Don't worry. I'm not here to read your last rites. Do you remember meeting me earlier?"

"I remember sitting in the churchyard."

"At least we know you haven't lost your marbles," remarked the familiar voice of Alan Truman who appeared carrying two cups.

"The reverend made a discreet phone call asking me to call in because your boys are in France right now with your sister who has been on the phone several times asking me where you are."

Grant buried his face in his hands and groaned.

"You're welcome," scoffed Truman. "I told them a last-minute emergency came up, and you'd be there tonight."

"Thank you," responded Grant, looking up. "Did

she say anything?"

"Yes, she'll still kick your arse for not telling the boys where you were."

"Ah, em, gentlemen."

"Sorry Vicar," responded Truman, handing the tea to Grant. "Might I suggest, once you've drunk that, we rearrange your trip to France so you can have a family Christmas and thank the vicar here for her intervention."

*****

Truman could not fathom why Stuart would leave his house and walk to the cemetery unless he had drunk too much. When they entered the house, Truman decided it was the time for a conversation about his drinking.

"I don't know what you were thinking last night. But I blame the drink for your midnight venture."

Stuart stuck his hands in his pockets. "I think we can say you're right again."

"Stuart, this drinking of yours is a problem. Every morning you smell like a brewery. Your eyes are barely open. You're dishevelled. It's time to give the booze up. I know you miss your wife, but life must go on. Drinking isn't going to ease the pain; it only dulls the pain."

"OK, I get that. Starting today, it's a wake-up call. I can't go on like this." Stuart could feel the pangs of addiction kicking in.

"Well, consider this; in my opinion, Zodiac is leading us in circles; to counter that we need you to lead."

"I hear you."

Alan nudged Stuart bearing a wry smile. "You never cease to amaze me. You visit your dead wife, fall asleep in a graveyard and end in the arms of an attractive vicar."

"It was her sofa."

"Said the actress to the bishop." Truman shrugged with a laugh and continued while Stuart rolled his eyes. "What can I say? She's an attractive-looking vicar. She's single?"

"Really?"

"She wasn't wearing a wedding ring."

"What's that supposed to mean?"

"Nothing. Just an observation – that's all!"

20:00 Hrs

Alan Truman waited until Stuart left in a taxi before dashing indoors into the warmth. Outside, the temperatures plummeted below zero promising a frosty Christmas. Heading into the kitchen, he opened the fridge wanting a much-needed snack. A block of cheese, he thought toastie; however, there was no bread.

What about crisps and nuts?

His mobile vibrated. Glancing at the display panel which showed an 'Unknown' caller, he answered hoping it was nothing important needing his attention.

"Detective Alan Truman speaking."

There was background noise before the caller spoke.

"I'm watching you!"

Uncertain whether it was a joke, Truman turned to the windows before responding. "Who is this?"

"I said – I'm watching you."

"Are you playing a game, Stuart?"

"NO! He's on his way to France."

"OK. If you're watching me, where am I, and what am I doing?"

"You are standing in the kitchen next to the fridge," a pause followed. "It looks like you're hungry. Don't let me stop you from eating."

The hair on Truman's neck bristled as goosebumps tingled along his arms.

Who is this?

Opening the front door, he heard footsteps on the other side of the hedge and rushed to the gate colliding with a woman walking her dog. Apologising profusely to the startled woman he gazed left and right along the street, his breath lingering in the frigid air.

"Where are you?" asked Truman, his patience running short.

"I'm behind you."

All he saw were streetlights and driveways, no one nearby with a mobile.

"Where are you?" asked Truman. "It's too cold to be playing games."

There was a sudden roar of an engine followed by an array of lights that lit the street, leaving Truman mesmerised as a 4x4 sped by and turned right.

Rushing indoors to get his car keys, he pulled the door closed. Once in his car, he drove at breakneck speed trailing the 4x4 through the residential streets until the vehicle turned into a single-track road and powered away. Truman wary of oncoming cars dropped back and stopped when the lane widened at a junction. He switched off the engine, hoping to hear the 4x4.

Where the hell did he go? How can a vehicle of that size and noise disappear?

The answer came when a set of blinding lights reflected straight off his rear-view mirror into his eyes. Before he could start the car, the 4x4 rammed him and pushed him forward at an increasing speed. Truman gripped the steering wheel; to hold his car straight he placed the car in gear and released the clutch. As the engine turned over, he spotted a farm gate. At the last second, he swung the steering wheel right, crashing through the gate, bringing his vehicle to an abrupt halt while the 4x4 motored on.

Frantically turning the ignition without success, Truman abandoned the car. Ducking through a gap in a hedge, he found his feet sticking in the soil. About 100 metres away, he could see house lights. Aware that his feet were sinking into the damp soil, his chances of placing distance between him and the road were fading.

Behind him, there was a screech of tyres, a door opening and closing and then a powerful spotlight swept the field, forcing Truman to keep low.

The cold, which he tried to ignore, soon numbed his face, hands, feet and chest. The residual heat absorbed by his body in the car soon dissipated. With each breath, he lost more heat. As an increasing gust of freezing wind swept over the field, the colder he became. His breath hung in the freezing air as he moved towards the house.

It was a relief when the 4x4 driver turned his engine and drove off. Truman used the last of his dwindling energy to stand and head for the building ahead. Somehow, he kept his legs moving until he stumbled and fell in the courtyard against farm machinery triggering the security light. Moments later, the owner appeared and helped him inside while his wife called an ambulance.

CHAPTER 26

2015 | Aquarius | Jan 20 – Feb 18

Jan 21ˢᵗ | 09:30 Hrs

With Acting DI Truman recovering from his injuries and DCI Grant attending briefings and meetings, Detective Sergeant Franklin had assumed temporary command of the Zodiac case.

In the far corner of the central office, a police officer called across to Franklin, "That was a call from the Middlesex General Hospital. They have a patient with a knife wound in his shoulder."

"Give it to CID?" suggested Franklin. "You know the rules."

"It concerns us because the patient claims Zodiac stabbed him and murdered his mate, Huey!"

Franklin gazed across the floor, spotting DC Johnson.

"DC Johnson. How do you fancy meeting a criminal?"

She stood up, tying back her long blonde hair.

"Fancy starting in at the deep end."

She smiled, showing mature confidence. "I'm game if you are."

They walked out towards a car.

"You came to us with good recommendations."

"I was a police constable for five years and completed my detective training two weeks ago."

"The word is you had a notable clear-up rate?"

"Yes, more by luck in two cases."

"Good for you. However, this is a huge step up. If you have any questions, doubts, or worries, you talk to me."

"OK. Understood."

"What made you become a police officer?"

"When I was fourteen I spent an evening in a police patrol car. It petrified my mother. But I went home in one piece and joined the police a few years back."

A dealer's story

Paul Drake, the alleged Zodiac victim, was well-known to the local police for drug dealing and petty crime.

When Franklin and Johnson flashed their warrant cards, Drake sat up. Tattoos covered his entire torso extending to his arms, body and neck. Noticing their interest, he winked towards Johnson. "I have tats lower down if you'd like to see them, darlin'?"

Janine screwed her face to answer, "Tattoos do nothing for me, and I'm not your darlin'."

"You can come back later for a private view if you like when Mr Happy here is gone."

"No, thanks," scoffed Janine.

"What about you, Mr Happy?"

"Keep yourself covered," responded Franklin, "else I'll do you for indecent exposure."

Drake scoffed, "Yeah, right!"

"If you're wasting police time with allegations about Zodiac stabbing you," retorted Janine, "I know a place where your tattoos might be of more interest!"

"I knew the name Zodiac might get you running." Fixing his attention on Franklin, he waved him closer. "Before we start, can you tell me, have we met before?"

"I doubt it 'cos I'm new to the area," responded Franklin. "Remember we're not from the social to discuss welfare, and we're not solicitors here to discuss your compensation claim. We need quick answers."

"Awight, awight. Zodiac's in an abandoned building on the Park Royal Industrial Estate."

Janine eyed Drake carefully.

...*Is he taking the mick or is he bang on the truth?*

"Can you describe Zodiac?" asked Janine, hoping to drill down further.

"Describe him? We never saw his face. He wuz always wearin' a baseball cap with shades, even at night-time! I'm tellin' ya. The dude is a psycho."

"How did you meet him?"

"After Archie Suggs was topped, the Pakis and

Albanians moved in. Them people have major ambitions, innit. Anyone messes with them get done big time. You know my meaning, innit?"

"I've met their type before." Franklin checked Drake over. "Little boys full of piss and vinegar embracing a dangerous world. They won't last long."

"You ain't met these geezers, man," responded Drake, determined to make the two police officers understand. "They're fuckin' men'al and would do your granny if you didn't pay up; fuckin' immigrants ruining this country and killin' the trade for our homegrown boys 'cos we can't make a decent living. When we sold the last of Archie's stash, we found us a new supplier who tells us he's supplyin' high-grade uncut shit at a high-grade price, except, as we later find out – it's a shitty cut."

"What's the name of this supplier?"

"Foreign names I can't pronounce. I don't get personal when we meet 'cos they get suspicious, innit. We pay the price to collect the product then walk away; no questions asked."

"What about your new customer?"

"He found us and buys smack. Summat like two days later he calls wanting more. But when he comes swaggering up, he accuses us of murder!"

"Who did you murder?"

"He sez we killed his girlfriends 'cos our smack was shit."

"And then what happened?"

"Like – yeah – he goes men'al, innit. When I get to close for comfort, he stabs me in the shoulder, but it's only a gash. He leaves me like in a heap of rubbish before murdering my mate Louis. So, I crawl away, innit."

"Why didn't you help your mate?" scoffed Johnson.

"I wuz dying."

"You weren't dying," criticised Janine, "because you're here now – alive."

"Innit true," pouted Drake, sucking through his teeth, "these days you bitch coppers have no sympathy. Your men'ality is summat like a prossie doing smack while the punter is on the job!"

"I'd stop before I drag you to the station for questioning," proposed Janine, leaning over Drake. "If you're telling us a story, I'll have you charged with wasting police time."

"Except I ain't leading you a line, innit."

"OK, Paul. Did he tell you he's Zodiac?" asked Franklin, certain it was another story by from the public domain to get attention.

"While he's prodding Huey with a blade, he's askin', 'Ave you 'eard of me? – I'm known as Zodiac.'"

"Are you sure?" prompted Johnson. "He could've been anyone."

"Yeah, sure like. Innit just the thing coppers say. Don't believe the drug dealer. He's trashed, innit. I ain't deaf and I 'eard what I 'eard. The mad dog was Zodiac – innit!"

*****

Out in the corridor, Franklin pulled Janine to one side.

"Is there a possibility Zodiac might not only be killing women but also doing drug dealers?"

"OK, if he is – where do we start?" asked Janine. "I don't think Zodiac deals drugs unless it's a cover. Does it sound like he buys it and passes it on to friends? We need to find these women."

"OK. Let's get the word out to fellow officers who might come across two women who died from a drug overdose poisoning. The link to Zodiac might be tenuous, but we can't afford to overlook much now."

Park Royal Ind. Est., London NW10 | 16:15 Hrs

Despite the doubts, that Zodiac was guilty of attacking Drake – DCI Grant, Franklin and Janine Johnson set off with three uniformed police officers following to the alleged crime scene to check his claim out.

The crime scene which Drake described was a disused former factory unit, a dilapidated building on the verge of collapse. Armed with torches and little else they stepped inside the building where the smell of glue and urine hit their noses.

"What a mess," uttered Grant. "Condoms, syringes, and what is that mattress used for?"

"Sex," quipped Janine. "Could be lumpy and a passion killer."

"Oh look," quipped Franklin, placing his torch beam on two rats grooming themselves on the mattress, unperturbed at finding themselves in a beam of light. "We have celebrities taking a bow."

When Franklin crunched something under his shoe, he lowered his torch to see a living carpet of cockroaches scuttle away. Scratching his leg with vigour, he called out, "I think something has crawled up my leg."

"Maybe you should've worn bicycle clips!" smirked Janine.

"I don't own a bike!" replied Franklin, tailing Grant through a doorway followed by Janine who flicked a switch. After buzzing and crackling, a bright fluorescent glow lit the room.

On the damp blackened walls hung torn posters and Pirelli calendars of barely clothed women. In an adjoining room, a pool of black liquid covered the concrete floor. Grant peered up. As he did the hairs on his arms bristled. His facial muscles twitched.

Avoiding a gasp of sheer disbelief at what he saw, he found his throat so tense his voice disappeared. Suspended from the rafters by ropes tied to his feet and hands was a disembowelled naked man. The killer had sliced away the flesh on his back to represent wings and nailed both flaps to the ceiling.

Middlesex General Hospital | 22:10 Hrs

A police officer entered the Accident and Emergency department and followed the direction boards until he saw a lone police officer standing outside a room.

"I'm looking for Paul Drake."

"Yes. You must be my relief," answered the constable, checking his watch before replying.

"You're early. I was expecting someone else!"

"He's on a domestic. I'm the nearest officer to the hospital – control asked to come straight over."

"Suits me," replied the constable. "I'm off. So, until tomorrow morning, Drake is all yours."

January 22nd | 22:00 Hrs

Jack, earlier that day packed a large suitcase, informing Richard that he was off to Australia on business for three weeks. With the house to himself, Richard stretched out on the sofa. The last few days had been a revelation in terms of Jack's behaviour and his total disregard for close friends was obsessively bugging Richard. Never had he witnessed such callous disregard towards friends.

Two evenings earlier they arranged with Helen to have a meal at her Chelsea home (where Davina spent 90% of her time). The evening entailed laughter and mirth until Davina wanted something extra to help the night swing.

"Jack, darling," murmured Davina, "did you bring your usual after-dinner desserts?"

"Oh yes please," spoke Helen. "We will get high and have fun," she whooped, twirling her arms, "and party – party – partay."

Jack handed over three packets of white powder to Helen and Davina. Together they went through the motions of creating two lines each. They rolled up banknotes and together snorted the heroin. Taking deep breaths, they giggled, feeling the rush take effect.

As their senses dulled, their blood pressures peaked, blood flowed from their noses followed by simultaneous hyperventilation as they both struggled to breathe.

"What the hell have you given them?" questioned a stunned Richard. "Who supplied you? It's lethal."

"New supplier," answered Jack, calm as his friends struggled to breathe.

"Call an ambulance to get them to A&E," argued Richard, dropping, gripping Davina's hand. "Jack, what are you doing? Help them!"

"I'm not risking it; the cops could ask questions. I bought defective stuff, they used it and now they're dying."

Jack watched in disbelief as Davina and Helen slowly succumbed to the poison they had snorted. The last thing he expected was Jack to let them die.

*****

Richard tapped his fingers on his chest as the ITV newsreader reported two murders; a man in an unused building; a second man killed while under police guard in a hospital – sources confirmed a connection between the killings.

The report never sank in until later that evening as he watched a late movie. Jack had strolled into a hospital and murdered the dealer who sold him the crappy drugs.

Why take such risks? Could he not wait until they released the dealer?

It begged the question – something on his mind for ages.

Who is Jack? I share his house, but we only speak when he wants and he never talks about himself or others. He's killed Archie and two drug dealers I know of; talk about mind-boggling. I've met no one like Jack before. His attitude is schizophrenic. When he's with friends, he's the life and soul of the party, but behind closed doors, there's a sinister side to his personality. I'd say he's destructive, arrogant, and considers himself above most people and is self-centred. But what does he do besides manage three or four properties? He's a millionaire but never talks about business interests. That door off the kitchen, which he keeps locked. What does he have down there? Why does he keep disappearing down there? He doesn't want me down there.

Secrets?

Does he have a secret room full of personal stuff? I'll call Daley and see what we can find. If anyone can, he can.

Meet Daley 'The Hack' McCarthy

During his school years, bullies singled Daley out because he was different. Despite their constant threats, he provoked them with gestures and words that stung more so than any physical action. So, it was no surprise that Daley spent his out-of-school hours avoiding the bullies to prevent violence.

"Bullies…" rasped Daley one day to Richard. "Anyone who has a gram of sense knows bullies rely on support from weak-minded followers to change allegiances if they know they won't get hurt."

Daley's motives were to make the lives of the bullies difficult. He watched from a safe distance as they chased after him, getting nowhere. However, when they did catch him, Daley was ready for a beating. It never stopped his determination to get further under their skin. It was a battle of wills which the bullies were losing. They could not keep up with Daley's smart war of attrition. Daley played two sides against each other. The result was a violent gang bust-up in central Glasgow.

When Daley was fifteen, a psychologist took him out of school. His lack of social skills, erratic behaviours and ability to function at a high level were due to Asperger's syndrome. From that point, Daley had a purpose.

In his case, the teachers made no sense. They spoke in monologues and endless tones that showed no enthusiasm. At sixteen, after failing his exams, he left school. He aimed to learn a skill to earn a good living. School, in his case, was an abject failure.

No one saw him for ten years. The headline news featured a young Scottish entrepreneur. He had proven his credentials by saving a Scottish bank from a cyber-attack, saving millions of pounds sterling. He was the talk of the town, a hero, and that was to change Daley's life.

When Richard caught up with him, he could see the transformation. Daley had found his world but his ideas and principles had changed. Daley spoke of hacking sensitive government networks. The other was his growing support for social 'revolution' to unite the workers and overthrow the masters. In part, he funded left-wing anarchist groups, using the money he stole from banks.

CHAPTER 27

24th January | 09:30 |

The Hack is on the Job

Standing side-by-side in the L-shaped basement, Daley unwrapped a packet of chewing gum and placed two sticks between his teeth.

"If you think he's disappearing under the floor, there's a trigger here to release a hidden door."

"I'm certain about that."

"You take a seat while I look. I want you out the way."

*****

Richard sat on the concrete floor, reading an article on Scottish castles. He was drifting off to sleep when Daley, who had been quiet, called out, "I have found the key."

Richard ignored the words, aware that the floor beneath him was moving. Springing to his feet, he watched a hidden door open to a ninety-degree angle.

As the whistling of hissing air filled the room, a frustrated Daley popped his head around the corner. "Whoa, check that out. Where does that go?"

"There's a flight of stairs leading to a door."

Daley chortled, jumping down the steps to stand before the door that swung open, activating a set of lights in a good-sized room.

"My friend," whistled Daley, "this is one hell of a panic room."

"A panic room," murmured Richard, looking at a set of photographs hanging on the white-coloured walls.

"Yeah," confirmed The Hack, absorbing his new surroundings, "if burglars broke in, the family can come down here and wait in safety until the cops arrive."

Daley stopped next to two server rack cabinets holding unbranded servers. After checking them closer and with palpable excitement in his voice, Daley remarked, "Who is your man? – He's a geek of the highest calibre. I bet your bottom quid these servers are his designs because there is no visible branding – what's more, I betcha the design for this hardware is stored in there. I'm going to find it."

"Go ahead," prompted Richard, "see what you can get. Try not to disturb the room. Jack has an instant memory recall."

"He won't even know I was here," whispered Daley, checking out his surroundings.

*****

Eight hours later, a smirking Daley bypassed the inbuilt security, giving him access to the design specifications for the software and hardware and various bank accounts holding vast sums of money.

"This is my Magic Wand," interrupted Daley, "and I hope this works!"

"What will it do?"

"Your man has designed a sophisticated operating system. Very secure and way beyond what I've ever seen or created."

Attaching a portable hard drive, he continued to speak. "I'll load a Trojan Horse into his computers to gather the data I need to access his accounts."

"Is it your design?"

"I needed something quick and got this from an unnamed source who told me some techie working on advanced coding and technology designed it. It works like a charm."

"Sounds good!"

"So, tell me, pal," queried Daley, "when you have what you want, what's your plans?"

"Och aye." Richard rubbed his hands. "I can see my ambitions of buying a Scottish castle getting closer by the day."

The Hack smiled. "You've been talking about a castle since you were a wee kid."

"It's my dream." Richard paused and changed the subject. "Em – what's your cut? You've never said, and I've never asked."

"I won't take from you. You always stuck by me when every other kid was shoving me around."

"Thank you. Talk about sentimental. But you know, I don't like bullies and you at the time looked vulnerable."

"I take this amount from banks each week and donate part of it, not all of it, to left-wing revolutionary causes worldwide. The banks are funding the revolutions that will bring them down. When they do, we'll distribute the wealth to the poor and then hold the bankers to account for past discretions and crimes."

"The revolutionary council will find them guilty and execute them by a firing squad!" suggested Richard.

"Something like that," smiled Daley, using his hand to mimic a shooting gun.

"What about the new technology?"

"State property. No commercial gain."

"I don't know whether you're serious or joking," queried Richard. "It all sounds extreme."

"Pretty! It won't be pretty when the revolution comes. Blood will flow until people comply with the aims of the revolutionary council."

The Hack's face lit up as he changed the subject. "You enjoy your share, while you can, because when the revolution arrives, a revolutionary government in waiting will topple the democratic government. The workers will gain the upper hand when they seize the means of production. We'll seize the wealth of the greedy banks and create an equal society subordinate to the State."

No chance – that will never happen… "Did you find anything else to interest you?" queried Richard.

"Server schematics, the code and the design of many a smart gadget."

"Can you use it?"

"Yes," agreed The Hack, "but I also know people who'd pay millions for this technology."

"Would they be radicals and revolters?"

Ignoring Richard's sarcastic question, he checked the progress on the screen. "I'm still downloading any information that might be of use. I'll leave my calling card. When he logs on next, my mobile will receive an alert. I'll begin the countdown."

"OK, but before you go, can you decrypt stuff I can use?"

"Like what?"

"C'mon," gestured Richard, "give me a moment to myself. You can do this at any time. Allow me some discretion."

"Of course," winked Daley, "it's not my business. I'll free his encrypted drives. Then it's up to you."

I know who you are – now

As much as he admired Daley for his achievements, there was a limit to how long he could tolerate his company. Daley talked about technology always. Richard was curious to know who was shaping Daley's ever-expressive opinions on radical left-wing politics. Once upon a time when the subject raised its head, Daley would wander off. Not interested.

Jack shared several similar traits. Technology and money. He talked but erred on caution. His eyes were dim – a lack of light. When he spoke to people by phone, he showed a lack of tolerance. If they did not understand what he was saying, his sarcasm knew no limits.

Richard surfed through multiple articles and personal papers. On the verge of boredom, he found newspaper articles about Zodiac. What was Jack's interest?

News Flash

1993 – *Zodiac* – *The serial killer has killed again. Police found a 20-year-old city worker in her home, murdered by a single cut to her neck. The police have confirmed the investigation is ongoing and hope to make an arrest soon. Separate sources confirm Zodiac covers his tracks.*

October 1993 – *Following a fire at Broadhurst authorities believe up to 17 patients have died. Police, fire and rescue have so far found ten bodies. Because of the severity of the burns, identification may take some time.*

October 1993 – *Broadhurst Hospital* – *East Wing* – *The local police and fire brigade have concluded their search for bodies. A spokesperson confirmed three of 17 patients remain missing. An expert believes the weight of the falling masonry crushed and burnt the bodies.*

November 1993 – *Broadhurst* – *the authorities, after consultation with the relatives of the deceased, have confirmed the names of all 17 patients who perished in the fire. The police have identified seven bodies by using dental records and visible body markings. Three patients remain missing.*

December 1993 – *The police have released the names of the 17 patients burned to death in Broadhurst. They have confirmed that three bodies still are missing. There have been recent suggestions that three inpatients may have escaped. Staff at the hospital have denied an escape because of internal processes and checks.*

Police do not consider the three missing patients dangerous.
Geoffrey Taylor 19
David Fish 22
Alan Turner 25
Jason Cooper 19
Mark Jones 30
Alex Winton 33
James Foster 19
Angelo Ferraro 26
Raymond McCoy 18
Jack Thompson 36
William Knowles 35
Joseph Moreno 21
Xavier Donaldson 26
Kevin Davies 17
Steve Taylor 39
Oliver Maxwell 22
Muhammed Assad 30

There was no Jack – but he knew the name Raymond McCoy. He turned up one evening while he was watching a YouTube video on his smartphone.

"Can I help you?"

"Is James in?" asked the caller with an intense

stare and smelly breath. "I need to see him."

"James?" responded Richard, looking confused. "No James here."

"Who lives here, then? Has James moved?"

Raymond glanced the caller over before answering. "I live here. Who are you? Maybe I can pass a message on?"

"If James shows tell him Raymond from Eastview Flats in Hackney called."

News Flash

August 17, 2014 – 'The Tanners' – The search for the six teenagers extended to a local landmark. A local dog walker reported the smell of rotting flesh. The forensics team found the six teenagers and five bodies wrapped in heavy-duty cellophane hidden.

August 22, 2014 – 'The Tanners' – Police have still not identified the five bodies found in 'The Tanners' who they believe disappeared in 1992. Police are asking members of the public who reported missing relatives during that time to come forward.

September 4, 2014 – The police have confirmed the identities of the missing six teenagers. Rumours continue to suggest that more bodies lie in tunnels running below 'The Tanners', a building the owners abandoned many years ago.

October 2014 – 'The Tanners' – Once the focal point for village gossip. Villagers claimed children and prostitutes were available for participants.

December 1993 – Following the murder of Pauline Carrier, and death of her husband, the local businessman

Jonathan Carrier, 'The Tanners' has been boarded up to prevent trespassers from entering.

May 2000 *– 'The Moscow Times' – Valentin Lenevski, a prominent Moscow businessman, attended the funeral of his only daughter yesterday. An unknown UK national murdered Yulia. Authorities believe he was using a false identity.*

Why does Jack collect newspaper clippings about a large house named 'The Tanners' and a Russian Oligarch who lost a daughter in tragic circumstances? Should I call this Lenevski and ask the question? But what If I'm wrong. But then again, does it matter?

Jan 27ᵗʰ | 16:45 Hrs

An excited Marietta Reilly tidied up her desk and switched off her laptop. That evening she and her friends were out clubbing for her birthday. Tomorrow afternoon she was flying home to Ireland for a week.

Jan 28ᵗʰ | 09:15 Hrs

When the birthday girl awoke, her head throbbed with the hangover from hell. Her eyes flickered, trying to pierce the overwhelming darkness.

Where am I? she thought, trying to move her arms which like her legs were bound.

"Help!"

There was no answer.

"Help."

She could hear nothing and see nothing.

What did I do? Why am I here? Are my friends playing a joke on me?

"OK bitches, you've had your fun, get me out of here NOW!"

She waited before yelling, "Joke's over, get me outta here now, bitches. You're scaring me."

So she continued without receiving a response.

She drifted in and out of sleep, aware that someone with rough hands lifted her head to drink. The taste of cold water moistened her dry lips and satisfied a deep thirst.

After licking her dry, chapped lips, she croaked, "Why am I here? My family expect me home for my birthday!"

When the 'b' word entered her head, her stomach churned. Her head filled with dread at what would happen.

Was she a prisoner of Zodiac?

Her heart lurched, and her elevated mood soon lapsed as she screeched an outpouring of panic. There, next to her was the man at whose expense she and her friends made jokes. Beware Zodiac man; he's coming for you. It was all a joke except now, it was no joke. She was his captive and knew how the story ended.

"OH, MY GOD – OH, MY GOD, OH, MY GOD – YOU'RE HIM, AREN'T YOU? YOU'RE HIM! YOU'RE THAT ZODIAC KILLER!!" she screamed.

11:00 Hrs

In County Mayo, Ireland, Aine Reilly sat awaiting a call from Marietta to say she was at the airport.

As the hours slipped by with no word or message, Aine's instincts told her all was not well. With her husband out on the farm and not answering his mobile, she called her nephew who worked for the local Garda who contacted the Metropolitan Police.

Two hours later two Metropolitan Police officers called at her flat where they found her packed case, passport, and birthday cards on the dining table.

When the police contacted Aine, she packed a bag and left a message for her husband to reach her when he could.

17:15 Hrs

Franklin was holding a brief meeting with the Zodiac team when the news about Marietta Reilly broke. His first thought was to contact the BBC to consider a televised appeal.

Two hours later, armed with photographs and personal details of Marietta – Truman made the televised appeal while the team waited at ZHQ to answer the phones. Within minutes of the broadcast, her friends called in with their vague recollections of events. One friend of Marietta replied with: *I didn't know where I was and how I got home. It wasn't my birthday, so I didn't have to worry.*

Despatching two officers to the club staffed by non-English-speaking cleaners, they spotted CCTV that covered the front entrance and lobby area.

22:00 Hrs

Franklin's mobile shrilled as he ate a sandwich. Taking a quick slurp of his tea, to clear his mouth, he answered the call, "DS Franklin."

"DC Hayder here. We've watched the VT. While we can identify her entering the premises, we can't ID her leaving."

"Are you sure?"

"We've spent hours examining the VT. Between us, we agree. She never left the premises; the only other exit leads to an alley not covered by CCTV."

"Have you searched the premises?"

"Yes, the entire building. She isn't here."

"What's your next move?"

"As this is a crime scene the club can't open tonight, and we need more officers over here to question the staff. The head doorman told us they checked staff in and checked staff out through the main entrance. Security did a final sweep of the premises at 0400 hours. The place was empty!"

Jan 30th | 08:30

When DC Nicola Paige called Janine, she reluctantly climbed from bed and drove to SW3. Parking beneath a streetlamp, she admired the white stucco-fronted facades with their black railings.

Outside on the steps and windowsills were flowerpots large and small, an attempt to bring a touch of the countryside to their affluent London street. During the summer the blooms added colour to the road, and no doubt would bring bright smiles to the faces of the residents.

With a ground level and another two levels above Janine could only imagine the size of the interior rooms that placed the size of her pokey North London flat into perspective.

She hurried along the pavement to where she could see two police officers standing. Showing her warrant card, she entered a large reception hall where DC Paige was reading a message on her smartphone.

"Janine, how are you? And welcome to 'how the other half lives'."

"You called to say you might have found the two mystery women I was asking about."

"The owner of this house is Helen Mortimer and her close friend Davina de la Riviere. We have another team at her house, going through bits and pieces."

"Who alerted you?"

"We received a call from an accountant friend of theirs named Clodagh Laugher. She'd been trying to contact them. She got worried and called in."

"So, what's killed them?"

"My thoughts right now. They overdosed on a lethal batch of cocaine. The police, paramedics and hospitals have reported an increase in deaths of users. We have five similar cases on the go. We're trying to track these dealers down."

"An overdose you're saying?"

"More likely hypoxia caused by an overdose of the drugs or poisoning. Drugs like heroin and morphine are depressants. The drug slows their breathing and heart rate. When they slipped into unconsciousness, their depressed body forgets to breathe, and they die."

"You sound like a doctor."

"I've seen a lot of this in recent months." DC Paige frowned. "Lives cut short in their prime with drugs and alcohol."

"Anything else?"

"Yes, that's why you're here. We believe our women had guests who left them to die. Our CSI fella suspects someone has cleaned this room and the kitchen to remove any evidence."

"Covering their tracks?"

"In the dishwasher are four plates, four bowls and cooking utensils, all clean. We found food packaging in the bin. The weight of the chicken suggests a meal for four."

The suggestion was correct. Jack waited until Richard left for work before returning to Helen's home. Once there, he cleared away the remnants of the meal and washed the plates and utensils before drying them.

"Are there any drugs around the house?" queried Janine.

"Nothing, not even a trace on the glass-topped coffee table."

...Spotting traces of powder, he took care to wipe the table

over to remove any evidence of heroin…

"Someone has something to hide, but who?" Janine scratched her forehead, glancing around at the lounge before continuing, "This male friend you mentioned, do you know who he is?"

"Nope. They spent time together with a rich guy. No names, where he lives. Nothing. They described him as fun and sexy."

"Why did she want them?"

"Investments."

"OK!"

"Anything else you can tell me?"

"She also told us that neither women have social media accounts."

…Despite nagging from their friends, social media was not their thing. Helen and Davina preferred to meet their friends face to face.

"Did they own mobiles?"

…Davina and Helen never succumbed to the trends of modern society and never used their mobiles to pose for selfies although when asked, they pouted with friends who took selfies. Weeks after meeting the friends he gave them both mobiles. All communications between them would be through those mobiles. He quickly found the two mobiles and stuffed them into his pockets. Later he would wipe them …

"Yes. We've bagged all the technology for examination."

…In the dining room, lay his two dead friends who had provided him with an open, outgoing, sociable reputation. The dead were of no value. He needed more 'friends' who didn't ask

awkward questions about his life…

February 3rd

On his last visit, he brought water and food that didn't taste right, but she was hungry. As the all-consuming darkness surrounded her, she tossed and turned while her body rejected the food.

11:00 Hrs

Stopping at McCoy's front door, Richard noticed a pungent odour. From inside the grunts and groans of a porn movie were clear and what he assumed was Raymond's heavy breathing.

After three raps, the shrieks stopped. When the door opened, Raymond stared at him. When recognition set in, he spoke. "I recognise you. You answered the door that evening when I called around to see James."

"James?"

Shaking his head, he raised his hand and snorted. "Come in."

Richard crossed the threshold, conscious that the offensive odour was growing stronger. His eyes opened in disbelief. There was rubbish covering every inch of floor space with narrow paths through to the bathroom. Richard crunched on something underfoot. He avoided looking but followed Raymond to a sofa as the distinct smell of urine and faeces wafted under his nose.

"Where is James?" asked Raymond.

"I don't know a James, but I know a Jack Kruger. He owns Eastview." Richard somehow avoided the temptation to cover his mouth and nose to block the smell.

"Who is James?"

Lowering his voice, he peered at Richard. "Do you keep secrets? I can't speak until I know you won't tell."

"Yes. I won't tell."

"OK. Two decades ago, James and I were patients in Broadhurst. We both suffered from severe depression. We discovered we had much in common and spent hours talking."

"What is Broadhurst?"

"A hospital for people with mental health difficulties."

"James was in a mental unit?"

"Yeah. James was an intellectual soulmate. We both understood science, technology, and we'd play maths games. It helped pass the days. But there was an edge to James. As if he was looking for something. When my aunt and uncle mentioned my scholarship to attend the Massachusetts Institute of Technology, he asked a lot of questions."

"What was his interest in MIT?"

"I'm not sure," answered Raymond, sipping a dark liquid from a plastic cup. "I think he had a place at a university, but something serious happened to him."

Guessing there was a story somewhere, he posed the question. "Were you discharged?"

"One day maintenance men arrived. Later in the day, there was panic when the men discovered they'd lost the keys to doors which were kept locked. A nurse found the spares. Panic over. The next evening after the staff changed shifts and did their inspection rounds at 10pm, James 'escaped' every other night returning before the shifts changed.

"…Then in October 1993, his father came to visit with bad news."

"What bad news?"

"He wouldn't say. The next day he said, 'Mission accomplished. It's time to go.'"

"Go where?"

"I wanted out, and James was my lead."

"Why did you want to run the risk of leaving?"

"I planned to confront my aunt and uncle. Nicking money from me… We were ready to go. That's when Jason turned up. James let him come. From day one, he hung around like a bad smell. I always got the impression Jason guessed what James was planning. When he saw us ready to move, he turned up. James led us downstairs into a basement and left us for a short time before he returned and walked us out through a fire door into the grounds. We walked out."

"You walked out?"

"Yes. To avoid attracting the bloke on security we walked along the back streets until we reached a car park where James had a 4x4 parked. We then drove to 'The Tanners'."

"Is this 'The Tanners' out in Bucks?"

"Yes, we showered, changed our clothes, we played computer games, ate steak and chips and drank wine. When I switched on the TV, the news was reporting an explosion at Broadhurst. The wing where we slept had collapsed after an explosion, killing seventeen patients…"

…Richard showed no outward reaction…

"…It also meant we could not show our faces. Technically we were dead. We risked arrest and imprisonment if caught. Jason didn't grasp our situation. He threw a fit and decided he wanted to go home. Jason had a temper and a nasty edge to him. James convinced him of the situation and promised to drive him home the next day. The next morning, I couldn't find them. I never saw Jason again; I asked no questions."

"Do you have any relatives?"

"My parents died in a car crash. My Aunt Maureen and Uncle Percy became my legal guardians."

"Where are they now?"

"No idea; they disappeared. I don't care. I'm sure they were accessing my savings accounts set up by my parents."

"OK, what happened with James and you?"

"I lived in 'The Tanners'. James would come and go; a year later, he moved me here with an income."

"Why do that?"

"To avoid signing on for welfare and keep a low profile. It was five, or six years before I saw him again. I thought he might be dead. After a short visit, he disappeared for over thirteen years. When he turned up, he looked ill."

"What happened to him?"

"No idea. I don't ask questions. He offered me a Job in Tremors, collecting and washing glasses."

"Tremors," muttered Richard. "That's where Marietta Reilly went."

"Do you know what happened to her?"

Raymond replied without hesitation, "I acted to save her life but also to set James up."

Richard cocked his head. "Tell me?"

"James has an office close to Tremors. I have keys so I can clean the office. When he left for Australia, he forgot to lock his spare keys away. That gave me access to other stuff. I looked through his drawers. I found a list. It gave him away."

"Who is he?"

Raymond checked his visitor over. Was it a good idea to reveal his secret? Would it help him? Since making the discovery, he was bursting to tell someone.

"That he's Zodiac!" blurted an eager Raymond, unable to contain the news.

Richard stared agog; did he hear Raymond correctly?

"Ja – Ja – James," stuttered Richard. "James is Zodiac?

…His suggestion makes sense. Jack has newspaper cuttings about Zodiac.

"In his safe. I found the names and photos of Zodiac victims. His next two victims – Marietta Reilly and Carol Schaeffer."

"Go to the police. Explain everything; It might be your only chance to get rid of James."

"I can't. Me – I'm dead and have been for over two decades. If the police find me, I'll go to jail."

"What about the list and photos?"

"They're in my wardrobe."

"Put them back," advised Richard. "If for any reason, the police came here and searched your flat, you'll be answering difficult questions."

"OK." *I didn't think of that.* "I'll do that. James is smart. If I grassed, he'd go into hiding, so deep they won't find him. And he'll destroy the evidence. Then one night, I'll see him standing by my bed – end of."

"You're treading on dangerous ground. If this goes wrong, you could end up behind bars."

"Yes, I know. I want to get rid of James. Be free. He's been a burden on me for many years."

"How did you sneak her out?"

"She tripped in a corridor and knocked herself out. I put her in a cleaning trolley and left by a rear entrance and brought her here."

"No one stopped you!"

"I was pushing a trolley and nothing else."

"Is it far?"

"Not far. I came in through a fire exit on the ground level. It's dark around there, and you can't see much. Come with me. I'll show you Marietta."

Raymond led Richard down six flights of stairs, along a passage through two locked doors which he opened and let Richard peer inside. There, on a mattress was a naked woman who he recognised as Marietta.

"That is her?" spoke Richard, clutching his smartphone thinking photograph.

"Look – but don't disturb her, no photos," warned Raymond as Richard stood over her noting how thin and ill she looked.

"We have three days before James returns, he boards his flight on the 5th." Richard swallowed. "Listen carefully. We need to move her when James is on his flight back to London not before he boards the flight. If he did we could lose him down under. In the meantime, I hope Marietta will survive another two nights?"

Feb 4th | 18:05 Hrs

Watched by Stuart Grant, Alan Truman peeled two small potatoes then prepared greens while stirring a chicken dish he was cooking.

"How are you feeling?" asked Stuart, spotting Truman grimace as he moved around.

"Shook up would be about right?" Truman pointed to a box of painkillers. "He did a good job and knocked me around a bit. I didn't think I'd make it."

Truman peered at his old friend. "So, you never told me what happened when you got to your sister's house."

"I dried out by avoiding the wine in her cellar and stuck to water."

"Yeah, I've noticed how much sharper you are, and there's no lingering smell of alcohol on your breath."

"I'm no longer tired."

"Good for you." Alan checked his watch. "Carol is late."

"She's not that late!" reassured Stuart, checking his watch.

"That's the point; she's never late, always early!"

"I've known you for over thirty years. I've never seen you cook."

"Neither did I. My mother bought me a recipe book to save my money disappearing on takeaways. I followed the recipes and found I could cook. Carol likes my cooking."

"I'm glad to hear it."

"If you and I went down that road, we'd be here for the rest of the year sampling my food!" scoffed Truman.

"Whoa… you know me better than I know myself. All those nights out drunk as newts."

"And how many bedrooms did we wake up in belonging to people we'd never met!"

No – no," countered Grant, "you did that, not me. I was respectable and almost married."

'OK," Truman stroked his chin, "I'm trying to remember her name."

"Whose name?"

"You know her name."

"Who are you talking about?"

249

"You know, what's-her-face."

"What's her name?"

"Forget it," laughed Truman, "I can't remember her name either."

"You're making this all up, aren't you?" wailed Grant as Truman broke into a fit of laughter.

"When did we last laugh?" suggested Truman. "These days, we never stop working."

"Indeed!" declared Grant. "We've got too much serious crap going on these days."

"We're big boys now," responded Truman as his mobile shrilled.

Grant listened as Truman conducted an animated conversation before placing his mobile into his trouser pocket.

"What's up?" asked Stuart.

"Carol is at the nick. She told me weeks ago that a tramp followed her. That tramp approached her earlier and said 'Zodiac' was coming to kill her."

The custody suite

Jake Miller, the custody sergeant, smirked as another drunk who called him every name under the sun was led to the cells.

"Jake, I bet you've heard it all before," suggested Truman, stepping forward.

"I have, and I'll hear it all over again." Jake glanced at Truman and Grant with a knowing glint. "It's been a long time since I saw you two. Can we expect a

Laurel and Hardy show? Or have you given that routine up?"

"Not tonight," countered Grant. "We have someone we need to see."

"Let me guess – I bet your visit involves that fella in cell two."

"Who is he?" asked Grant. "Did he give a name?"

"No," called Jake, "he kept muttering indecipherable language," breathing in, he gestured around the suite, "and as you can tell, his body odour lingers."

"Did he have anything on him?"

"A wallet with a £5 note, a key and nowt else and his address is a secret."

"Can we see him?" asked Truman, gesturing towards the cells.

"Be my guest," offered Jake as the doors to the custody suite swung open followed by two police officers escorting another drunk.

Feb 5th | 09:00 to 09:45

Truman and Grant decided to question the prisoner while Carol's recall of what he had said was fresh in her mind.

In an adjoining observation room, Franklin, Hobbes and Dr Pitcher gathered. McCoy sat with a duty solicitor as Grant and Truman entered. After explaining the preliminaries, Truman began.

"For the tape, could you tell us your name, please?"

"No comment!"

"Do you understand why you are here?"

"No comment! Next question."

"Where do you live?"

"It's a secret. No comment."

"Do you know Marietta Reilly?"

"No comment."

"What about Carol Schaeffer?"

"No comment!"

"Why were you following a woman earlier this evening?"

The prisoner lowered his gaze and coughed openmouthed. The smell of his breath permeated the air.

"No comment."

"You told her Zodiac was coming."

"No comment."

"Are you the man known as Zodiac?"

The question provoked a more extended, angry response. "NO – I'M NOT HIM! Why do you ask?"

"You told the woman Zodiac was coming. How would you know?"

"I am not him. I have never touched the woman. That was someone else."

"Who is that person?"

Tapping his head, "I don't know," he shouted. "Anyone in there? Anyone in there – who is the Zodiac?"

He fixed Truman with an abrupt stare before continuing. "My memory is a haze, boss; I remember little. I have voices in my head."

"Why did you mention Zodiac to the woman outside the tube station?"

"Did I? Don't know, boss. I'm tired and want to go home."

In the adjoining room, Frank Pitcher turned to Hobbes.

"Can we stop this interview?"

"Why?"

"He isn't Zodiac, but a mentally ill man and can't manage the questioning. But here's the good news. I think he knows who Zodiac is."

"How can you tell that?"

"It's obvious, his reaction when asked about Zodiac. He doesn't know what to say. He looks scared and vulnerable. This man has neither the intelligence nor the ability to murder women and evade the police. Also, might I suggest that he's about to explode?"

The prisoner let out a holler and banged his head off the table and followed through with headbutts to two officers who moved in to restrain him.

Pitcher shouted an unheard warning as more officers entered to help subdue the prisoner who screamed and wailed his discomfort until the weight of numbers pressing into his back caused him to slump unconscious.

A furious Pitcher left the safety of the room to

join Grant and Truman. "That is not Zodiac," he barked, "and we haven't got a clue who he is."

"Are you sure?" scoffed Truman.

"Look, you may not think much of profilers like me. Believe me, that man, NOT YOUR MAN. My belief is he knows Zodiac. Now, because of excessive force, he's out for the count!"

11:45 Hrs

Grant and Truman were sitting in silence in the ZHQ holding cups of coffee when a grinning Superintendent Hobbes entered the office.

"Gentlemen – gentlemen, good morning to you; I can guess what you two are thinking."

"That's very astute," mocked Truman.

"Today I have good news and good cheer!"

"Christmas was five weeks ago."

"An officer took a call this morning from the neighbour of the tramp you arrested."

"What's the punchline?" asked Grant.

"The tramp's name is Raymond McCoy. He lives in a four-storey block of flats called Eastview in Hackney."

"Is this a joke?" interrupted Truman with a hint of sarcasm. "Raymond McCoy as in our Zodiac McCoy?"

Hobbes scoffed with a throw of his head. "Would I lie about something as serious as his name?"

13:15 Hrs

Grant, Franklin and Truman arrived at McCoy's flat. Waiting in the corridor was a middle-aged black man with greying Rasta dreads.

"You came at last. It's about time. We've been complaining for months."

"What's your name, sir?" asked Truman.

"Patrick de Sousa."

"We can't do anything about the smell," responded Truman. "We would like to know his name and what he does."

"Know him – as in his name – NO – we don't see him, but we hear him. We know when he goes out because he slams his door and we can't hear no more television and moaning and groaning."

"Have you complained to the landlord?"

"All the time and they do nothing. He's noisy and a risk to our health. He watches porn movies all day – all that huffin' and puffin' from the TV and him. One of these days he'll pull it off. Then bang goes his pleasure. So, we want him out because he's a nuisance and smells."

A second resident appeared and greeted De Sousa with a handshake before introducing himself.

"I'm Jimmy, can I help?"

"Can you give us any information about the gentleman who lives here?" prompted Truman, ready with his notebook.

"He's no gentleman, man; he's a sicko. When I

saw him arrested near the tube station last night, I called the police to ask why. But they wouldn't tell me. He stinks, he's noisy. We can't sleep at night with the noise."

"Ya see, I'm not the only one who wants him gone," added de Sousa, spotting the key in Grant's hand. "If I were you, I wouldn't open the door without a mask."

"Why?" asked Grant, turning the key. "He isn't in."

De Sousa and Jimmy stepped away as Grant pushed open the door releasing an overpowering stench.

"You smell now what we smell all the time?" quipped De Sousa. "If you catch a disease, go to the hospital straight away. It might be deadly!"

"And you three might be the antidote!" added Jimmy with a laugh as Grant stuck his head around the door noting piles of rubbish including half-eaten takeaways covered in a mould and still in their tin foil.

Closing the door, Grant faced his colleagues.

"I'll call SOCO and let them do the dirty work because I'd rather be able to eat tonight."

*****

When three SOCOs arrived carrying their equipment, Grant and Truman prepared to re-enter the flat wearing protective suits and face masks to filter out the smell. Franklin, in the meantime, spoke to the residents, all of whom had a story about Raymond McCoy.

Inside the flat Truman stood before a gleaming 50-inch television and a Blu-Ray DVD player sitting on a clean wooden TV stand with two drawers. Opening a drawer, Truman selected a DVD and placed it into the tray. The opening sequence told him it was a porn film.

Grant ventured into the bathroom. Scattered all over the tiled floor lay crunched toilet paper and pornography magazines. Carefully lifting the toilet seat, he squirmed at the putrid black mess that met his gaze.

"How does he live like this?" commented Truman. "He's got a massive collection of porn mags and DVDs. He must wank all day!"

"I've no idea," replied Grant, following Truman to the bedroom. Apart from a bed a with crusted sheets there was a large wardrobe. Wondering what to expect Grant opened the door and peered from top to bottom. At the base was a box containing photographs. Grabbing several from the top he thumbed through the photos, recognising the faces of four women.

"Alan, he's got pictures of Zodiac victims here, taken in the street or sitting having lunch or a coffee with a friend."

"Do we have a game-changer here? A solid reason to charge our man?"

Stuart held two photos side by side.

"You're not going to like this."

Truman stood over Grant. "What are you talking about?"

"Your Carol, he's got a photo of her, coming out pf Aldgate and another leaving her flat, the other woman is Marietta Reilly," he replied, handing the photos to Truman.

"Why would he have these if he isn't Zodiac?" quizzed Truman. "Do we have a result or not?"

"What's Carol's birthday?" asked Stuart.

"April 2nd."

"She's an Aries. We need McCoy conscious because Carol isn't about to become one of Zodiac's victims."

"OK, OK," responded Grant, "I know what you're thinking. But, let's step back here. If McCoy, as Dr Pitcher says, is not the Zodiac, then who is he and where is the real Zodiac?"

23:20 Hrs

Raymond's arrest meant Richard had to act. He had a plan; to recover Marietta from Eastview and hope no cops saw him. Then place her in the lobby of Highgate Court. It would be the best place. He had visited the flats with Jack on business and knew the six-digit PIN to enter the rear door of the building. CCTV did not cover that area.

If it worked as he hoped police attention could turn to Jack. Else make an anonymous call.

February 6th | 03:30 Hrs

When his mobile rang, Stuart glanced at the front panel. The call was coming from ZHQ.

This better be important. Why ring so early?

When the caller told him Marietta Reilly was safe in St Thomas's hospital Stuart toppled from his bed!

Highgate Court | 11:30 Hrs

While DCI Grant drove to the hospital to speak to Marietta Reilly, the rest of the team stood in the lobby of Highbury Court.

"Gather round, please," called Truman to his team. "The DCI has gone to the hospital. We need to begin by speaking to the residents."

"Janine. You're speaking to Mrs Kaplan. She reported sighting Marietta."

*****

"Come in, my dear." Mrs Kaplan waved Janine through to the lounge. "I've been expecting you. Take a seat. I'll make some tea and get a plate of biscuits and cake."

Janine ran through the questions she had in mind until Mrs Kaplan returned with a tray of tea and biscuits.

"What can you tell us, Mrs Kaplan?"

"I was going to the utility room with my rubbish when I saw her shivering in the lobby. I could see she only had a sheet to cover her. Being cautious, I decided against talking to her. So, phoned the police. When I went to see how she was, she'd gone."

"She's now safe and sound in the hospital," replied Janine with a smile.

"Oh, that's good to hear. The radio news reported

this morning that Zodiac kidnapped her – such a horrid man."

"How would she have entered the foyer without a key, Mrs Kaplan?"

"Unless you live here, you can't just walk in. The front entrance needs a security key. If you lose it, the managing company will give you a signed letter for a specific locksmith. By presenting it, you get a new key cut. If you enter through the rear entrance, you must enter a six-digit PIN. If you don't remember it, you can't get in."

"What about visitors? How do they get in?

"Unless a resident buzzed her in, I don't know how she got in. We have CCTV overlooking the main entrance but not the rear. If there's any suspicious activity, a security guard will arrive."

"Who looks after security?"

"Good question…" mumbled Mrs Kaplan. "Oh, yes, two words combined into one – 'Secureye'. The managing company uses them to keep us safe, so they tell us."

"Have you lived here long?"

"Over fifty years."

"Do you know your neighbours?"

"I'm the chair of the residents' committee, so, I can introduce you to them all. There's Mr Hanson in number three and Miss Knight in six, have lived here for years. Like me are also pensioners. The other tenants are mature couples and one young couple who moved in not that long ago."

Mrs Kaplan shifted in her chair and leaned forward. "If you're wondering if any resident here knows her, or is responsible then I cannot answer that."

"Do you have any empty flats?"

"Only the suite on level five," mumbled Mrs Kaplan. "The man who owned it died two decades ago. It's been empty ever since."

Picking up a lever arch file from the nearby chest of drawers, she placed it on her lap.

"In this file, I have the contact details for all current and former residents, including their addresses, next of kin. For obvious reasons." Finding the correct page, she handed the file to Janine. "Those are the contact details for the gentleman who lived upstairs – Jonathan Carrier."

"Jonathan Carrier!"

"He died alone in that flat. The police told me he'd been dead for over a week before his cleaner found him. He had problems at home and staying here was a permanent arrangement. Before the problems, he returned to his family home at weekends."

Questions piled up in Janine's head.

What should I ask first?

"Before moving here, where did he live?"

"Oh. In a large house called 'The Tanners' in Bucks. A prominent place, I believe."

"The Tanners?" queried Janine. "I've heard that before."

"Yes… it was in the news. About the teenagers who disappeared," prompted Mrs Kaplan. "The police found them all dead. When the BBC reported the story, I thought of Jonathan and how he'd be turning in his grave."

"What did he die from?"

"Unfortunate events. First – someone murdered his wife, followed a day later by his son burning to death in a horrendous fire at Broadhurst Hospital."

"Sorry – step back – his son died in the fire at Broadhurst. What was his name?"

"I can't remember the name, but I stuck several newspaper articles in the folder about the story and the death of his wife. Some bastard murdered her in King's Cross and left her in her car."

Janine turned the pages of two articles describing the fire and murder.

"Was the murderer caught?"

"Not that I recall… but to finish answering your question. After Jonathan's death – it was a non-stop procession of comings and goings. First, the cleaner, the police, his secretary, and undertakers. A solicitor whose business card I attached to the page."

Mrs Kaplan paused. "The last caller. He got me thinking."

"In what way?"

"He said he was Jonathan's half-brother. He'd arrived from Africa… South Africa… mmm."

"The half-brother?" asked Janine, checking the list of names. "Did he upset you in any way?"

"No. Of course not. And he stayed on for a few weeks to save on hotel bills."

Mrs Kaplan crunched her lips. "He said he was from Africa. But there was something familiar about him. In fact, at first, I thought it was the son. But it couldn't be because he died in the fire. But despite the darker skin, he looked familiar, also creepy. I printed his name in there somewhere. He met with the solicitors to sort out the finances. The brother, no doubt, inherited a fortune. Convenient, I thought. I wrote all their names in case anyone else called by."

"Jack Kruger?" suggested Janine.

Mrs Kaplan gave a reassuring nod. "Yes, that's the name. As I said, creepy."

*****

Thanking Mrs Kaplan for her time, Janine headed to the foyer where Franklin and Truman were talking to a security guard who handed over a DVD.

"Do you have keys to the flat on floor five?" asked Janine.

"No," replied the security guard, "why?"

"Why are you asking?" probed Franklin as Truman displayed a look of curiosity.

Pulling Truman and Franklin to one side, she explained her conversation with Mrs Kaplan.

"Maybe she met Kruger before and didn't remember," scoffed Truman.

"I doubt that," remarked the earwigging security guard. "He's our boss. I know Mr Kruger only arrived in the UK after his half-brother died."

"Did he tell you that?" queried Janine.

"Yes!"

"Where is Mr Kruger?" probed Janine.

"He's away on business abroad. I think he's back today."

"We need access to level five," demanded Franklin. "Pronto, if you please."

"I'll call a locksmith," moaned the guard, "because if you damage anything, I'm responsible. This job only pays minimum wage."

12:00 Noon

Jack Kruger followed his chauffeur through arrivals with a mind in overdrive. On the flight, a live Sky News broadcast announced the capture of Zodiac and how his latest victim escaped his clutches.

The news boards outside WH Smith displayed the headlines in large black letters:

'Zodiac Captured' and 'Marietta Reilly Found'.

Confused, he read the various newspaper headlines.

How has it come to this? I've been set up. But who's responsible?

He looked right and left as an uncanny feeling settled.

"I get the feeling someone is watching me."
…Jack… Jack.

He glanced towards the first level. A man, wearing a baseball cap and sunglasses, was looking in his direction.

Who is that?

Every honed instinct in his body warned of danger. He sensed the cold gaze of a predator upon his back; not an animal, the human type like himself that would show no mercy.

"Sir." The voice of his chauffeur. "Are you OK? You've gone pale."

Jack swallowed before answering. "I'm tired. It was a long flight."

"I thought you flew business class with proper beds."

"Yes," he replied, glancing towards the gallery. The predator was gone.

Once in the back seat of his car, he switched on his tablet to read the news about Zodiac. Two articles later, he had more questions than answers.

What is going on? I know her, even met her briefly. Everything is safe in my office. Not even Raymond has access.

Then he twigged.

…The keys to the office. I didn't pick them up. Shit. Raymond has set me up. How dare he? Did he do it on his own? But who would help him?

As his chauffeur turned onto the M4, a black BMW X5 pulled alongside. Sitting at the wheel was the baseball cap man. The predator was closing in, bringing death in his wake.

Tick-tock – tick-tock.

*****

On entering his panic room, he knew Richard and someone else had been inside. The lingering scent of the soap Richard used and the sniff of mint chewing gum.

265

Switching on his personal computer to examine the security logs, he leaned in, searching for a note in the boot logs. He saw nothing. That only heightened his suspicions. Highbury Court came to mind. Switching on a TV, he watched the news. Top of the report was Marietta Reilly. Her escape, according to the press, was miraculous. Would her flight lead to the arrest of Zodiac?

I wasn't here. I've been set up. By who? Can I expect the police to call?

As CEO of the management company that owned the building, the police would be seeking a conversation. That would require charm and tenacity. There was no mother to give him an alibi. But he had an alibi – Australia. It was time to face the questions. He grabbed the keys to his Toyota.

Let's get it over with!

Outside his front door, he looked left and right. Starting the vehicle, he looked ahead. Less than ten metres away was the baseball cap man.

Who is he? Do I confront him? What the hell does he want? Is he stalking me?

It was then his mobile rang to distract him. Baseball cap man walked on without staring back. The caller was his head security man. Could he come to Highbury Court? It was urgent.

A step back in time | 13:00 Hrs

The responding locksmith opened the door within minutes. Truman entered, followed by five officers.

The first impression was a time machine. Everything belonged to another era.

"All of you. Look around. See if there's anything to find. My hunch is this place is clean."

His team scattered, leaving him to take Janine aside to the lift.

"Call the solicitors who managed the legalities and follow up on Jack Kruger and Jonathan Carrier. We need further insight into who they are or were. The events all seem coincidental and worth checking out."

Engrossed in her mobile, Janine stepped from the lift brushing against a man. With an apology on her lips, she stopped.

He looks familiar. Where've I seen him before?

She was on the verge of asking as the lift doors closed.

On the fifth floor, the new arrival entered the suite. He could hear voices but see no one. He glanced at the furnishings, the décor and brushed his fingers against the wall and the sofa before standing before a solid oak wall cabinet. He looked at an empty bottle of whiskey and a tumbler sitting on the middle shelf.

Voices coming from an adjoining room prompted him to declare his presence. "Hello, is there anyone here?"

Truman turned towards the door. The voice was familiar. Peering around the door, he viewed the newcomer who seemed at home strolling around the lounge, touching the furnishings with a knowing smile – time to say hello.

"I'm Detective Inspector Truman. Can I help?"

"Ahh, hello… I'm Jack Kruger."

Jack Kruger? …Janine mentioned that name less than five minutes ago.

Truman moved toward Jack Kruger. With every glance, he could see familiar mannerisms; akin to a friend he no longer recognised. His instincts were screaming like the robot in the TV programme 'Lost in Space'. Warning – Warning!

"How can I help?" asked Truman.

What do I see here? Who is this bloke? Could this be our man?

"My company owns this building. When I got home from Australia earlier this morning, my head of security rang and told me to come over."

"How long were you in Australia?" asked Truman, aware that two of his team were standing close by. Like him, they were staring at Jack Kruger trying to work out in their heads why he looked so familiar.

"Four weeks on business. I have witnesses. But, have you spoken to the residents?"

"We're doing it now. So far, we've no reason to suspect anyone who lives here." Truman moved closer to the visitor. "As you've been out of the country, I'm not sure you could tell us what's going on."

Truman stopped speaking.

…Stop talking. Don't give away what you're thinking here, Alan… Steady as she blows…

"Do you have a contact number, in case we need to ask you a few questions maybe today or tomorrow? We will see you again?"

"Call me anytime. I'll be available," offered Jack, handing over a business card.

"Before you go, sir, just one thing to ask."

"Yes?"

"Don't leave the country!"

Truman followed Kruger and watched him leave by the stairs. Behind him, one of his team offered thoughts. "He looked familiar. I couldn't work out why."

"Ditto. I think he's the missing link in our investigation, and we'll cross paths again soon."

"You seem certain, Inspector."

Truman touched his nose. "Copper's instinct."

When a smiling DCI Grant stepped from the lift, Truman asked, "Who did you pass on your way in?"

"People loitering in the foyer." Grant paused. "Why? Are you referring to anyone in particular?"

Truman frowned. *What am I NOT seeing? What am I missing? Copper's instinct. I'll work it out soon enough.*

"Let me update you on the morning's activities."

*****

Calling ahead to the solicitors to outline how vital her query would be, Janine sat opposite a dapper Derek Chambers, a senior partner in a firm of City of London based solicitors.

"I believe you oversaw the estate of a Mr Jonathan Carrier who owned Carrier Properties?" began Janine. "I'm hoping you can help me with enquiries."

"When my secretary mentioned your query, I

cleared my desk. It's a matter that has weighed on my mind for years. I'll be glad to share it with you. Oh, before we start, would you like coffee?"

"Please, milk with no sugar."

Chambers picked up his phone just as his secretary entered with a pot of coffee, which she placed on the desk.

"I swear she's psychic," remarked Derek, glancing at Janine. "I think it, and in she comes." He glanced at Janine with a half-smile. "Just to make you aware, I have something to confess!"

"Will it involve your arrest?"

"Not very likely," he answered, pouring the coffee. "I also hope you can solve a career-long mystery for me regarding the names Jack Kruger and Jonathan Carrier."

"What would that be?"

"Jonathan Carrier was a client. We had reason to suspect he had connections to crime syndicates who used his Buckingham home as a base for debauched activities."

"Would that be 'The Tanners'?"

"The same, however, our senior partners back in the days were nervous about said connections. They were discussing how to end their relationship with him because of the damage such a relationship might yield. Then the news came he had died. It was more like a burden lifted rather than a shock to the partners."

"You have a reason to remember this case?"

" Yes, for many reasons. I recall around three weeks

after Mr Carrier's death a Mr Kruger arrived in this office claiming to be the half-brother of Mr Carrier. Amongst the papers he had with him were letters, written by the brothers discussing becoming partners in business. We had heard of Mr Kruger because a former associate of our firm drew up the preliminary agreements for Jonathan Carrier on transferring shares to Mr Kruger, until he arrived here we'd never met. He was in shock to find his brother Jonathan had died."

"What were you thinking?"

"When he spoke, it was like he had prepared for the meeting in advance, rehearsed if you like. I did note his accent kept slipping between a well-educated English schoolboy and a poor imitation of a Southern African accent."

"You didn't think he was genuine?"

"Yes... I've been visiting South Africa for years as I have family out there. Mr Kruger was keen to discuss what he'd left behind in South Africa. However, the more he spoke, the more suspicious I became."

"What was he saying?"

"South Africans have a unique greeting which is 'Howzitt?' or they may ask you in Afrikaans 'Hoe gaan dit?' That means – how are you? When I greeted him as such – let's say he looked confused...?

"...His home address according to a letter he had was close to Pretoria. The name of his street was an Afrikaans word; however, his pronunciation was way off the mark. Also, he kept mispronouncing the names of local places. So, as he would inherit a profitable private business and Mr Carrier's well-earned personal fortune, I did two things. I appointed a tracing agency to find any living relatives in Zimbabwe, and South Africa but alas there were none…

"…A death certificate came to my notice for a Jack Kruger who died in a car accident in Pretoria. The police report clarified that the body was beyond recognition. The only means of identification was a burnt identity booklet. When we asked Mr Kruger for his opinion, he explained that burglars broke into his house and stole personal items, including his ID and car…

"…The South African police assumed the dead man in the wreck was him. So, I extended the search. However, the partners were getting impatient. They pushed me to accept that Jack Kruger was who he was. He had in his possession letters, ID, legal documents and private letters written between himself and his brother."

"What happened next?"

"By the time we completed the paperwork, Jack Kruger had moved to the United States. We never saw him again."

Chambers reached into a drawer and placed a large folder on his desk. "The information you want is in this folder. There's another matter I must mention."

"Which is…?"

"In Jonathan Carrier's last will he named his son – Martin – as a beneficiary. Now, here's the thing. I met and spoke to Mr Carrier, as did the partners. No one knew he had a son. He never mentioned anything. We arranged a search of birth and death records and couldn't trace Martin Carrier. There was nothing on record either. My guess is he bypassed the system. For the record, Jack Kruger didn't know either."

With a nod at Janine, he asked a question. "Do you know?"

"I spoke to a Mrs Kaplan this morning, a Highbury Court resident. She explained Mr Carrier had a son who died in a fire at Broadhurst Hospital."

"The mental health facility?"

"Yes."

"I didn't know that."

"After Carrier died, Mrs Kaplan said there was a list of visitors, including Jack Kruger. When she met him, she thought it was Mr Carrier's creepy son. However, he was dead."

"Interesting."

Derek opened the folder, with a comment. "I wasn't aware of that, but I remember the fire as it caused a lot of concern and debate about the safety of patients and the rickety Victorian buildings."

Derek rubbed his forehead. Janine could see the guilt and concern written into his face. His initial thoughts were correct. But the firm's partners placed him under pressure to complete the paperwork.

"If I were you, Mr Chambers, I'd let it go. It happened a long time ago."

"My suspicions were right… OK – let's discuss the businesses and see if that can help you… Kruger had no intention of continuing the business without his brother as he didn't have the experience to run the company. He said they'd planned to counter the behaviour of Mr Carrier's deceased wife. As both were dead, he instructed us to sell the business. Soon enough, the vultures were gathering to pick at the bones."

"What do you mean?"

"The news of Jonathan's death spread like wildfire. Other companies were circling hoping to pick up a few bargains."

"And did they?"

"NO. Everything went at a price dictated by the market. Kruger kept three residential properties," mumbled Derek, handing a list over to Janine. "Highgate Court, a five-storey block of luxury flats in Chelsea; 'The Tanners', a large family home in Bucks; and Eastview, a block of flats in Hackney. I transferred ownership to a new company named Tanner Trust Properties, set up in the Cayman Islands. That was that – he left the UK."

Derek Chambers folded his arms and took a breather while Janine scribbled her notes.

"Finally, a word about Jack Kruger. Back in 2004, South African police arrested a group of alleged mercenaries. The SA government deported them to New Guinea. The court found him and others guilty of trying to overthrow the government and they were sentenced to life imprisonment. However, a decade later, the New Guinea government granted them a pardon. Do you know about it?"

"No. I can't say I do."

"Last year, while listening to a radio broadcast about British mercenaries active in Africa, the broadcaster mentioned a familiar name."

"What name?"

He tapped the keys on his laptop before pointing to a headline.

'Foreign mercenaries released from an African jail.'

He gazed at Janine with puckered lips before pointing to a photo. "That is Jack Kruger who was here. I recognised him straight away."

"So, do I," mumbled Janine, "I passed him this morning in Highbury Court."

13:10 Hrs

"I have news," announced Janine, bounding into the ZHQ prompting Grant and Truman to look up from their desks.

"Good news?"

"Yup. I spoke to the solicitor who managed the estate of Jonathan Carrier after his death and the role of Jack Kruger, whose name was on the sheet of paper Mrs Kaplan provided."

"That's interesting," remarked Truman, "we met a Jack Kruger at Highbury Court this morning. He returned from Australia this morning."

Janine recalled her interview with Mrs Kaplan and Derek Chambers; the brothers Jonathan and Jack, Martin the mystery son and the link to 'The Tanners'.

Grant clasped his hands. They needed something from this line of inquiry. "A name for the impostor would help. Did he have one?"

"No, he didn't, but I have a theory?" suggested Janine.

"Tell," urged Grant. "I'm all ears."

"I think this Martin somehow assumed the identity of his father's brother – Jack Kruger, then moved to the USA."

"Hello,' reacted Truman with a broadening smile. "That's the Kruger we met this morning."

Grant rubbed his chin, pondering over Janine's theory.

The team need a break. Anything that moves the investigation forward has merit.

"One more thing – before I left. Mr Chambers showed me an article on the web from a South African newspaper."

Janine sat at a vacant computer. Pulling up the article, and the photograph, she pointed to the screen. "Jack Kruger was in an African prison for ten years."

"Whoa. That's who we met this morning. Jack Kruger."

"Is that him?" asked Grant, feeling a shudder at the sight of the face.

Truman observed Grant's reaction as he added, "I'll contact the South African newspaper to see if they can send a better picture."

"Sir, I think a visit to Princes Risborough will help us."

"Sir, I think a visit to Princes Risborough will help us," suggested Janine. "First, to get more on the bodies found in The Tanners. They could be the missing pieces of the jigsaw."

2004 | June | The African adventure

Leaving Russia using a private charter, he had time to think. What had happened to Yulia was a mystery. Try as did he could remember nothing after falling asleep. He also had a small problem about where to go. However, a recent email from a South African business contact gave him an idea. A South African Bank needed a software security consultant and were offering an extendable three-month contract. After tidying up his affairs through his lawyers, the next day he boarded a flight to Cape Town. In between work assignments, he drank beer, ate at restaurants and swam in the sea.

One hot Sunday friends invited him to a braaivleis. With steak, boerewors, salads and alcohol aplenty, it would be a long hot day in the sun. The massive consumption of alcohol gave rise to engaging conversations such as travelling through Africa to the Egyptian coastline at Alexandria.

The idea appealed to him. He was up for a challenge. Two weeks later, he bought a Land Rover and drove north without a plan or route in mind. He intended to follow his nose and absorb the various cultures, sights and sounds Africa could offer.

Three months later, he drove into a remote South Sudanese village. Along the red dusty roads, and the village itself were fruit and vegetable stalls. Colourful garments hung off makeshift rails and billowed in the breeze. Long horned cattle roamed freely munching on what grass they could find, while the goats fed upon the trees scattered throughout the village. His arrival was greeted by a local missionary and a team of medics who offered him temporary accommodation in return for any help he could give.

Straw huts of varying sizes were dotted randomly. Out in the distance stood a larger building – a church, he guessed. He had been nowhere near it to ask. Occasionally a group of men would walk through the village bearing arms. Their angry faces showed the ravages of war. Were they in place to offer protection or keep law and order in what was a chaotic country?

On the fourth day, he ate breakfast with the aid workers before heading to the market. Somewhere in the distance, he could hear shouting and popping sounds. Then came an explosion. When the people ran in random directions, and the popping sounds became weapon fire, he took cover behind a wall.

Bullets and grenades came closer with each second. To stay there meant injury; at worst, death. Jack looked for cover. But, before he moved, a white soldier dressed in camouflage headed in his direction. As the soldier slid towards him, he asked in a clipped English accent, "Sir, how's the heat out here?"

"What's going on!"

The soldier pointed towards a bullet-riddled brick shack.

"Can you run to that building, or must I carry you?"

"I can run."

"We have thirty seconds before all hell breaks loose. When I say run, you run as though Satan is banging your arse. We'll take cover in there."

The soldier grabbed his arm and together they ran toward the building as bullets whooshed overhead nearby. Inside the building, they dived to the ground as the battle intensified. The soldier drew his pistol and aimed it toward the door.

"If any bastard comes in here with a weapon, he's dead."

It never happened. They kept their heads down while armed insurgents ran by but never stopped to look inside. When the bombing and shooting stopped, the devastation and death left an eerie silence. A thin woman stooped by years of heavy labour hobbled along the road with a walking stick wailing her concern at the empty stalls as a warm breeze drifted along the dusty street.

The staring, lifeless Eyes of the Dead caught his glances. Nothing or no one could harm them. Their lives ended without warning. Soon the villagers would collect their dead and lower them into graves. Family, friends and relatives would mourn their passing as the gravediggers covered the bodies in the red earth.

In the distance, a motley collection of white, black and Asian soldiers gathered. They talked amongst themselves as the soldier approached them, shaking his head.

"This would've been far worse if we weren't here."

"T-I-A, boet!" shouted a South African holding an automatic weapon across his chest. "T-I-A – This is Africa, a beautiful and dangerous country, where nations fight wars; life is cheap and remains the warrior's last frontier."

"Who are you?" queried Jack.

"I'm Major William Heathcoat. These men are

soldiers of fortune."

"You're mercenaries!"

"Men who lost their way but found excitement to feed our greed for war and money."

2004 | December | Arrested

The following evening, he found himself back on South African soil in Cape Town. With his Jeep damaged beyond repair and his belongings scattered he took William Heathcoat's offer of a flight to Cape Town.

"What were you doing there?" asked Jack as they sat in a hotel bar drinking cold beers.

"We were in the middle of evacuating VIPs who rebel forces had cut off. They attacked us with bigger numbers than we expected."

"Who are you?"

"I was an officer in Her Majesty's Special Air Service, SAS. After I retired, a large security organisation approached me because they liked my sniper skills. So, I accepted the role."

"I thought the SAS were Black Ops specialists?"

"We are, but nevertheless, I'm a trained sniper, I could take an enemy soldier out in the right environmental circumstances from 1,500 metres."

Six black men carrying papers and wearing smart suits drew Heathcoat's attention. When they approached his men, he turned to Jack.

"Don't ask me why – get yourself clear of this

building and leave this country. Go, get away from here."

Two men blocked Jack's escape and forced him against a wall. Minutes later, a shouting match between the suits and mercenaries led to a fight. As the fists and boots kicked in, it took only minutes for the armed police to arrive and take control.

In a glare of publicity, Jack, Heathcoat and five others appeared in court. The New Guinea government wanted the men extradited as mercenaries. They supplied illegal weapons to a group whose aim was to overthrow the legitimate African state of Equatorial Guinea.

Five weeks later armed guards placed them on a flight to New Guinea. Jack pleaded innocence. No one was listening. What would happen once they got there? Only time would tell.

Beaten then found guilty

Once behind the high walls of the notorious Black Beach Prison on the island of Bioko, there would be no respite. All prisoners were easy targets for the vicious jailers who interrogated them at every opportunity. Armed guards dragged them from their cells in the middle of the night with threats of execution. Only when the trial date neared, did the guards ease up. The prisoners must appear fit to appear in court.

On the day of their appearances in court, the judge announced the men guilty of being mercenaries and sentenced them to life imprisonment. Once behind the prison walls of Black Beach, the guards placed them in separate wings.

Two months later, they opened his cell door and led him through to the courtyard with his fellow prisoners, where he sought shade against a wall. He watched a guard open a locked gate through which a gaunt figure, dressed in green and clapped in irons shuffled. As the man approached, Jack stared upwards blinking against the sun as the man stopped only feet away.

"How's the heat out here?"

"T-I-A!"

2013 | December | Freedom

Heathcoat had run out anecdotes and preoccupied his time thinking about his family. Jack thought Heathcoat might be doolally, constantly muttering about a chance to sleep in a comfortable bed. When the governor announced the Red Cross were on-site, there came an opportunity to change their routine, if only for an hour.

A guard led Jack and Heathcoat to a small room with a table and three chairs. They spoke of repatriation to the UK. Freedom. A way out beyond the prison. Days later, their lawyer Joseph Mbela arrived and took Jack and Heathcoat aside. Using a handkerchief to wipe his face and bald head, he sat.

"Good news for you."

"Are we getting out?" asked Heathcoat. "I don't think I can continue here forever."

"Negotiations are underway. We hope to have you both out of here and clear of the country within two weeks."

"Who has initiated these negotiations?" asked a curious Jack. "And how do we know this isn't a ruse to move us from one shithole to another shithole?"

Mbela leaned over the table. "We don't know. Those details are not available to us."

"Give me your best guess."

Mbela stared at Jack. "Listen, Mr Kruger. Be thankful you're to be released unless you want to remain in this place. When I defended you ten years past, you, my friend, looked and roared like a lion." Mbela paused and took hold of Jack's arms. "After ten years here, you have withered. Today you are more like a goat with little strength and a small voice."

"A goat?"

Mbela leaned even closer. "Mr Kruger do not turn away opportunities. Freedom is yours with a presidential pardon. Leave this place. Don't argue semantics."

Heathcoat responded with his view. "He's right. Let's take what's on offer and go. I want to see my family. Go home, enjoy a pint down my local. Whoever is behind this, I don't care. I want out."

All went quiet. Their routine continued. Then, without any warning, the guards collected Jack and Heathcoat from their cells. A representative from the British Embassy met and spoke to the men for five minutes before signing a document. Within hours the men were safe in Kenya.

*****

In between medical assessments and debriefings, they lazed about in the sun. When the question of repatriation arose, Jack opted to finish his African adventure. William Heathcoat wanted to fly home to be with his family. Under an African sun, they exchanged memories. Africa had proved to be a harsh mistress. Heathcoat had nothing but admiration for Jack. They survived a brutal prison regime and could tell the tale. Watched by Jack, Heathcoat climbed into the Embassy car.

Jack travelled to the Masai, where he spent the next two years watching the setting sun and walking a separate path to the nearby bar. One day he awoke and decided it was time to go home. He could not delay whatever the future held. A week later, with the hand of death waiting on the horizon he flew into London.

CHAPTER 28

Friday | 13th February | 11:35 Hrs

The Archives

Eleven months after their visit to tidy the basement, Vicky walked in and glanced around with a sigh. They had delayed the task until they had no choice. Two hours after starting, Vicky sat down exhausted. Behind her was a pile of bulging black bags full of paper selected for shredding. When her smartphone buzzed, with a text message, she answered before jumping onto social media to see who was doing what. With little activity amongst her friends, she whispered, "I love Mondays."

Staring at the last filing cabinet, she opened the bottom drawer and pulled out the files to dump into a black bag. Then, wedged at the back was a thicker file held together with crystallising elastic bands. Vicky grasped the file and pulled whereby the folder fell apart spilling a ream of completed application forms.

Picking up the forms and placing them on her lap, she read the name, Harriet Adams. In the centre pages, someone had scrawled the word 'Leo' across the two pages with a black fibre-tipped pen. She read the second form: Freda Lowe – Pisces, followed by Patricia Hugo – Aries. "I know those names," exclaimed Vicky just as Moira walked in.

"Are you talking to yourself?"

"I found these application forms bundled together in the drawer," exclaimed Vicky excitedly, handing them to Moira who looked through them as Vicky's face lit up. "I'm sure these women were victims of that serial killer bloke – Zodiac."

Do you know this man?

When Grant and Truman arrived at the rear entrance of Heathland Properties, two members of the company's security team led them to Moira and Vicky who were waiting amongst the boxes.

"Hello, I'm DCI Stuart Grant, this is DS Alan Truman. I believe you have something for us?"

An excited Vicky responded by handing over the files. "Yes. I found these in the drawers. I recognised the names of the women. They're Zodiac's victims."

Grant checked the names against a list on his iPad before remarking, "That's how he did it!" Passing the file to Truman, he turned to Moira. "Whose writing is this?"

"It belongs to Martin Carrier."

"Do you know Jack Kruger?"

Moira looked at the police officers with a frown. "You're asking a lot of questions about dead people."

Grant tapped his iPad. "Can I show you photos?

Tell us if you recognise the man."

A puzzled and confused Moira took hold of the iPad and pointed straight to a photo. "That's Martin. I recognise his eyes. When was this taken?"

Grant scrolled the screen to show the African newspaper photo. "What about him?"

There was no hesitation in her reply. "Without a doubt, that is Martin."

Truman and Grant glanced at each other, prompting Moira to ask, "That is Martin, isn't it?"

"That is Jack Kruger, taken a few years ago."

"But Jack's dead!"

"Yes, he is, but we believe Martin didn't die in the Broadhurst fire. He used the fire and later resurrected himself using the name Jack."

Moira sat shocked and shaken as she glimpsed between the photos and Stuart before commenting. "I can see a similarity between you and Martin."

Grant smiled and looked at the photo. "I can't say I see it."

"From where I'm sitting, you do."

Truman looked closer at the photo while Grant wandered off with his mobile in hand to call ZHQ. Looking agitated, he held a brief conversation before re-joining the group.

"I've sent Hayder and Ronson out on a mission. I asked they call back tomorrow with answers."

Feb 14th | 15:55 Hrs

The Zodiac team were summarising their leads and thoughts when Hayder and Ronson returned to ZHQ.

Hearing the clump of their feet, Grant ushered them forward to ask the initial question, "What have you found out? Tell us?"

"At Broadhurst, we met Flora Gibson, former nurse, who worked there when the fire broke out. She didn't know who we were talking about until I showed her a photograph."

"What did she know him as?"

"James Foster – he also had a nickname – but she can't remember what it was."

"Foster," mumbled Grant with a discernible frown. "Where did that name come from?"

"That was the name given by his father at patient check-in."

"What was his father's name?"

"She never met him, and the fire destroyed most of the records. Flora remained adamant James was up to no good."

"Such as?"

"She explained that his admission was an attempted suicide. He alleged suffering physical and mental abuse by his mother. However, she thinks his attempted suicide was a ruse to get away from his mother. She also swears blind he had sociopathic tendencies. While there, he became good friends with a fellow patient named Raymond McCoy."

"McCoy!" gasped Franklin as Truman moved to a nearby computer.

Yes," continued Hayder, "he and James Foster were in the same place with a third patient who hung out with them – Jason Cooper."

"Who was he?" requested an impatient Grant.

"I'll get there soon enough," implied Hayder, refusing to be rushed by a senior officer. "Flora told us she watched Foster when McCoy's aunt and uncle arrived. He always sat with them discussing Raymond's background."

Ronson interrupted with a comment. "She suspected Foster was storing mental notes about McCoy's life."

"Did she alert a doctor?" queried Grant, writing notes.

"Yes, but they did nothing. Flora always suspected the fire was a deliberate act of arson. She made it clear to the police that Foster may have started the fire to cover his escape."

Grant folded his fingers, conscious of a common theme developing – missing and dead people...

"...And as we know," disrupted Truman, "in the fire's aftermath the fire and rescue people never found three bodies. I think Janine's theory has substance, that Foster fella escaped with McCoy and Cooper."

"...Before I get to McCoy... Jason Cooper lived with his parents in a remote farmhouse in Wiltshire. We talked to a local constable who confirmed their disappearance in November 1993... When Mr and

Mrs Cooper didn't collect their weekly orders from a local shop, the owner called the police. They lived in an isolated house with no close neighbours and no friends. Despite police requests for family and friends to come forward, no one did. The case fizzled out. In 1996 a local farmer bought the land at an auction…

"…Back to the McCoys – we travelled to Tring. They lived in a cottage close to the Grand Union Canal. We met the local police sergeant who said the couple had a cruise booked but never boarded the ship and no one has seen them since."

Hayder handed over a copy of a newspaper clipping.

"The sergeant sent us that by email. Their disappearance was a talking point for months because they were active within the village. Police divers dragged the canal and nearby reservoirs. No bodies were found."

"What about the nephew, Raymond?"

"We asked, but he couldn't remember any mention of the nephew in any capacity. However, last year, he met a woman who claimed she was a former CIA agent. She was searching for a Raymond McCoy, a former engineering student at MIT."

Grant raised his hand while Truman spoke. "He was an engineering student, you say?"

"Yes. McCoy completed a four-year degree in electrical and software engineering… why – what's up?"

"I think we have our man," mumbled Grant, glancing around the room. "Continue with your report."

"The local police gave us her number. She was

more than willing to help – she's in the next room."

Dr Pitcher raised his hand. "What do you say her name was?"

"I didn't."

"If she's got something to say," advised Grant, sensing it was coming together at last, "get her."

Ronson left the room and returned with a tall, slender and statuesque woman in her early forties. With her hair tied back, exposing an attractive square face, the men at once sat forward while Pitcher stood, shook her hand and spoke to the audience. "I must point out that this lady and I have met. I have an idea about what she'll tell you."

"Why haven't you mentioned it?" queried Truman, thinking they had missed an earlier opportunity.

"You'll hear it now... I assume."

She opened with a courteous, "Good morning. My name is Sheila Dean. I'm a former CIA operative, and many years ago, I participated in a mission in Moscow that could relate to your investigation...

"...In 1999, my team was tasked to locate two former MIT students – Raymond McCoy and Francis Brooklyn-Harris. I believe you are aware of the facts.

"I believe the FBI had McCoy on a watch list for alleged deviant behaviour. However, in 2005, there was a hacking incident at NetEye involving sensitive classified data. Their security didn't notice what was going on until it was too late...

"...Their security specialists found sophisticated Remote Access Trojan Horses transmitting data in small packets, hence why the hack remained unnoticed for some period…"

Truman grinned as he made a quick-fire comment. "Sounds like a James Bond film."

Sheila reacted with a stern headmistress-type stare. "If only. I deal with real life, and it gets serious. My team spent months listening and analysing information. We tracked the alleged NetEye hacker to London. At the time he was communicating with a Russian woman named Yulia Lenevski."

"I've read about that name before," queried Marian Knowles, a detective constable. "Wasn't she the daughter of Valentin Lenevski, the Russian Oligarch who has masses of influence in the Kremlin?"

"She was. That was our concern," confirmed Sheila. "The hacker was flying to Moscow to meet Lenevski. We had every reason to believe he was selling sensitive data to the Russians. We alerted our Moscow branch who followed Miss Lenevski to the airport. She met a man. However, the passenger manifest had no Raymond McCoy or Brooklyn-Harris listed."

"Who was he?" asked Grant.

"We didn't know," responded Sheila. "The names on the manifest contained no one we knew. Our mission was the hacker, and the only way to capture him was to break into Yulia Lenevski's apartment. When they returned home, the team waited; Yulia rumbled them and activated her smartphone which sent a Help message to her father. One agent tried to stop her and in doing so 'accidentally' killed her. They panicked and left the hacker lying unconscious on the bed."

Harry Pitcher cut in. "If the Kremlin discovered that a CIA snatch squad had killed the daughter of a Russian businessman instead of a hacker, the US government were facing a diplomatic bust-up with lots of red faces in Langley answering to a humiliated President."

"Hang on a minute here," interrupted Grant. "What's this got to do with Zodiac?"

"An anagram." Sheila wrote a word on the interactive board: 'Ikra@zed.cillo.'

There were moments of silence before Marian Knowles spoke up. "The first four letters I-K-R-A 'Ikra' is Ukrainian for caviar."

Truman turned to look at her with raised eyebrows.

"I read Slavic languages at university and spent a year in Moscow. To help me learn Russian, I read the Lenevski story in an old newspaper." Turning her attention to Pitcher, she continued, "And 'Ikra@zed.cillo' rearranged spells Zodiac@Killer!"

"That's right," confirmed Sheila, "the hacker used that code word to access the NetEye database and extract the information. At the time everyone thought it was an access password, no one noticed it was an anagram.

"...After the confusion, we returned to Langley and were all given desk jobs. After two months, I resigned. My belief was if terrorists or shady governments bought the technology, there was a real threat to life. I contacted Valentin Lenevski as a journalist. When the subject of the Englishman came up, all he said was – Jason Cooper used a false name."

"Did Lenevski have any idea who Cooper was?" asked Truman.

"No, but I still think it was Brooklyn-Harris or McCoy using the name Jason Cooper."

"You can rule out McCoy and Cooper," prompted Truman. "McCoy's under police guard in hospital and the real Cooper died over twenty years ago. But, is Lenevski still going?"

"He's in his late seventies now. A man mentally crippled by the death of his daughter. His wife died a few years ago. But given his mindset, he still seeks revenge on Cooper for murdering his daughter."

*****

When Sheila Dean left, there was a buzz of excitement. When the incoming call tone of the audio-visual system shrilled, DC Johnson appeared with a woman standing next to her; they all turned forward.

"Hi, this is Doctor Barbara Filkin, a forensic pathologist who managed the team that did the autopsies on the five mystery bodies and the teenagers found at The Tanners."

"Good afternoon," responded Barbara. "I have little time, so I'll be quick. I have the photographs and details of the autopsies and follow-up notes. I hope to tie up loose ends for you. It would be good to think we're solving one part of the mystery. To make this easier, I'll split the screen so I can talk through what you can see...

"...The background is this; police found six dead teenagers and five other mystery bodies, forget the bodies found deeper in the tunnels; they are another story. We're concentrating on the five bodies as no one seems to know who they are but what we know could be useful to you."

"OK, we get that," answered Truman.

"I will point out that because the environment was dry, the bodies have mummified."

Two mummified bodies appeared on screen… labelled one – male, and two – female…

"This information is important. The forensic team found no means of identifying the bodies – no names – no passports, driving licenses, bank cards, or travel documents. That suggests the murderer wants his victims to remain unidentified… hence the labelling you can see on screen…

"…Here we have a man and woman in their late fifties or early sixties. We did toxicology tests. Both died after ingesting potassium cyanide."

"Is it a painful death?" asked Grant.

"No, it's quick and painless." Sheila paused, expecting more questions. "We found two suitcases and two travel bags that suggest our couple were off on their holidays. In their bags, was a 'Daily Mail' and a 'Woman's Own' both dated November 1993…

"…About the packed clothes, we contacted the various retail outlets that sold the clothing. They confirmed that all the clothes were on sale twenty or more years ago. That fits with the magazine and newspaper."

The screen switched from bodies one and two to three – male, four – female and five – male.

"Both the male and female were shot at close range to the back of the neck. We suspect the man on the right pulled the trigger then committed suicide. He bears the classic signs of suicide. A bullet entered under his chin and exited through the top of the skull. Someone took the bodies to 'The Tanners' post-death because we found no evidence of dried blood and no weapons in the fridge or in the cellars…

"…We took DNA samples. We know the male and female left, are brother and sister aged between thirty-five and forty-five years of age. Next to them is their son."

"An incestuous relationship?" queried Franklin.

"Yes. We believe the murderer placed the five bodies in the refrigerator around the same time."

Grant stood, knowing the answers they sought were in place. "Thank you, Barbara and Janine, for calling in. You've been a great help."

"I hope you get your man," remarked Barbara as she left Janine on the conference call.

Franklin jumped in, "It's got to be the Cooper family. My bet is the other couple could be Raymond McCoy's missing aunt and uncle?"

"There's a theme evolving," stated Grant, striding to the whiteboard, "and it's dead relatives. If there's no one alive to identify you – or knows you – that means you could assume a new identity."

"Makes sense," suggested Truman, half-reading an article on the computer screen and half-listening.

Grant chose his words. "Based on DC Johnson's earlier theory that the son Martin Carrier assumed the

ID of Jack Kruger, let's say Martin escaped from Broadhurst with McCoy and Cooper." Grant glanced at his audience. "So, what is the question our predecessors always asked about Zodiac and victim number eleven?"

"Was there a twelfth victim?" responded Hayder who continued in full flow. "If he could leave and enter Broadhurst without the staff knowing – it gave him the perfect alibi and the opportunity to kill his mother close to her birthday. But, for obvious reasons, he didn't leave the usual trinket to identify the killer as Zodiac."

"Excuse me, people," intruded Truman, "I've found articles dated October and November 1993. Pauline Carrier and her murder. She was found dead inside a Range Rover that belonged to her husband, Jonathan Carrier. The police spoke to him – but had an alibi."

"I think we have our answer to a long-standing question about the twelfth victim," suggested Grant with the hint of a smile. "The twelfth victim was his mother."

Truman used the word 'happenstance' to describe the moment. For months the team had toiled away looking for answers. Now, by chance, Marietta Reilly, a Zodiac victim, had turned up in a building belonging to Jack Kruger, now their prime suspect.

Was it a coincidence? Grant and Truman thought so.

Did a third person help McCoy and place Marietta in Highgate Court to bring Kruger into focus?

Janine announced, "I have news. On the day

before the teenagers disappeared two constables stopped at a mobile café on the Dennenmiss Road where they noticed a Toyota Land Cruiser parked up. One officer wrote the registration number but never followed up. He has just done so. Its registered keeper is Jack Kruger. His address is in Belgravia."

23:45 Hrs

DCI Grant was on his way home when he received a call to tell him that ANPR had picked up the Toyota Land Cruiser belonging to Jack Kruger heading towards 'The Tanners'.

He pulled up in a lay-by and called Truman. "Do we go in tonight or wait for tomorrow?"

Truman clucked before replying. "He knows that house, we don't. If he sees them coming, it could become a cat-and-mouse chase. We don't know what he'll do when cornered."

"I'm sending six officers out to work in pairs and watch over 'The Tanners' and make sure he doesn't run during the night. Tomorrow we get him."

At home, he settled to watch TV with his mobile charging nearby. What followed was a long night before finally, he would meet his nemesis face to face, meaning a personal mission was ending.

*****

Earlier that day, Jack Kruger, knowing time was up, left his Belgravia home to drive 'home' to 'The Tanners'. Over the last few days, the baseball cap man whose eyes behind the dark glasses were following him, his presence was unsettling, signalling a life-ending scenario. It was death stalking him, watching and waiting. The final blow would come without warning.

Inside 'The Tanners' he sat by a window, to write letters to his solicitors and business partners. There was no time for explanations. The revelation would be a talking point around the board rooms for months, with endless disputes regarding the ownership of his hardware and software. Placing the envelopes flat on the desk, he took a long look outside before retiring to bed.

Time (tick – tock – tick – tock) was ebbing.

*****

Inside a one-person tent, dressed in army fatigues overlooking the 'The Tanners' sat a man. He fingered a black case, which he opened. After checking the relevant parts were in place, he assembled an AX50 anti-materiel .50 calibre sniper rifle.

CHAPTER 29

1993 | November |

Final Thoughts

Four weeks after his 'death', he let himself in through the main door of his dad's top-floor London flat in Highbury Court. He had thought of visiting Jonathan but, how would he react to his resurrection?

Jonathan had always helped him during painful periods. When the bullies appeared, he hired a former soldier who taught him how to defend himself in ways he never thought possible – not only self-defence but attrition, simple bomb-making and survival skills.

To help Martin – Jonathan hired a private tutor who introduced the world of science and technology.

The only negative was Pauline. A desperate maligned woman. Her existence had shaped him: their words and their deeds. His attitude towards people changed as he sought to repeat the violence.

His dad provided a significant opportunity. The

application forms held the information he needed; names, date of birth and addresses – the question was, where were the applicants now? If they asked why he was calling his answer would be easy. He worked in Personnel. If there were suitable vacancies, he'd ask if they'd be interested in a job at Carrier Properties. If so, their details remained on file.

In the corner stood a desk and a telephone with a view of the main doors. Should anyone enter, he would replace the receiver.

Over the next few days, he built up a list of victims who answered his questions without a hint of suspicion.

They were his chosen targets to satisfy his lust for death and disorder.

A final conversation

Out in the corridor, he heard the faint 'ping' of the lift then approaching footsteps. He hid in the second bedroom and watched a tired and drawn Jonathan enter. Dropping his briefcase, he headed straight to a wall cabinet and grabbed a bottle of Scotch and a tumbler.

Switching on the television, he slumped onto the sofa, poured a considerable measure of Scotch and gulped it down before placing the tumbler aside to stretch out. Soon he fell asleep.

Jonathan was a shadow of his former self; Pauline's antics had taken their toll. His thick brown hair appeared lank and thin while his lined, weary face showed how Pauline and friends had broken him.

An intense, loud action scene on the TV stirred Jonathan, who snuffled before sitting up and rubbed his chest before his reddened eyes slowly fell on his son.

"For a ghost you look lifelike for a ghost!" wheezed Jonathan, rubbing his chest.

"Please call me Martin. If you don't mind."

"Pauline never liked the name your mother gave you. Too common, hence why she liked your middle name, James. I take it as you're alive, you haven't met Pauline along the way."

"No."

"Pity," smirked Jonathan, "I'd like to know how death suits her."

"I'm sure she fights the fight."

"I despised her for the way she used criminal gangs against me!"

"Why didn't you stop her?"

His face contorted with anger as he spoke with palpable emotion and bitterness. "Pauline countered my moves. Any move to divorce her meant 'Game Over'. Her gangster friends had the means to destroy me."

"So, you let me suffer at her hands."

"I repeatedly offered to take you away, but she threatened to tell the police I was a paedophile. Pauline used you against me. A bargaining chip. While she cavorted with gangsters, thieves and treacherous bastards, you were beyond my grasp."

Martin leaned forward, catching Jonathan's alcohol

breath. "This is not a dream. I am alive; like you."

Words hovered on Jonathan's tremoring lips. "You killed her, didn't you?"

"Did I?"

"I know you for who you are, my boy."

"And who am I?"

"Your route into Broadhurst was not accidental. It was all planned; you fooled the authorities and me. I think you found a way out of Broadhurst and murdered Pauline days after her birthday. My question is this. Why did you not kill her earlier? It would've saved me unnecessary stress."

"Why didn't you put a stop to it all?"

"I've told you, she had powerful, nasty friends."

Jonathan grabbed his chest as he gasped and coughed while his eyes turned red and weepy.

"I killed her in her Range Rover. She shouted and squealed because there was no big boy gangster to protect her. I used my knife to silence her by slitting her throat. The light in her eyes as she slipped towards death. Then she uttered the name Arthur, her beloved."

"The irony is this, Martin, had you said something about killing her off, my silence was a given. You did me a favour."

…Martin responded with a shrug.

"…I've not forgotten how distraught Pauline became when she received news about the Arthur Suggs murder…"

The coughing and chest rubbing continued…

"… I had Pauline sectioned to silence her and to protect you."

"I remember."

"Tell me, did you kill Arthur Suggs at the grand age of sixteen?"

"I needed the practice."

"I had my suspicions I wish I had been there to see it."

Martin smiled. "There wasn't much blood," smiled Martin. 'He died in pain."

"Pauline told me you hung out in Aylesbury, Oxford getting up to no good."

"What else did she tell you?"

"Local stories of your indifference to people, moulded by the evil events in the house. But, as for those local lads who beat you up, how did they never identify you as their attacker?"

"I wore a black mask and dark clothing as my Israeli mentor taught me."

Jonathan suddenly gasped and turned a deathly shade of pale and grasped his chest. "Ahh, my time for penance is here." Jonathan broke into strangled laughter. "Your secret goes with me to the grave. But be careful. Events can catch up with us."

"Maybe…"

"Look in that mirror and ask yourself – who am I?"

"I know who I am!"

"What are your plans?"

"I'm off. The United States calls. Someone has provided me with an unexpected opportunity."

"Is he still alive?"

"Yes! I plan to take his place at MIT in Massachusetts. In case you're curious he's too ill to go. It would be a waste not to grasp this opportunity."

Jonathan smiled and turned to make himself more comfortable. "I, too, am ill. I don't have long. Pauline gradually killed me. My heart still beats, but my spark for life blew out. No matter the weather – I see a grey day."

"What about the time before Pauline?"

"Contentment skulks as a memory. As the days pass by, my life runs like a movie. The ending draws closer, whereby my reality slips away. So, no, I wait for Abaddon carrying his sword, awaiting my final penance and confession before his long, cold arm of death takes me somewhere suitable."

He pointed behind Martin before gripping his shoulder. "After I die, check the safe in my bedroom." Jonathan sighed with a smile. "Also, I have left you a trust." Breaking into a mocking laugh, he continued, "But, you're dead. How will you explain that one? Oh, to be a fly on the wall to hear your story of resurrection. Somehow, I'm sure you'll work it out. When you do, you'll be a wealthy man."

*****

Martin gawked at the cold body of Jonathan. For all his earthly troubles and fears, he was now beyond harm. Martin touched Jonathan's still chest before holding a loose arm to thumb the cold dead skin.

In the background, a ticking clock served as a reminder that time never stopped. In the streets below, cars moved, people walked, talked shop. Life continued.

Martin ate breakfast mulling over the fact he was now alone. With no 'Father' or 'Mother', brothers or sisters – no one close knew him. He could be anyone he wanted to be. What a prospect!

I'm a wealthy man. But I died in a fire. I can't reappear. There's no way I can front this out and explain my reincarnation. I've denied myself a considerable fortune through circumstance.

In the safe were two box files. Contained inside were house deeds, birth and death certificates belonging to four generations of the Carrier family who migrated to Southern Africa in the late 1890s. They settled in Rhodesia and grew tobacco crops.

One death certificate grabbed his attention – Jack Kruger – Jonathan's half-brother – the same mother but a different father.

One day Jonathan received the news from South Africa that Jack had died in a car accident. Jonathan flew out for the funeral and on his return, he placed a folder full of papers into the safe. In those papers, Martin found Jack's birth certificate, his death certificate, a valid Zimbabwean passport and a South African passport.

Letters between the brothers outlined Jack's plans to move to the UK and setup a business to counter the threat from Pauline. In his will Jonathan had left the entire business to Jack Kruger, plus a substantial trust fund payable at twenty-one for himself.

Within seconds an idea was forming.

Can I get ALL the money? I have nothing to lose, so I tell myself. But if it goes wrong, the game is up.

Fate was on his side. In the second box was an agreement for transferring shares from Carrier Properties to a company named 'JK Properties Limited'. A swift check of the share certificates confirmed that Jack Kruger, the director of JK Properties, owned 49.9% of Carrier Properties with stakes in related Carrier subsidiaries. Martin grinned from ear to ear. It was all playing into his hands.

A sense of rejuvenation took over when he checked Jack Kruger's birth date. There was only a five-year age gap. In his mind, a plan was forming. After comparing Jack's passport photo and his face in a mirror, would it be possible to assume the identity of Jack Kruger and grab the inheritance?

Nothing was beyond the realms of impossible. Prepare the story, stick to the script and remain confident. It was a case of Jonathan's solicitors believing he was Jack.

Meeting Raymond and later... Jason

Meeting Raymond in Broadhurst proved to be a pivotal point in his early-stage plans. When Raymond mentioned MIT, an incredible bonus, he made plans to gather personal information from Raymond and his aunt and uncle. If he was to become Raymond, he needed to know his subject. He could then, with confidence, take Raymond's place at MIT.

His observations of Maureen and Percy led him to conclude they were controlling, sarcastic, cruel and unforgiving towards Raymond. Their visits coincided when the subject of money arose. He believed they were slowly bleeding Raymond for cash.

Two days after the fire he drove an agitated Jason 'home'. His parents went into meltdown, wondering what evil forces had saved their son from the fire. His mother smacked her head twice while screaming hysterically. Eventually calming down she ranted, "You can't be alive. Did you NOT die in that fire? How did you survive?"

"I'm alive," whispered a smiling Jason, his eyes darting between his parents. "Are you not happy to see me?"

Jason's mother tried to approach him, followed by her husband, almost pleading, "Please leave us, Jason, leave us; we can't look after you. Your death meant we were free from your tempers, your violence. We need to live here without you and the fear you create."

Jason's face turned bright red; his lips curled downward, his eyes narrowed as he turned towards a cupboard door, yanked it open and grabbed a shotgun and four cartridges.

"Put that back," advised his father, "it's loaded."

Jason ignored his father's order and scowled.

"Move outside to the back yard. We need to talk."

"No," countered his father, approaching Jason with flailing arms. "Since you left, we've had peace. We can no longer tolerate your disturbing presence."

Jason struck his father with the butt of the shotgun,

then grabbed his father's collar. His mother pleaded to stop but Jason was not about to listen and pulled his father to the tarmacked back yard and made him kneel.

"Don't, Jason don't!" screamed his mother as he placed the barrel of the shotgun in the nape of his dad's neck. Turning to face his mother, he smashed the butt into her face. As she fell, he pulled her kneeling next to her husband. To wails and cries of mercy, Jason, without a glimmer of conscience, walked behind his parents, lifted the shotgun to their necks and fired.

Without a flicker of emotion, Jason winked at Martin as he used his thumb to move the break-action and eject the two spent casings. Digging two new casings from his pocket, he reloaded the shotgun and closed the break before kneeling on the tarmac. With no hesitancy, Jason placed the shotgun barrel under his chin and pulled the trigger.

Jason's action was unexpected. It saved Martin the job of deciding their fate. What next: burn the bodies? No, bad idea. The police could identify Jason and start a series of questions surrounding their escape from Broadhurst. The cops might look to close to home. Too close.

His next move required planning and thought. He wandered into a barn full of machinery. Stacked on nearby trestles was an array of hand tools. Upright in one corner were rolls of heavy cellophane. In a second, he had an idea: use the cellophane to wrap up the bodies. The best place to store them was in 'The Tanners'.

After fixing a sandwich, he searched the house.

Amongst the papers, he found deeds, bank accounts, and building society accounts containing substantial sums. Finally, he wrapped the bodies in the cellophane and drove them home.

Killing Aunt and Uncle

He learned from their visits to the hospital they were soon to leave on a three-month cruise. At the time he thought it was a cynical, cruel move by the aunt and uncle. During one visit they seemed eager to tell Raymond their plans and produced a large brown envelope about that contained their holiday details. It became a non-stop boast of their holiday.

The aunt never stopped; she was a talking machine designed to wear you down. The uncle remained silent while listening to his wife. He recalled one of their visits to see their nephew.

"Look at this, Raymond." She waved a large brown envelope above her head. "We're going on a three-month cruise. Every day we will dock in a different country." She ruffled Raymond's hair. "We know you would like to come with us, but due to your illness, we can't get any insurance for you."

She pulled a sympathetic smile before changing the subject.

"But don't worry too much about our cottage, it'll be fine. On the evening before we leave, we're going to the local pub for a meal with Doug and his wife. We'll give them a key so they can pop around and keep the house safe. You know who I mean, don't you, when I say Doug?"

"As I've never been to your house…"

"It's a cottage, Raymond," interrupted his aunt. "How many times must I tell you? It's a chocolate box cottage."

An irritated Raymond raised his voice to make the point. "Nevertheless, I've never met your friends or neighbours, so no, I don't."

"No need to shout, Raymond. As you know, we don't like our neighbours," replied Maureen, placing the envelope on the bed. "Terrible people. We ignore them."

Raymond showed little enthusiasm as his Uncle Percy suggested they all get a coffee. Martin was quick to offer an excuse to watch television. He waited until they wandered off before returning to Raymond's room to grab the envelope. He pulled out the paperwork and checked the day of departure and their address.

If he was to become Raymond, travel to the United States, study at MIT, then Aunt and Uncle had to die. He needed no one around who recognised him.

*****

The day before Percy and Maureen's departure, Martin drove twelve miles to a village named Tring. He parked in a quiet country road. Thirty metres away stood a row of stone-built terraced cottages.

Raymond's aunt and uncle lived in the first cottage surrounded by a high wall and a large garden with masses of foliage about which Percy talked during their visits.

After Percy and Maureen jumped into their car to visit the pub as mentioned, he entered the cottage and mooched about looking over the half-packed suitcases, their passports, the cruise itinerary, foreign currency and various other items for packing.

In the kitchen, he tipped a small amount of white powder into a carton of milk before shaking it up. For good measure, he added the same powder to the water in the kettle; spotting a phone, he yanked the cable from the wall and left the cottage.

An hour later Percy and Maureen returned. If they didn't use the milk or boil the kettle, what would he do? Three hours later and close to midnight, the light in the lounge still shone.

Strolling cautiously up to the front window, he peered inside where Aunt Maureen lay slumped on the sofa holding a teacup. Percy lay on the floor with the telephone receiver in his hand.

*****

The powder had done the job. He was taking a risk using the Range Rover to transport the bodies to 'The Tanners'. Should the police stop him, what would happen?

Risky but necessary.

He took his time to collect items of value; birth and death certificates, passports, share certificates, bank account details, deeds to the houses and Raymond's paperwork for MIT.

"Be careful. With three names, don't forget who you are."

CHAPTER 30

Sunday | 15th February |

07:15 Hrs

Arising winter sun appeared over the thin white mist that covered the Chiltern hills. Rays of yellow light touched the earth, fields and hedgerows while grazing flocks of sheep and herds of cattle munched on the green grass, lifting their faces to feel the sun warm their faces.

The yellowing white walls of his childhood bedroom shimmied in the strands of the sun that reached through the windows. He did not sleep well. The night was long, silent. Two words came to mind when dawn lit the horizon: execution day. (Tick-tock-tick-tock.)

He stood and stretched his limbs while gazing at the winter skies lying over the Chiltern hills. Touches of frost glistened in the sun while two red kites flew high above the fields looking for carrion. After dressing, he sauntered outside into the weak February sun as a cold breeze brushed against his face, bare feet and hands. Doing his best to ignore the cold he strolled along an overgrown grassy path where he stopped to view 'The Tanners'.

"Dust," he whispered as if a close confidant stood nearby, "they'll demolish you to rid the world of my deeds. We lost our liberty the day we killed. Until death takes us, we live with lies, mistrust and more lies."

Not far away, two Irish setters barked and chased each other before stopping to sniff the air. Both dogs howled, creating a haunting sound that echoed over the fields.

On cue, a familiar voice spoke. "Martin, they come for you today."

Without turning or acknowledging the voice, he replied, "My executioner lies out there and won't miss."

"That is no forgiveness for the pain you inflicted. Look at your victims who stand and await your death. They don't wait to embrace you but lead you to the end."

"Go, Mother," he scoffed, "lead your death army away from here. Soon enough, I'll join you! But, before you go, I must ask – is death painful?"

"There is no pain. You'll fall asleep with scattered visions until your senses cease to hear and see!"

Closing his eyes to focus on Kenya, the Masai, Leboo and the dark red sky, he could smell the night air and hear the distant animals and the warmth of the red sun on his face. A rustling noise interrupted his thoughts. Before him stood Stuart Grant.

"Martin Carrier, I am Detective Chief Inspector Grant. I'm here to arrest you."

"My arrest," he folded his fingers. "Is there any chance of a promotion for this capture? I always believed in helping people further their career!"

"I have thought about this moment for a long time," replied Grant, "and now I'm here, standing before you in daylight and not in the dark I see you as you are – without your dark robes and mask. A mere man and nothing else."

Zodiac responded with a small bow as Stuart asked, "Are you Martin Carrier, AKA Zodiac or Jack Kruger?"

"When did I last use the name Martin Carrier?" he smirked. "I almost forgot who I am. However, why question my identity when you know who I am?"

Stuart stepped forward with a pair of handcuffs. "I'm arresting you—"

"Oh, come now," scoffed Zodiac, waving his hands. "What rights? I've abused the rights of people and taken their lives. I cannot demand rights."

"Everyone has rights before arrest!" replied Stuart, shaking the handcuffs. "Including you."

...The cool touch of his mother gripping his hand drew his attention. She pointed downwards. Repent – the irony?

Sparing the world one last glance, he prepared himself as folds of darkness wrapped around his consciousness...

A distant crack echoed, a whooshing sound, then a dull thump. When Zodiac stumbled but somehow remained standing, Stuart turned and screamed towards his fellow police officers who were keeping low behind the wall. "Who did this?"

Stuart stared on in disbelief as a second bullet hit Zodiac's head knocking him off his feet. Dropping to his knees he coughed and stared at the bloody mess. The bullet had taken more than half of Zodiac's head off.

It was not the end Stuart envisaged. It was to be a clean arrest, a drive into custody and charges laid out. Instead, he and the team could find themselves asked more questions as to why they did not arrest Zodiac earlier. It was never meant to be and somewhere deep in his conscience he knew that. Zodiac knew what was coming and welcomed death to escape justice and avoid the eternal publicity about his mental state.

...On the horizon, the red sunset and blood-red sky stretched beyond sight. The animals of the savannah moved together. They sought comfort and protection from the predators and opportunist killers that hid in the bush as night drew in. As the sun faded leaving darkness to cast its shawl, there was one last flicker of light on the horizon as Leboo appeared through the dark to ask, 'What is your story?' before all went quiet...

14:00 Hours, News Flash

We had unconfirmed reports that when police moved in to arrest Zodiac suspect, witnesses confirm hearing two shots. We believe Zodiac is dead.

*****

The jubilant Zodiac team popped the champagne. After eleven long months, their task was complete. Time to reflect, learn lessons and hope such an investigation was never required again.

Two men were missing from the celebrations. Grant and Truman stopped off at the morgue to see the corpse of Zodiac. They braced as the attendant drew back the sheet.

Truman gasped, as did Grant. Whatever they hoped to see was a lot worse than anticipated. Only the right side of the face remained intact with an open eye staring ahead while his lower jaw hung loose.

"What's left of his face tells us something," murmured Truman. "Did he know what was coming, and that he'd escape justice?" Glimpsing at Grant who showed no response, he continued. "A forensics team found where the assassin was hiding."

Grant still did not respond. A strong moment of anti-climax had descended. For so long, they worked hard to trace Zodiac, and now it was all over.

"An army expert measured the distance of the shot at around 2,000 metres. He suggested the sniper was possibly a Special Forces sniper."

Grant finally acknowledged Truman. "He's denied many people justice today with that act. I hope we have people out looking for him?"

"Yeah, it's already with Serious Crime. They'll let us know if they find something."

"There must be some evidence?"

"I'm only saying because the sniper's a pro. In the chaos, he slipped away. My guess is this – the chances of finding him are zero."

"Continue," urged Grant, "I'm listening."

"The ballistics expert found two spent Russian-made .50 casings at the scene. That suggests the assassin was a Russian."

"Russian," whispered Grant. "I think we've got the answer to our question. Valentin Lenevski had Zodiac assassinated for killing his daughter. The irony of it – Zodiac executed for a crime he didn't commit."

*****

Raymond stood in silence over a familiar bloodied face. With no signs of life, he looked ahead and beyond the skies. *I'm free now; I can live without looking over my shoulder.*

When his eyes opened in a strange environment, he saw a man standing close by wearing a blue top. Close by he could hear the beep of a machine and from his arm was a drip.

"Where am I?"

"You're in a hospital," came the reply. "How are you?"

"Is he dead?"

"Is who died?" asked the nurse as excited voices chatted from the corridor. Then an announcement on the radio followed.

"...Zodiac, the serial killer, was earlier today shot by an unknown assassin..."

Money – Money – Money

On Elbow Beach, Bermuda, lay Richard. When his smartphone pinged, he raised the screen to read an email from Daley.

Richard,

I hope Bermuda agrees with you and the sun shines for you. Have attached all the information you need to access all the bank accounts and investments in the name of Jack Kruger. I will send further details in separate emails.

I have what I need regarding the hardware and software designs. Let's say I have more than I bargained for and your ex-friend sure was a geek worthy of honour had he not turned into a killer.

I'm sure you'll hear of me soon enough and when you buy that castle invite me around for a few drinks.

Daley

CHAPTER 31

1972 | September

Lynn Foster regained consciousness with a vague memory of being thrown into the boot of a vehicle. From the sound of the engine, she was confident it was a 3.5 litre, petrol-driven Range Rover. But where were they going?

In the dark she could feel various items nudge against her; a pair of boots, clothing, a box of matches and a can of petrol. Then as the vehicle swerved something solid dug into her ribs.

She picked up the object and ran her fingers along its length, recognising the shape and feel – unexpected salvation.

When the vehicle came to a jarring halt, she focused on the juniors talking.

"Patience," she murmured, preparing her salvation. "At some point, they'll open the tailgate." She did not have to wait long.

When the tailgate swung open, with the juniors in her sights, she squeezed the trigger of a sawn-off shotgun. An enormous boom roared that left her ears ringing while the muscles in her right shoulder rode the recoil.

With no regret at shooting the two men, she swung her legs out of the tailgate. Both lay partially submerged in a water-filled ditch. Maurice moved his arms watching Lynn circle the ditch. "Please help us?" he begged.

"Why should I help? You were ready to kill me," she replied, taking hold of the petrol can with a shake before unscrewing the top.

"Please don't. Archie told us what to do."

"You stood by while Suggs raped me. Like cowards, you looked away!"

"Don't," pleaded Maurice, trying to raise his head, as she tipped the petrol out. "We didn't mean to hurt you. It was Arthur's idea."

"Too late!" Throwing the can aside, she struck three matches and threw them onto the ditch. As the surface disappeared under flames, she cursed Suggs and all the people who had used and abused her.

She hated them all.

Living for another day

After a restless night, Lynn strolled through the trees enjoying the peace and calming effect of the sunlight filtering through the trees. After months as a slave, a massive noise in her head stopped. Peace descended. She thought about going home to live a healthy life.

Hunger was tugging at her stomach. She had no money, coupled with the fact she had no idea where she was. The answer was close when she heard excited voices which she followed. She was on the boundary of a busy campsite: that meant food and money and a bath.

Dressed in torn clothes and wearing steel-tipped boots would only draw attention to her shabby appearance and if she begged for food, she risked the site owner calling the police.

By late afternoon, families cook their evening meals. A wave of aromas made her hungry. Patiently keeping out of sight, she waited for the families to head out.

She snuck into the tents, finding more than enough food, clothing, loose change, the odd banknote and a towel. She headed to the shower block where she ran a bath and as expected – used the bottles of shampoo and soap left by the campers.

It was pure luxury.

A week later, she sat in the Range Rover.

I can't live like this, going into the camp every night searching for food; sleeping in the back of the Range Rover with two dead men only feet away. What did I do to deserve this? What have I become? I've lost my humanity, killed two men, I've been used and abused, and I feel cheap and nasty, dirty. I must decide my next move, but where will I go? I've no choice but to call my sister and return home.

Walking to the public telephone box, she thought about what to say when Pauline answered the phone. It all went easier than she thought.

"Hello, Pauline Foster."

"Pauline, it's me, Lynn."

"Lynn… Lynn where have you been? For weeks

we had search parties out for you. Where are you?"

"Near a campsite now, but I was in London."

"London? What were you doing there?"

"I ran away to escape social workers."

"Dad continues to blame your disappearance on the social workers. He said they were holding you against your will. He told the media and anyone who'd listen, but, people stopped listening and thought he was mad."

"Do me a favour and don't mention me at all."

"Your secret's safe with me."

"OK. I'll come home."

There was a problem. She had no money.

Later that evening she waited until the manager of the social club locked up and drove home. She found an open window, squeezed through and took enough money from the till to buy a train ticket, a taxi, a sandwich and a bag of crisps along the way.

At home with sister

Lynn spent the first week more or less in her new bedroom asleep. When Pauline left the house, she ventured to the kitchen, grabbed a plateful of food and took it to her bedroom to savour the peace.

Over the days that followed, Lynn recited her story to a fascinated Pauline. It was clear Pauline had no interest in Lynn's life as a forced prostitute and the violence she endured; more so Pauline showed more interest in the gangsters and their lives. After telling her the stories, Pauline would dash off and make write notes, explaining her story would make a good novel. Nothing sinister in making notes.

*****

Lynn rubbed her tummy. "These pains won't go away."

"The pains you've had for two weeks?"

"Yes."

"Go to the doctor. Don't wait. Something might fall out."

"Don't," scolded Lynn. "You can be upsetting."

"Well. You know me."

"I'll see the doctor today. Get this seen to. It's possibly an infection of some kind."

*****

"What did you say?" asked a stunned Lynn. "Are you sure?"

"You're pregnant," replied the doctor.

"Pregnant," she gasped. "I can't be."

"You are," asserted the doctor.

"You must have it wrong."

"Are you all right, Miss Foster? You appear distressed about this pregnancy."

"It's unexpected. Not something I expected to happen."

"Without knowing when you last had a period, I can't say how many weeks along you are."

Pregnant. The word invoked anxiety as she stood

and gripped the door handle; gaping at the doctor, she muttered, "Thank you for your time, Doctor. I'm going home to decide my next move."

*****

"Well, what did the doctor say?" demanded Pauline as Lynn sat with a cup of tea.

"Well, what?"

"The doctor. What did he say?

"She… told me I'm pregnant."

"Pregnant! What are you saying here?"

Pauline appeared stunned at the unexpected news. After a long pause, she found her voice.

"OK, so, this child's father is a gangster who raped you. What about abortion?" queried Pauline as Lynn stared into space.

"The fact is right now," replied Lynn, "I'm thinking about my next move!"

The next day Pauline waited for Lynn to appear and when she did, it was question time.

"Have you decided?"

"Let me pour myself a cup of tea, why don't you?" scolded Lynn, gripping a cup and sitting opposite Lynn. "Right, I will tell you about my dream last night."

"What sort of dream was it?"

"About my boy."

"Boy? What boy?"

Lynn placed her hand on her tummy, "The boy in here… my tummy."

"The boy," interrupted Pauline. "What boy? Who told you it's a boy?"

"No one told me. I know it's a boy, I know – alright?" countered Lynn, avoiding a drawn-out discussion. "And when he grows up, he'll protect my family from evil. Sons do that for their mothers."

Pauline looked puzzled listening to Lynn continue.

"I believe the boy I'm carrying will right all the wrongs I suffered in the past."

"What are you chatting about?"

"My future lies in my womb. That's all I'm saying."

"So, you're keeping the gangster's baby? What happens if he turns out to be his father's son and becomes a gangster himself?" Pauline stopped talking to think. "That could be fun. He'll keep you in your dotage," chuckled Pauline, trying to lighten the tense atmosphere. "They call gangsters' wives 'Molls'. But what do they call the aunties of gangsters?"

Lynn ignored her sister, who continued to drone on.

CHAPTER 32

1973 | 1st April |

Meet my new man

Lynn was reading a magazine when an excited squeal made her jump. Moments later, an anxious stranger appeared. Before Lynn could ask who he was, Pauline was full of smiles. Gripping his hand, she spoke.

"Lynn, allow me to introduce you to someone special," gushed Pauline, brushing up against her companion. "This is Jonathan Carrier – who is something in the City." Turning to her beau, "Meet my sister Lynn who came home not so long ago."

"Pleased to meet you," she responded with a thought or two crossing her mind.

Why has Pauline never mentioned Jonathan before?

"Where did you two meet?" asked a curious Lynn.

"I met Pauline many moons ago at a party in the City... Our relationship was a slow burn until recently."

"Which city?" queried Lynn.

"City of London bash, The Square Mile, with a bunch of fellow directors. We were raising funds for a charity," replied Jonathan with a clipped accent bearing a slight foreign twang, "and Pauline was down there, ensuring all went to plan."

"Oh!" replied Lynn, with an approving look. "You're a long way from home?"

"Yes. But distance will not be a problem."

He is gorgeous. What has Pauline done to bag him? Is Jonathan a millionaire by chance? If so, I can imagine the tactics she used to snare him.

Jonathan was to become a regular visitor until May when they married at the Great St Bartholomew Church, in London, with a small reception at a nearby hotel.

1973 | 30th May

During a visit to Jonathan's 'posh' London flat Lynn's waters broke. He drove her to a private hospital where the staff rushed her to a maternity ward. Lynn was forced to admit she had not kept up her local appointments and had no idea how her pregnancy had progressed.

Twenty-four hours later a tired and tearful Lynn haemorrhaged blood and fell into a coma.

Pauline was sitting by her bedside reading a magazine when Lynn recovered. "You're awake."

Lynn tried to push herself up to gaze at her surroundings. "What happened?"

"You... passed out. The doctors had to take you

away."

Lynn's eyes reddened as she asked, "What about the baby?"

Pauline gripped Lynn's hand and sat on the edge of the bed and said, "Plural. It's babies."

"Babies?"

"When you passed out the doctor performed an emergency C-section. When they opened you up, they discovered you were carrying twin boys."

"Twins?" Lynn looked shocked. "Are they OK? Where are they?"

"The midwife will bring them in after they examine you. We all thought you'd die. Jonathan was beside himself because the boys would have no mother."

After a doctor examined Lynn, a midwife wheeled in the twins. After tearful introductions, she decided on their names. Stuart Philip Foster and Martin James Foster. Pauline held back on the quip to call either of them Arthur or register him as the father.

A doting Jonathan hired a part-time nanny and offered Lynn a self-contained flat with the suggestion she treated 'The Tanners' as her home for as long as she liked. It was clear to Pauline that when Jonathan sat with Lynn and the boys, he saw himself as a family man. He wanted children, but Pauline ignored the conversation. She had no interest.

Lynn soon found her routine. Every evening she sat with the boys and told them tales of magic, demons and wizards and the evil men who ruled the earth.

During the day, whatever the weather she walked the narrow lanes with her boys in the pushchair to a local farmhouse café managed by Mrs Eliza Grant, whose husband owned and farmed the surrounding land. There she spent an hour or more with other mothers while Eliza's children made a fuss of the boys.

Away from the malice and greed, her life had meaning and purpose. She was first a mother with two beautiful boys. In her head, she had their lives planned.

But, time for making broader plans was closing in. The heavy hand of fate bore down on Lynn when she awoke with a pain in her left upper chest and shoulder. When she could find neither her sister nor Jonathan, she sat the boys in their buggy and walked to the farmhouse café.

Eliza spotting Lynn's distress called an ambulance and settled the boys with stories and cuddles while the ambulance men took Lynn to hospital. The injuries inflicted by Arthur Suggs took their toll. Doctors worked to remove Lynn's spleen that ruptured twelve months after the first assault.

Lynn's unexpected death left Pauline and Jonathan in a predicament. That was the care of the twins. Despite Pauline possessing no maternal instincts, she, with Jonathan, assumed the role of parents to raise the boys.

Motherhood was draining Pauline. The twins were messing with her social life. Jonathan tried to persuade Pauline to keep going. He wanted the boys to remain under one roof.

Fed up with arguing, Jonathan called Eliza Grant

for advice. After a short conversation, and against his plans, she 'adopted' Stuart. To make him part of her family, she changed his surname to Grant.

Jonathan, recognising Pauline's hands-off approach to Martin's care hired a full-time nanny. Within weeks she packed her and left. Pauline resented their presence. Martin or James as Pauline preferred was to grow up surrounded by a motley collection of gangsters, thieves, perverts and people who cared not for another soul. It was to shape his ideas into the man he became.

Years later, 'The Tanners' remained a focal point for village gossip. There were tales of exotic parties, swingers and dungeons. The mysterious figure in black who beat up three local boys. Surely. Did he come from 'The Tanners'?

Despite the police calling and questioning the boy, they found no proof he had beaten up three boys. As for the rumoured scandals, such evidence was never forthcoming.

After the murder of Pauline, the deaths of Martin, and Jonathan, the scandalous tales, just like the white exterior of 'The Tanners', crumbled.

The murder of the six teenagers rekindled the earlier stories. Once upon a time, in an old white house, lived a dysfunctional family – so the story went.

2015 | 22nd January

As Thursday mornings went, he checked the clock and continued to lie in for five minutes before throwing aside the duvet to get up and shower. The house was spectacularly quiet. The reason was no wife and kids at home.

Downstairs the phone rang, prompting him to dash to answer. The caller who did not introduce himself asked if he would be interested in a contract and if so, he could meet two representatives at Embankment underground station that afternoon.

As a former Special Ops soldier, he was suspicious. On his arrival at Embankment, he spotted two men of Slavic appearance sitting outside a Starbucks. He guessed they were his contacts. Both looked uncomfortable and suspicious of anyone who came to close to their space. One was cleanly shaven. The other had a goatee.

Both men held up their hands as he approached. The goateed man stood and pointed to a vacant chair.

Heathcoat sat, smelling heavy tobacco breath on one of the men. "Right, here I am. How did you get my name?"

The goatee man spoke with a Russian accent. "You are William Heathcoat, a former SAS sniper with a known kill at over 2,000 metres."

Heathcoat smirked as he commented, "Seems your intelligence is up to date. From where you get that information?"

"We have our sources. In your mercenary outfit, you had maybe a Russian or two?"

"I prefer the term Security Company. Yes, we had one Russian." Heathcoat tapped the table. "He wasn't a bad shot."

"He gave us your name."

"Thank him for me." Heathcoat glanced at both men. Pointing at the silent man, he asked, "Does he not speak?"

"His English is not so good. When he has something to say, I speak for him."

"Who's the target, and who is Valentin Lenevski?"

"He is of no concern to you. However, as he's paying you the fee, he wants Cooper executed with two bullets."

"Can I ask who the target is?"

Goatee slid two photos across the table face down to Heathcoat. He gazed at the faces in the pictures. Bearing a poker face, he asked, "Who is he?"

Goatee folded his fingers with a knowing smile and looked at his silent companion with a nod. "We think you know him; a flicker of recognition crossed your face. Am I right?"

Heathcoat held the photos closer, allowing a brief smile of recognition. "He and I were together in an African jail for ten years. His name is Jack Kruger, from Zimbabwe."

The Russian smiled and met Heathcoat's gaze. "We know him as Jason Cooper, an Englishman, also a technical master who murdered the daughter of our boss Valentin Lenevski. Her name was Yulia; he killed her while they were together in her apartment. Later Cooper escaped from a secure unit by killing three bodyguards. If there were bullets in the gun, he would've killed Valentin."

William recognised the man in the photo as Jack Kruger but not the name Jason Cooper. At no time did Kruger during their conversations behind prison walls mention any such a deed, but then again, why would he?

"I know him."

"Then, you might be interested to know that he could be the serial killer Zodiac."

The accusation took Heathcoat by surprise. He glanced between the two men before uttering, "Zodiac... where's the evidence?"

Goatee leaned forward to whisper, aware that nearby coffee drinkers had overheard Heathcoat's statement.

"The name of the man who alerted us is Richard Deayton, who was most helpful. After a visit to Mr Cooper's home, we looked at what Mr Deayton had found. We advised him to settle any personal affairs and move far, far away before Cooper returns."

"Returns from where?"

"He returns to the UK from Australia on Friday 6th February."

William did a quick mental calculation. "That's ten days away. Why not let the police manage this?"

"Because Mr Lenevski urges you to assassinate him as revenge for killing his daughter."

"If you accept the contract, Mr Lenevski will pay you 10% of a five million fee upfront. The rest after you complete the job. Mr Lenevski would also give you the bullets and would like you to shoot the target at least twice. Mr Lenevski is anxious that Mr Cooper bears the pain of death as did his daughter Yulia."

"Can I trust Mr Lenevski?"

"Without a doubt! He would ask that you call him after the job and tell him that Kruger is dead."

"Am I to talk to him this Deayton?"

"No, don't approach him. He knows what to expect. If he should talk to the wrong people, we will deal with him."

"OK, understood."

"This afternoon I will have a courier delivery to your home the information you require about the target and the man who tipped us off. Mr Lenevski will look forward to hearing from you."

*****

William could not accept the fact that Jack, or Jason was Zodiac. Together they spent many hours in an African jail talking and keeping each other company. Oddly enough he could never recall Jack talking about any special woman in his life.

In the package Goatee had delivered the evidence was there in black and white. It left him wondering how Lenevski's men had obtained the evidence so quickly, while the UK police appeared to flounder?

He knew of Marietta disappearing after a birthday night out. But Jack was out of the country. He did a search on Google and soon learned that Highgate Court belonged to a company owned by Jack Kruger and also owned the Tremors Nightclub through a company based in the Cayman Islands. However, he was not listed as a director.

William after a lot of thought guessed someone else had learned Jack's secret and decided to set him up for the final fall. There was no doubt that he was to be the man who would finally stop Jack... or was that Jason?

To see Jack one last time, he waited at Heathrow's T5 and watched Jack exit Arrivals. After so many years Jason, or Jack still looked the same, just a little bigger. There was no mistaking his eyes that could hold you in a conversation. Shaking his head, he looked ahead to the job of taking Jack down. He could not afford to miss. Two clean shots to end a life. After all, he was doing it for the money.

He pitched a one-person tent, aware of the police presence. Using his sights, he guessed 'The Tanners' was around 2000 metres away. To make a successful shot would depend on the weather. At 6am, the four teams of police officers moved on to meet their colleagues pulling up in an assortment of police vehicles.

As light broke on the horizon, Jack appeared and wandered around the grounds. Heathcoat looked down his scope and placed the recoil pad against his shoulder; primed and ready.

Detached and focussed on the task, it was a case of pulling the trigger. Jack's destiny was in his ability to make a clean shot. The target was already dead in his mind. Now was the time to fire!

Squeezing the trigger, the bullet hit Jack in the chest. He loaded the second bullet and squeezed. Jack hit the ground.

"It wasn't personal, Jack. We had a true friendship in Africa. Your company was the best. A lonely Russian made an offer I couldn't refuse. I only did it for the money!"

CHAPTER 33

1500 Hrs GMT | Calling Moscow

In the *Rublyovskoe Highway* area of Moscow, Valentin Lenevski sat listening to a classical music concert with his eldest son Yevgeni when the telephone rang.

Valentin plucked the receiver with a shaking hand.

"It is me, Valentin. Calling from the UK. How are you?"

"I await your news."

"The man who killed your daughter is now dead."

"One or two bullets?"

"Two."

"Thank you!" replied Valentin, replacing the receiver as his eyes filled with tears. Father and son embraced.

"That is the news I wanted to hear for so long. Justice for me is served."

Yevgeny held his ageing father's face. "Go to bed, Father. You're tired and it's been a long day."

"Yes. Time for sleep."

Valentin shuffled away watched by his son. He was happy. He visualised the bullets striking his daughter's murderer and the sight of Cooper lying dead. Before pulling the duvet over, he held up a photo of Yulia in her graduation gown. Kissing the picture, he laid back. He missed her so much.

After a restless hour, he fell asleep only to awaken an hour later from a vivid dream where Yulia walked with him through a green field. A sudden tightness in his chest made breathing almost impossible. With a smile he let go to fall asleep one last time.

CHAPTER 34

Parting Words

Dear Stuart,

I'm writing this letter because soon I will be dead. I travelled a road where fate decided my death in a green field where I lived as a child.

One of your questions must be – who am I?

I was born on the 31ˢᵗ of May, 1973.

If you have not guessed, you and I are twins.

As our Aunt Pauline Carrier, née Foster, could not cope with two babies, the Grant family took you as one of their own. That decision saved you from my world of the violence and pain that shaped my life.

Our Aunt Pauline married Jonathan Carrier, a property millionaire. She could fleece him while she consorted with degenerates.

One evening Arthur Suggs and friend Dave Davis arrived at a party. Suggs filled Pauline's mind with tales of gangsters and villains, leaving her in constant awe of him. He told a story that intrigued me. I soon realised the story was about our mother.

Arthur Suggs made her an offer she turned down. In doing so, he raped her and assigned two men to bury her. If Pauline knew to whom he was referring, she never said a word.

The decision to make Arthur pay came on Archie's 16th birthday. Arthur paid for his deeds, as did his best mate Dave Davis, a paedophile. I must now confess to murdering his son, our half-brother, using the same method of rope torture.

I am now dead. A man like me set me up for the finale. Allow me to predict an event.

Listen out for the English rose who rises from the depths of a Scottish loch.

Finally, the bodies in the tunnels below 'The Tanners'; they are youngsters smuggled into the country and murdered. I'm sure once the authorities release the information, the sleep of the guilty will be disturbed.

We're all architects of our private hell. No one can hurt us as we've hurt ourselves.

Farewell!

Martin James Foster

News Flash

May 2015. Members of a scout group called the police to a campsite at Asheridge, near Chesham on Wednesday. Two Scout Leaders stumbled across two bodies buried in a bog. A senior police spokesperson made clear there was an attempt to burn the bodies.

June 2015. The police have named the two men found in a bog as Maurice Gooch (19) and Herbert Miller (21). Families reported both men missing in 1972. A police spokesperson suggested they were driving a stolen Range Rover. During the chase, the men escaped.

EPILOGUE

Lightning lit the sky; thunder cracked while he walked home from the nearby shops carrying milk and bread. Across the road, a figure in black approached, causing his heart to thump.

When two arms appeared and pushed the hood back, he sighed with relief, recognising the Reverend Josephine Hooper.

"If you ever visit your wife's grave, my door is always open for tea or coffee!"

"I'll do that."

Josephine raised her eyebrows. With a wave of her hand, she continued her way.

If she looks back, then she's interested, thought Stuart.

Seconds later, she did.

ABOUT THE AUTHOR

Michael Clark was born in Newcastle-upon-Tyne in 1959. Up to the age of five, he lived in Hobson, County Durham, before the family moved to Burnopfield. He attended the local primary school up to the age of ten. Many of his primary school teachers recognised his comprehension skills at an early age and allowed him extra time to finish his written work, recognising his ability to tell a story. He has a collection of poetry and other short stories he hopes to publish.

Michael has had various careers. Since 1996, he has worked as a freelance technical author within the Information Technology sector. He has blogged about technical authoring for many years and contributed articles to LinkedIn. Articles have discussed the good, the bad and long-running problems associated with technical authoring and personal observations about the workplace.

Family-wise, in 1969 with new opportunities on offer the Clark family relocated to sunny South Africa and settled in Kensington, Johannesburg. Michael attended Hillcrest Primary School, Jeppe High School and Studywell Tutorial in Central Johannesburg. In January 1978, he returned to the UK. Michael has always held a passion for writing.

His interests include photography, an eclectic mix

of music, foreign holidays and cruises. He holds a Bachelor of Arts degree in Contemporary History and Humanities Computing from the University of Hertfordshire and has lived in the County of Bucks for almost fourteen years.

Printed in Great Britain
by Amazon